EXTREMOPHILE
VIOLET RAIN
BOOK 2 OF THE UNWINDING

JULIANA REW

Cover Art by Keely Rew

Extremophile: Violet Rain
The Unwinding Series Book 2

by Juliana Rew

Copyright 2020 Sophont Press
ISBN #978-1-7362848-0-3

Discover other titles by Juliana Rew:
(1) The Unwinding: Gin's Story
(2) Erenarch Academy: Under the Dragon Banner
(3) Daris Moon
(4) Miranda of Daris
(5) Mountain Ma'am
(6) The Adventures of Mountain Ma'am

Cover: Keely Rew

www.julianarew.com

Dedication

In gratitude to everyone who's made us feel like part of the family. This book's dedicated to baby Cassandra. May we all grow BIGGER.

Contents

Chapter 1. Slow Stepper 7
Chapter 2. City of Fallen Angels 23
Chapter 3. Never Speak to Strangers 33
Chapter 4. Baby Blue Chasm 47
Chapter 5. Grounded Fears 63
Chapter 6. Native Cuisine 79
Chapter 7. The Drive 87
Chapter 8. Playground 91
Chapter 9. Flight 111
Chapter 10. The Search 119
Chapter 11. The Devil's Circle 129
Chapter 12. Competition Is Good for You 141
Chapter 13. Not Feeling Myself Today 155
Chapter 14. An Orphan of the Storm 171
Chapter 15. Lay Your Money Down 179
Chapter 16. Regeneration 191
Chapter 17. It's Just Us Now 201
Chapter 18. If They're Hungry Enough 217
Chapter 19. The Sinister Corridor 221
Chapter 20. The Jeweled Cave 229
Chapter 21. Artifacts 235
Chapter 22. Be Yourself 243
Chapter 23. Who'll Stop the Rain? 251
Chapter 24. Memories Are Made of This 259
Chapter 25. Coming to an Understanding 267
Chapter 26. Planetfall and Eternal Refuge 275
Chapter 27. The Return of the Watchmen 283
Art Credits and Acknowledgments 291
About Juliana Rew 291

Chapter 1.

Slow Stepper

"The crossover is extremely dangerous," the leader of the Watchmen said. "Bravery is required to undertake this test." Strong praise from Yverra, who normally seemed a rather cold fish. Yverra's reflective gold-rimmed eyes fixed her with an unblinking stare. "Ready?"

Violet Rain ran her fingers through her cropped purple fringe and pulled her long dark hair into a ponytail. At least she wouldn't have to take her clothes off, because she wasn't going into a wormhole this time. The Watchmen had ridden ten wormholes to get to their station this far out. She closed her eyes and nodded.

Violet felt herself leave her body. That was an illusion, of course; her body was still in the same spot, cradling her brain within its delicate cranium, as always. She'd left her personal projector in the lab, where it handled all the necessary computation for the illusion. But her human brain was pretty good at imagining all sorts of things she hadn't really experienced, even as a virtual reality expert back in 25th century Los Angeles. She'd held a position of rather high responsibility keeping life in the megalopolis on an even keel, but the reality there was just that—virtual.

She hovered near the Boundary. Microscopic particles of cosmic "dust" were the only detectable matter, along with a few infinitely remote stars.

"Release the water," Yverra ordered, her voice becoming fainter. Probably Violet's "hearing" would be the first to go. No problem. She would still sense vibrations.

The truce between Violet's universe and its jealous brother remained in place. The two universes had warped around each other in a Yin Yang pattern and exchanged stable nexuses as hostages. Each now hid a nexus from the other deep within itself. *Don't destroy my baby, and I won't destroy yours.* That in itself should have been sufficient to keep the two siblings from constantly going at each others' throats—and it was—until yet another universe had popped out of the Hatchery. Now the Unwindings were beginning again on the universe's outer boundary, as both matter and some different form of matter annihilated themselves on contact. The Watchmen's "safe vantage" on the edge of the universe was no longer quite so safe. Application of copious amounts of dark matter from the Hatchery was a temporary fix, but basically they were in trouble again.

Violet merged her consciousness with one of the sleeping dust motes and could smell the water as it sprayed over her. *Choi-oi,* it was delicious. She couldn't actually taste it, but she could sense it reinvigorating her like a drink of her favorite brew from Echo Park. Soon she would absorb enough moisture to reproduce, and even to move. But that would take a little time. One by one, her eight legs began to unfurl and plump up like the Marshmallow Man. Arduously, she tried moving one of her newly swollen members. They didn't call these tiny Earth-bred creatures "slow steppers" for nothing.

☯

Violet Rain was glad to have a job as an honorary Watchman. In fact, she was glad to be alive at all. Her particular timeline since the 25th century had been destroyed, but at least the Watchmen had diverted the Unwinding long enough to let Earth take another path. Their universe still existed, and Violet still had her ancestors. Yverra's Watchmen hadn't been so fortunate. Emperor Calaneris had destroyed their civilization with a dimensional mine.

The idea was to make a little reconnaissance trip for security purposes. No retaliation on a fellow universe, or anything like that, just a little harmless spying that might prove useful someday. The multiverse was a politically complicated place, and the Hatchery didn't favor one universe over another. The Hatchery could do just fine without *their* little universe. There would be plenty more where that came from.

The inner edges of the Yin Yang were considered impenetrable, unless you wanted to risk destroying both universes in a rather unpleasant conflagration. The two had understandably developed a real aversion to each other. Besides, that was the whole point of the truce. Nobody in or out.

"If we could just beam your awareness across the boundary, we could teach you to use quantum entanglement to travel anywhere, anytime," Yverra had said. "But, entanglement alone can't carry information, it takes something lightspeed or slower to do that."

That's when Violet had proposed using *tardigrades* as vehicles. Yverra initially dismissed the idea, because the creatures were microscopic. Scaled up to human size, they would be crushed by their own mass.

"No, we need a solution that is scale-invariant," Yverra said.

"Then what about the other direction? What if I was physically as small as a waterbear?"

"Hmm, I'll think about it."

Yverra was a capable leader, but sometimes she wasn't much of an idea person.

Violet summoned Yverra to the lab.

"I think I've got something that might work," she said. "We had a huge biological databank back on Earth, which we used to create all sorts of virtual realities. For over 500 million years, Nature did a remarkable job engineering the phylum *Tardigrada*, but I've deconstructed the genome and generated a new intra-species hybrid small enough to do the job without setting off the burglar alarms. Here, take a look."

Through the scanning electron microscope, the projected cryptobiotic critter looked like nothing so much as a piece of dust.

"It's virtually hollow," Violet said. "A molecule of water will easily fit inside, activating it. But even fully distended, it's still so small that it's practically undetectable, unless you're looking for it."

"It does sound promising," Yverra said. "And it is hydrophilic. It reminds me a bit of the creatures where I come from. What will you call it? Isn't it an Earth custom to give new species a Latin name of some sort, usually in recognition of something or somebody important to the discoverer?"

Violet could swear fluently in French, Vietnamese, and Korean, but her Latin was... sketchy. Surprised by Yverra's knowledge of her planet, but grateful for the reminder, her thoughts turned to her parents, her family, and the multicultural melting pot that had been her Los Angeles neighborhood as she grew up. God, she missed green grass and trees. After a moment, she said, "I guess I would want to name it *Milnesium angelensis*, in honor of my home town."

"*Angelensis* it is," Yverra said. "This will be top secret, you understand. Everyone would probably be quite resentful if they knew they were being spied upon. If we ever need to do so, we can frame it as a *fait accompli* and convince the universes to behave diplomatically. It's in their interest as much as ours."

🍥

Call them what you like—moss pigs, waterbears, whatever. The *Milnesium angelenses* were tardigrades, or "extremophiles," capable of living under the harshest possible conditions. Hard vacuum, temperatures near absolute zero, pressures six times as high as the deepest ocean, ionizing radiation, total lack of water. They could go into hibernation and reawaken years later when conditions improved. Violet hoped her disguise as a sentient waterbear might just be what was needed to get across the Y-Y Boundary.

Now feeling comfortable in her "sea legs," Vi began to freestyle toward the Boundary. At less than a hundred Angstroms across, counting her skin, she was larger than a *mycoplasma* bacterium, but more usefully equipped with inflatable water wings. She pinched off her first tardigrade embryo. Backpedalling against the flow, she reeled out a filament of sticky silk from her central thorax and began attaching embryos along its length like beads on a rosary. It wasn't so easy to stay back of the Boundary. Sparse as the region was, literally everything in Creation was rushing that direction. She stopped at a hundred embryos.

"Who's your mommy?" she murmured. "Or maybe that should that be, 'who's your daddy?' Ha, either way, it's me. Good old parthenogenesis." The Hatchery would be envious.

She'd convinced Yverra this was yet another reason this species could be useful—no need for sexual reproduction.

And I'm just the right parasite, Vi thought wryly. Still technically a virgin. Not that she couldn't handle the real thing if it came up. Being a waterbear was just another alter ego. It seemed like everybody in L.A. had at least two avatars, to help keep their public and private lives separate. She was accustomed to dealing with different forms of reality, and sexuality was just one aspect of it. With a PhD from UCLA in VR Engineering, she had even done postdoctoral work setting up the Mars Colony VR. That place was certainly a passion incubator, with its low gravity and close quarters...

"Violet, are you paying attention? What's the status?"

"I'm here, Boss. Rainbear's brood's online," Violet replied.

"All right, start pushing the rope."

A joke from Yverra? Unheard of. She'd been high priestess of her people, used to handing out orders with little evidence of a sense of humor. Violet emitted tiny bursts of hydrogen and steered the thread orthogonal to the best known location of the Boundary. She latched onto the end and pulled it taut as it approached oblivion.

Until recently, the universe had naturally expanded outward at an accelerating rate. But now it showed great restraint, not infringing on its neighbor, in return for the same favor. Nonetheless, Vi could feel an attraction, an *urge,* to get BIGGER.

With Yverra's help, Violet's little monsters were going to try to slip across the Y-Y Boundary into the Yin Universe without it noticing. The Watchmen had gained their nickname by their ability to hack and shift time. Hacking was an old Earth term referring to mechanical wristwatches. If you pulled out the winding stem, the second hand stopped; you could push it back in to set the time exactly. People first used hacking watches in wartime to synchronize battle plans. Bank robbers also were quite fond of hacking watches.

"Number one coming," she announced. "Hack away."

The stars winked off and back on.

Did it get through? After much looking, she saw it. *Merde.* Burnt to a cinder. And still on this side.

12

"Umm, maybe you need to change the interval," Vi suggested to Yverra.

Sixty-eight waterbear cubs later, no luck.

"Let me be the first to thank you for suggesting using decoys for the first tests," Violet said. She would have been well and truly fried by now, if it hadn't been for Yverra's caution.

"I'm tapped out for ideas," Yverra said. "I'm asking Benrus and Ralff if they have any further suggestions."

"Hello, Violet? Benrus here. There's been a complication we hadn't expected."

"Yes?" Ben and Ralff were skilled time-displacing physicists who, like Violet, had been invited as honorary Watchmen by Yverra following the destruction of their timeline. Vi expected the problem to be something like an inability to perform quantum entanglement on the other side. But it wasn't that.

"The extremophiles weren't time-oxidized; they were crushed. There's a wall."

"Crushed? Out here in vacuumland?"

"Our universe's pent-up expansion is being walled against by the Yin Universe along the inner Y-Y Boundary," Ben explained. "It's possible the Boundary's becoming unstable."

"Then maybe we can find a chink in that wall," Violet said.

Yverra interrupted. "Perhaps. Regardless, we're going to need something tougher than baby waterbears."

Violet thought about the Yin-Yang Boundary, first suggested by her twelve-generations-back grandmother Virginia Sun-Jones. It would be a shame if the truce wasn't going to work out after all. And with a third universe in the picture, things were already starting to get hairy. But the usual duality of yin and yang could also mean interconnectedness.

"Come on in," Yverra said.

"But—"

"That's an order."

Back to the drawing board. Violet arrived back in her body in the space station. The station was close, but not too close, to the Boundary. Yverra, Benrus, and Ralff were huddled together with their backs toward her, talking animatedly, but eventually Ben noticed she was back.

"Water?" the tall alien offered, holding out a cup. She still wasn't used to his lack of a mouth.

"Yeah, right," Violet said, swinging her feet off the VR couch and standing. "What's next?"

"Something more pressing, "Yverra replied. "It looks like we've had another incursion. We're putting the cross-universe reconnaissance on hold while we construct a stasis field."

"You mean like the one we made as the hostage for the Yin Universe?"

"Yes. I think it's good insurance to have a lifeboat."

Violet knew Yverra was extra wary and highly loathe to repeat previous mistakes. But hiding in a stasis field didn't sound like a good idea to her. Once inside one, you couldn't tell what was happening outside. No light went in or out while it was operational. You'd just as likely step outside and find that the universe had ended billions of years ago. Better to hang out with the universe and watch it wind down slowly. Or blow up suddenly. Whichever.

"I'm still not convinced a strategy using some sort of "vaccination" maneuver wouldn't get us across the boundary relatively safely," Violet persisted. "It worked for the hostage exchange. There might be a little immune reaction at first, but then the Yin would have the right antibodies."

The three ignored her, already immersed in their next technical challenge.

"Um, okay, then, I'll leave you guys alone to design the lifeboat, while I do a postmortem on the tardigrade project."

ॐ

In her sleeping quarters aboard the station, Violet tossed and turned, going through the steps over and over in her mind. *Bo-tay,* Totally stuck. She felt like a college student who had crammed too much in at the last moment and then failed the final exam. Not that she'd ever had that experience, but she'd dreamed about it. Finally deciding that sleep was not forthcoming, she rose, threw on a mini *hanfu*, and padded down the hall toward Yverra's room. All the rooms on the space station were identical, like a budget hotel. Bed, bath, flat screen tv, lava lamp optional. She knocked on the door. A light turned on, spilling across her feet.

"Come in." Yverra sat upright on her bed, still fully dressed in frogskin leather garb. Mystical symbols bio-fluoresced faintly on her sleeves. Violet suspected that Yverra never slept, simply keeping up the pretense by staying in her room at night. There was no telling with amphibians.

"Can I talk with you, Yverra?" Yverra patted the bed, and Violet sat beside her. "I know I'm not a physicist like Ben and Ralff, but I wasn't very happy with how today's test went. I felt like you didn't trust my instincts, and that you bailed out before we had a chance to complete it."

"I didn't think we were getting the desired results, so I called a temporary end to this experiment. It doesn't mean we can't try other things."

"It's just that you don't seem to recognize that I spent two years managing Los Angeles Commercial VR, and I learned something along the way about thinking on your feet to save struggling projects," Vi said.

Yverra's unblinking metallic gaze was a little unsettling. Impassive, even cold.

"I'm sorry your feelings were hurt," Yverra replied. "Actually, it's just the opposite of what you suppose. I value your confidence and creativity more than you know, and I'd hate to lose you. I need you, Violet. If left to my own devices, I would have lived out my reign all alone and heartsick in another dimension and never been involved with traipsing the universe. And another thing: I probably appear much older than you, but I'm not your mother. I wouldn't even know how to be one. Nevertheless, I do know how to teach you to be a Watchman."

Violet was speechless at this unusual outpouring. Although she was still miffed that Yverra had ignored her, she also felt a little guilty that her idea hadn't worked out. This was her chance to prove herself useful, to become one of the team. She hadn't meant to turn this into a childish relationship squabble.

"That sounds good," she finally said. "But, may I suggest something?"

"Of course."

"Could we be partners, instead of just teacher-pupil?"

"I'll think about it."

☺

A burst of hard gamma radiation had wiped out the anchor span of the Rainbow wormhole, uncomfortably close to the station.

"I don't want to move the station if possible, because it is so ideally located," Yverra said. "It's only ten or twelve jumps to either the Boundary or through time to the Big Bang. Unfortunately, it's as if this new universe was purposely targeting us."

"We got into trouble originally by infringing on the Yin Universe's territory," Violet pointed out. "Maybe it's a misunderstanding."

Yverra demurred. "No, in that case, we were just naively expanding without knowing the consequences. This time the new universe is the aggressor."

"What do you think its beef with us is?" Violet asked.

"I don't know yet, but I'm going to visit the Hatchery to see if I can get a better idea. At the very least I can obtain more supplies of dark matter."

"We seem to be everybody's misfit brother, don't we?" Violet said. "Well, good luck."

At least with Yverra preoccupied elsewhere, Violet reasoned, she could resume her tardigrade mods. She had a good start. Maybe a few additional tinkerings would do the trick.

Who was she kidding? No one but a ghost could pass through solid matter. For now, she'd have to concentrate on improving the creature's agility and mobility. She tried narrowing and lengthening the rear two pairs of legs to resemble those of waterstriders, then covering them with hairs constructed of carbon nanotubes. Conceivably, it could walk on the wall, instead of smashing against it with a splat.

Within a few hours Yverra returned.

"I've got some bad news," she reported. " The Hatchery says it is powerless to completely prevent damage from new incursions and suggests we take whatever measures we think appropriate. I'm going to finish working on the stasis lifeboat. Get ready to bring whatever supplies you need. We leave in an hour."

"*Merde*," Violet mumbled, as she headed for the lab. It would be impossible to pack up all the tardigrade equipment. She'd have to settle for a small sample. With an unsteady hand, she poured crystals into small vials and set them in a pile atop her carefully folded hanfu. No way was she leaving without the hand-embellished silk robe her mother had given her.

A cacophonous creaking rumbled overhead. The station was beginning to break up.

"This is it!" Yverra shouted. She began chanting, as the symbols on her sleeves glowed more brightly. An eye-watering bright spot appeared in front of her, which she enlarged with hand gestures. "Everyone get in!"

Ralff and Benrus leaped inside first, followed by Yverra.

"I'll be right back," Violet said. "I forgot something." She turned and ran to the VR projector pod to grab a travel eyepiece. As she reached in, the entire station imploded.

Violet felt herself leave her body. Did she still even have a body? She reached out—yes, she still had her senses, so her body must still exist. The station was gone, and she streaked through a vast desert of darkness, gathering momentum. She'd been flung clear, but why was she still alive? Somehow, she had piggybacked onto a waterbear. Some cryptobiotes must have spilled onto the VR table. But there was no Ben here to offer her a spritz of water. She wouldn't be moving or swimming anywhere, except to certain death at the wall. She cursed herself for delaying foolishly, being unprepared yet again. In a way, it was comforting. She wouldn't have very long to think about the error of her ways before she was ground into nothingness.

♋

Violet didn't know how much time passed, but she knew it was growing short. She could feel the pull increasing.

The pressure mounted exponentially. If she had a head, it would have given her the universe's biggest migraine. A wave of what could only be called nausea shuddered through her, though she had no gut to empty. Gravitational forces beat against her like Godzilla stomping through Tokyo. She hadn't expected to go out as a *Milnesium angelensis*, though. She would miss Yverra

18

and the Watchmen. They'd helped fill a void left by the people who had loved her, the family that had meant everything. Now no one would remember her.

Suddenly the turbulent pull ceased. She floated weightless, surrounded by abyss. Where had the wall gone?

To her shock, a rather reptilian-looking hand reached out and grabbed the anterior side of her upper segment. Yverra yanked Violet back into the space station, where her body stood beside Ben and Ralff. Violet blinked.

"Yverra! I saw the station destroyed! Then, I hit the Y-Y Boundary wall, and I didn't die! How did you find me? How did you rescue me? Where—?"

"Saving you was the easy part," Yverra said. "We are simply in another dimension, one much like our original. We can join up with the original shortly, since the timeline wasn't completely obliterated. I've been remiss in teaching you how to timeslip. It's something most Watchmen can do from birth. The better question to me is, how did you get beyond the wall? I had nothing to do with that. In fact, we had just sealed the lifeboat, when the Hatchery contacted us and said you had created a breach in the wall and were in the Yin Universe in violation of the truce. Speaking of breaches, I really must find out how the Hatchery keeps finding ways to contravene my stasis bubbles. At any rate, we popped over there, retrieved you, and here we are."

Violet wasn't exactly sure yet how she had survived the wall, but she briefed her fellow Watchmen on her latest mods to *angelensis*. And while she had gained a new appreciation for Yverra's caution and judgment, now that the Hatchery had caught her red-legged on the other side of the Boundary, the jig was up, spying-wise.

"Once we explain we meant no harm, I think we'll be all right," Yverra said. "We merely took appropriate measures."

"Yeah, there's an old saying that it's better to beg forgiveness than to ask for permission," Violet replied.

"We've won a brief reprieve," Yverra said. "Why don't you get some rest, and we'll resume in the morning?"

Violet couldn't argue with that. She stumbled down the hall to her room, prepared to sleep the sleep of the dead. Disbelieving, she touched her carefully folded *hanfu*, sitting in its usual spot of honor by the bedside. Thank goodness it hadn't been destroyed in this dimension. She switched on the antique lava lamp replica—really a VR projection—and watched, mesmerized, as the wax melted and rose in blobs in the oil. The vision she craved began to resolve itself, a verdant vista, complete with an inviting wrought iron and wood bench. Violet sat down, closed her eyes, and turned her face upward to let the sun warm her face. The Earth's sun. *Her* sun…

☺

When Violet arrived at the lab eight hours later, Yverra, Ben, and Ralff were already hard at work. She again wondered if they slept at all at night. She shrugged. So what if she needed more sleep than them? Pushing down her automatic guilt response, she stepped in.

"Good morning, Violet," Ben said, pulling a chair out. "We're just starting to configure the new specs. Oh, is that a new outfit? The shoes are a very close approximation to the color of your hair. New artificial shade?"

That was as close to a compliment as Vi was likely to get, at least until she could explain that it's impolite to inquire if a lady's hair color is natural. Furthermore, anyone should know that purple wasn't a natural hair color.

"Yes, very nice," Yverra said, not looking up from her microscope.

"*Sumnida*, guys," Violet said. "What's new, Yverra?"

"We have temporary safety in this new dimension, but it is just a matter of time before the incursions begin again. We're not very far removed from our original timeline."

"Well, let's get going, then," Violet said. "I know it's been slow in coming, but I have a feeling we're on the right track. These little guys have an even stronger survival instinct than we do, and I'm starting to be able to put myself in their place for real."

"Quite perceptive," Yverra said. Violet had never noticed before how expressive Yverra's voice was. And her gold-lidded eyes were not really so alien, once you got used to them. For once, the gaze that held her seemed—approving.

"You know, Violet, between your new multiverse surveillance method and my dusting off some rusty dimensional transfer skills, I think we make a pretty good team."

"Thanks," Violet said.

Yverra stuck out her webbed hand. "You're quite welcome... partner."

21

Chapter 2.

City of Fallen Angels

The sun was shining, as usual. Another day of perfect L.A. weather. Violet's friends were busy drinking their breakfast, also as usual. The perfect weather was an illusion, the never-ending drought camouflaged by a massive VR projection over the metropolitan area.

Violet kept an eye on the myriad projection requests that she juggled. The idea of a holographic lounge had been around for a long time, but everybody had their own idea of what should be in it:

Little girls seemed to be partial to unicorns. Two suntanned high-adrenalin junkies were surfing 50-foot waves off Hawaii. Waves like that were rare in real life, but Violet tweaked the oxygen content of the water in case one of them took a spill while she wasn't looking. A breathing mask would conveniently appear within easy reach if that happened. Lifeguard duty of a sort. A history buff dressed in medieval armor brandished a heavy broadsword imbued with magical powers so he could defeat any comers on his quest for treasure.

Violet took pride in making her customers' VR adventures exciting. She quickly selected a likely opponent from the VR library of European and Asian dragons, adding a weakness against magic, so the swordsman wouldn't end up roasted like a pig on a spit. Or frightened to death by an overly realistic and dangerous VR experience. What the mind believed the body followed. Of course, she had to also track the psychological profiles of her customers. It was all too easy to plot your own suicide in VR. Violet hadn't had a death on her watch—for at least a month.

In spite of the idyllic surroundings her clients enjoyed, this was a high-stress job, keeping all the clients on this channel happy and quiet. Just a matter of fulfilling every desire of 100,000 people. "Your order delivered in 30 minutes, or it's free," was the old motto. Nowadays people expected their orders to be both instant and free. She wasn't always instant, but she was one of the best, and she'd been glad to get this gig.

In virtual reality, it was possible to become an entirely different person. Everyone carried a small computational projector that created scenery and even new virtual bodies for their wearers. Violet sat at the holographic console in a large computational and data storage warehouse, keeping her finger on the pulse of public opinion and making ratings match the popular desire.

Violet received an invitation to wildly popular actor Manny Chen's party for his "closest fans." His newest movie rose to the top of the ratings the minute it came out. Sure, he was a famous thesp, and he'd won a lot of Proppies, true, but did he have to talk about himself *all* the time? No reason she couldn't drop in to the party for a bit and schmooze with the celebs. She slipped into a silk dress and materialized in Manny's living room, where he had already launched into a tale about his latest role in a medieval Chinese actioner series for the Starwriter Ranch Studio. A small crowd of fans, mostly female, had already gathered, jockeying for spots to sit on Manny's plush oriental carpet.

Manny stroked his long white beard. "Yes, then the village summoned me to be their hero. I wasn't sure I could do it without the aid of a dragon. There were at least a hundred bandits perched all around the valley, and there was just the one of me."

"Tell us, oh wise one, what did you do next?" Violet muttered under her breath.

"Of course, I had the magic staff. I struck the ground with it twice, and the earth shook, dislodging half of the miscreants who hadn't been paying attention."

Violet couldn't help being sucked in. She'd been responsible for setting up the Kirk's Rock backdrop and earthquake effect, and it was no small feat to divert enough power to the Ranch without alerting all the little old ladies who monitored energy expenditures. Which was better—trying to save the earth, or trying to make it go away in people's heads?

"So, you didn't need a dragon?" she prompted.

"*Au contraire,* I most certainly did," Manny replied. He took another swig of his kombucha drink. A cross between chai and beer, the drink had a powerful kick of probiotics and hot ginger.

"Yum, this stuff is heavenly," he said, "both nutritious and mood-improving." He took a big bite of the spicy food on his plate, a cultural leftover from most Angeleno's Hispanic/Asian heritage.

"As I was saying, fifty or so of the bandits were swallowed up by the earth. The remainder began uttering untranslatable imprecations and waving their swords."

Violet smiled. The "untranslatable" cursing was just a bunch of loudly pronounced words in various languages that she had mixed into an angry-sounding mélange for the show. She thought it would be fun to become Manny's foil.

"Was this where the dragon comes in?" she asked coyly.

"Patience, my little flower," Manny cooed. "I first decided to bring my alternate avatar in for a little consult."

"But, isn't your avatar a meek janitor-type fellow? And blind, to boot?"

"Yes, of course. How do you think I am able to infiltrate the underworld? Nobody is afraid of Ragged Beggar Fo-Lon. Although they should be..." he said, adding an echoboom to his voice.

25

Violet looked around at Manny's groupies on the floor. Two of them were hanging on his every word, like he really did all this stuff. *Get a life,* she thought.

She was being uncharitable, she knew. Most of these girls' lives were virtual, and few had ever been "off the Ranch," officially known as VR Channel 16747.

It was just easier for the population to stay in their appointed city dwellings, which freed up land for agriculture. Here on Channel 16747, you didn't even have to leave your habitat to go to the park. There was a park right "on the grounds," with trees, grass, and birds. Even a bench to sit on for those who wanted to cogitate a while. The park was a copy of a real park that used to exist; it was just "enhanced" a little. One of Violet's favorite creations was a cyclocross race track around the perimeter. If you were up for a little competition, you could don some elbow and knee pads and jump on a shiny mountain bike.

Late in the twenty-first century, AI and VR had advanced dramatically, allowing governments and individuals to easily modify information on the networks to their own liking, until at some point no one knew what was real and what was not. The ideals of democracy had come crashing down, replaced by the promise of utopia. A pioneer in the VR field, Janus Parker, had first proposed the idea of "gated" reality. Only a select few, trusted, individuals could control virtual reality channels, because only they had access to the network and, hence, to "real" information.

Violet had jumped at the chance to take this job, even if it meant leaving Mars Colony. And John-Paul. He too was a VR expert, and they had become close while helping set up the Martian VR channel.

"Are you sure this is what you want?" John-Paul had asked. He didn't seem to get that her VR career was important to her. Though they both had a lot in common, like coming from patriarchal families and love of Asian culture, they each interpreted their roles differently. He went along with the flow, while she preferred to swim upstream.

So far Violet really liked living on Skywriter Ranch, even if most of it was a highly compute-intensive illusion, populated as it was with all these creative types, actors, directors, special-effects folks, and of course, techies like her. She was responsible for seeing that people lived their dreams—within reason. Tricking people's brains was her specialty. But it could be a bit lonely. She missed her and John-Paul's philosophical disagreements about whether what they did was actually ethical. She had argued that what they did was practical.

With the gradual global warming, population had been declining along with livable real estate. Skywriter was under frequent criticism from the environmental types, who argued against the use of VR due to its heavy power consumption.

She couldn't identify with that troglodytic attitude herself, since the sun was still shining and the fusion pumps along the coast were pretty dang efficient. Nobody drove anywhere anymore, so she didn't understand what they were complaining about.

Violet sighed and returned to reality. Or at least the Starwriter Ranch variety of reality. Off in the distance from her deck, she could see the local mountain range, the San Gabriel Mountains, again, tweaked to add just a little green to the nearly black pines hanging on to life near the top. Green was her favorite color.

Hanging out with flamboyant types like Manny, she had overcome some of her old inhibitions about dressing for success and now wore her dark hair long, with the bangs highlighted in purple. She liked to wear hanfu-style mini-dresses and high heels, all the latest fashions. But in spite of this she didn't have a new boyfriend. She felt a brief pang when she remembered her old friend on Mars. But there was no time for dating here, not enough hours in the day.

She time-sliced, stealing a bit of time to hear the continuation of Manny's story.

"Fo Lon's toe nudged the stick lying on the ground. He bent to pick it up and felt it with his fingertips," Manny said. "A smile lit his face, as his pale blue cataract-clouded eyes stared into the air. He sensed that it was magical, you see." The groupies nodded vigorously.

Violet nosed back into her multiplex feed. Not much would happen, plotwise, just Fo Lon hitting a lot of people with his stick and turning whole buildings into piles of toothpick-sized splinters. Entertaining, but all totally implausible.

She checked her queue. Still on top of things. Maybe she would check in with her buddy John-Paul on Mars. He still handled VR at the settlement. She'd shared the job with him, which was fun at first, her first real job after getting her PhD. But she'd transferred out of there when the Hollywood opportunity appeared. The communication delay to Mars made it feel like you were banished to a penal colony.

"Hey, John-Paul. Good to see you." Xoan was from the Philippines, but he preferred to be called the English equivalent, John. His normally immaculate slicked-back dark hair looked a little messier than usual. "What's up there? New virts are kind of slow right now, so I thought I'd say hi."

"Violet! How did you reach me? We've been trying to talk to Earth for days. Something is intercepting our communications, and we don't know what it is. Could you get in touch with Dr. Claveria and ask him to find out what's going on?"

"Sure," Violet said, threading in a comm line directly to her old advisor at the university so he could hear the conversation. She wasn't sure what John-Paul wanted with Claveria, though. She knew more than that old geezer...

"What's up?" she asked.

"Like I said, no Earth comm, and we've been having atmospheric anomalies. There's this wild green lightning hitting the dome right now. Some sort of electromagnetic interference, but nobody can figure out what it is and what's causing it. We're worried it's going to damage the life support systems."

"Weird," Violet agreed. "Are you getting this, Dr. Claveria?"

Claveria had introduced Violet Rain and Xoan-Paulo Hilario to Martian geology when they signed on as colonists but had never made the trip himself. He appeared on a side screen, looking like he'd been woken from a nap, his eyes puffy and gray. "Yes, thank you, Violet. Let me increase the resolution on my MarsSat network feed so we can take a closer look. My goodness, that is unusual. It's like Mars has a new planetwide aurora."

Violet was no expert, but one of the main things she remembered from orientation was that Mars didn't have a strong enough magnetic field to support a big aurora like on Earth, since its internal dynamo died out ages ago.

"Something is funneling huge amounts of solar particles right into the region where the Mars settlement is," Dr. Claveria added.

"Sorry to be pushy," Violet said, "I'm the one who called you, after all, but is this going to take long? If so, I'm going to have to request an okay to use these additional computing resources. I've just received some high-priority virt orders that need filling."

"Yes, can you please hurry?" John-Paul echoed. "Should we go underground?"

"I'm not sure," Claveria replied. "I'd recommend taking shelter, at least until we get this figured out."

29

John-Paul started to reply but was drowned out by a loud boom.

"Dr. Claveria's right," Violet said. "You'd better get to safety." As an afterthought, she added, "Hurry."

"All right, but we'll be out of communication again. We'll send someone to the surface every six hours, if we can. Damian! Let's get to the supply depot. It's got an underground shelter! Go, go, go! Talk to you soon, Vi. If you don't hear back, send help. Jesus! That was a big one. The supply dome just ripped open. Over and out." The communication ended.

"Do you think they'll be all right?" Violet asked Dr. Claveria. For once, she didn't care if the orders piled up or not. He frowned at her.

"There's something horribly wrong," he replied. "And it's originating from outside the planet." Abruptly, he cut the connection.

Though she felt a little guilty for taking time for personal calls, the situation on Mars did sound serious. Chastened, Violet returned to her job. Virt orders weren't just going to handle themselves. That's why she made the big bucks. Manny's voice at the Hollywood party drifted back into her feed.

"And so, the people offered a home to the heroic Fo Lon for saving their village, but he refused it, saying that he was happier on the road. Little Xu Lien ran up to him and presented a fragrant gold and pink rose.

"Ah the flower of peace," Fo Lon said, "may you all enjoy it forever."

Finishing his story, Manny sipped his drink and telegraphed an invitation with his eyes over the rim of his cup at Violet. *Tzao gao,* he was handsome, but she had work to do. She shook her head imperceptibly, and he turned his attention to the entranced female audience at his feet.

Violet rubbed her neck. She was beginning to get a sore throat. In the Mars excitement, she'd forgotten to take her antenvirals. She washed down two and took a hit of clean air. That plus her implant should hold her over for a while. She quickly cleared the backlog and sat back.

She'd gotten used to monitoring her vitals and meds, but the constant maintenance was a drag. For the umpteenth time today, she wished she didn't live in a post-apocalyptic world. Well, it wasn't really, but it was close enough. Close enough that nobody wanted to face reality. Especially the reality of what appeared to be happening on Mars.

Also, she was a little miffed that she'd missed the part with the dragon.

*****~~~~~*****

Chapter 3.

Never Speak to Strangers

Xoan-Paulo Hilario lay in the corner, gasping for what little air remained in the supply dome. It had been a mad scramble to get this far after the incursion of the weird green lightning into the Mars settlement.

"The main dome's down!" Damian had reported as they sat next to each other in the control center.

Xoan hoped the call he'd finally managed to make to Violet and Dr. Claveria on Earth wasn't too late. Violet was a bit of a flake, but she'd gotten more mature since she'd become a VR administrator in L.A. She still used his nickname of John-Paul, though, like she thought of him as some historical naval hero, or maybe a Pope. Who knew? Too bad. At one time, he'd thought she was THE ONE. Then she said she just wanted to be friends. He had wanted more. Exasperated, she had called him *collant.* He had to look that up. Now the best he could do was imagine that Violet still cared. He was counting on it.

The day had started off ordinarily enough. Not being much of a breakfast eater, Xoan balanced an insulated pod of coffee on the narrow ledge next to his monitor. Coffee was still an imported luxury, until the greenhouses could produce enough to satisfy the colony's demand.

"I see you brought me a coffee," Damian joked. "Where's the cream? Gotta keep my weight up, or I'll turn into a skinny scarecrow like you. You know you don't always have to wear your uniform to sit in front of a screen, right?"

Xoan came from a tropical climate, and despite his earlier training in Antarctica and no matter how warm they turned up the heat, Mars always seemed cold. The landscape here was actually quite similar to a desert on Earth. If you didn't count the lack of air, you might think you were in Iceland or another frosty clime on Earth. Reddish tundra stretched off into the distance toward Arsia Mons. Though they were near the equator, the ground was permanently frozen. From the colony's front side, the only landmark of interest was a volcanic dike with a flat top. The three main domes of the colony nestled alongside the base of a ridge, protected somewhat from the occasional storm. Though storms could blow through rapidly, the fine dust they kicked up tended to stay in the atmosphere a long time, lowering visibility and making EVAs more hazardous. Plans called for fracking equipment to dig tunnels to connect the domes, which would make it unnecessary to wear protective gear to move between them, but those construction materials hadn't yet made the six-month trip. Chunks of rock lay scattered across the plain, leftovers from some ancient volcanic eruption and a nuisance to those driving the rovers to gather samples. Shelter and essentials took first priority.

Luckily, coffee was considered one of those essentials.

Not being much of a breakfast eater, Xoan balanced an insulated pod of the hot, bitter stuff on the narrow ledge next to his monitor. Coffee was still an imported luxury, until the greenhouses could produce enough to satisfy the colony's demand.

Xoan had started to formulate a wise retort, when the violent electrical storm had knocked out the lights. They'd switched to backup, but the fix had only been temporary, with Damian's report of the demise of the main dome.

"Forserious?" Xoan muttered. Outside, brilliant lightning bolts exploded in the thin air, searing impressions on his retinas and illuminating the walls with a glaring green. Coruscating sparks littered the ground, the burning debris from the residential dome. The short-lived fires would soon be snuffed out by the lack of oxygen.

"Let's get over to the supply depot," Xoan said, clenching his teeth. If they were under attack, it had the advantage of being mostly underground, maybe out of sight of whatever terrorist organization had it in for the settlement. He hadn't heard of any nationalistic saber-rattling lately, so this warlike act was baffling. Who would spend a fortune on destroying a neutral, not to mention peaceful, scientific station?

He slipped on his breather and lightweight pressure suit and pressed his hand against the airlock door, before donning heavy gloves. Though the temperature outside was 50 below, a rather balmy summer day, there was no time to don a full Extravehicular Mobility Unit.

"Stick close," he advised his companion, crouching and beginning a clumsy running gait across the barren red dirt toward the partially hidden door of the supply dome. All around them, more domes exploded, then imploded.

The ground below his feet shook, throwing him onto his chest. The concussion sent one of his gloves flying off. Deafened, he crab-walked to look behind. Damian lay staring at the sky. Blood smeared his breather and seeped in a rapidly congealing pool from the back of his head.

Sickened, Xoan uttered a small moan. Damian was much too obviously dead. Feeling a stinging pain in his hand, Xoan clenched it against his side. Lack of atmospheric pressure would cause blood vessels to explode on any exposed skin surface. He crawled the last few meters to the airlock door, only to find its hinges loosened. His breather was damaged too; he could hardly get air into his lungs.

Clambering in, he pushed the red button to open the inner airlock door.

"Exterior door ajar. Close before equalizing," the motherlike robotic voice said—sensible, but in this case life-threatening. He would have to fake it out somehow, and quickly. He reset the door and put his shoulder into it, tapping the perimeter with his good hand to create a seal.

"Equalizing," the voice said. *Thank God.* As soon as the door opened a crack, he squeezed in.

"Error. Exterior door ajar. Close before equalizing." He'd just made it. The inner door closed with a snick behind him. He was trapped but glad to be alive and inside. He took off his breather to reserve his air supply. The air inside the supply dome was still barely breathable, but he didn't know for how long. He wondered how many casualties there might be.

The lower level contained a lichen farm, along with other tough "extremophile" species that had proven hardy on Earth. The plants produced oxygen, but not enough to make the lab atmosphere breathable. Experiments in terraforming were just getting started and were expected to take a long time. Xoan began to regret that he hadn't taken the time to put on an EMU. It would have made him independent of the dome HVAC systems, at least for a day or two.

He sat down in the corner, breathing shallowly, for all the good it would do. He remembered stories of the early Mars explorers, especially how Tom Howard had sacrificed himself to allow his shipmates enough resources to make it back home. Nowadays, nobody expected to go home. He'd signed a waiver. No reverse immigration. On the other hand, Vi had gotten a work visa to return to Earth. So the occasional rescue party could be expected, couldn't it? Probably not. People were expected to use VR to overcome any doubts or homesickness about leaving their home forever.

With VR, everyone here could choose the imaginary surroundings of their choice. The key word was imaginary. It took a great deal of computer resources to provide virtual surroundings for everyone, but Mars had that in spades, with one of the most powerful quantum installations and unlimited solar and fusion energy. The only resource they really lacked was water.

It became eerily silent. The lights flickered, then remained steady. Had communications returned too?

Xoan considered how to plot his last scenario. He'd record it, of course. Posterity might be interested, if only to find someone to blame. His father would like that. He'd leave a respectful and apologetic message, while hiding his terror and sorrow. He may as well leave one for Violet, too. They'd only done the deed in VR, and then she'd gotten cold feet, but their avatars had shared an unbreakable bond.

"Activate all comms. Begin broadcast, destination L.A. VR, Earth. Date July 1, 2416.

"This is Xoan-Paulo Hilario, Redstone Base, Howard Plateau, Mars. Based on satellite observations, we believe we are under attack by an unknown perpetrator, who is bombarding us with some sort green laser, or perhaps it is electromagnetic pulse radiation. At any rate, all of the domes are damaged, and I am trapped. I may be the only survivor." He paused and started a new message.

"Private message for Domingo Hilario, Manila VR Channel 736666. Subject: Mars disaster. Dad, if you get this, our Mars colony has been attacked. I think this attack must have been the result of treachery. All of our settlers were completely vetted before they emigrated, and security is the best that money can buy, so I can't imagine one of them is involved. Please find out who was responsible and bring them to justice. He's killed over 200 innocent, wonderful people. Message Send: Immediately."

Extremophile/Juliana Rew

"Private message for Violet Rain, Los Angeles VR Channel 16747 Administrator. Subject: Mars disaster. Hey, Violet, it's looking like I'm not going to be able to make it back to Earth, at least not in this lifetime, so please get this message to my father. And I just wanted to say, I'll see you on the other side. Love you, John Paul."

Xoan couldn't move. His hand was swollen and paralyzed, sticky, puce-colored blood gluing it to the floor. His failure to work out daily to keep up his muscle mass had caught up to him. But with the low gravity, it hadn't seemed necessary. Though it hurt like hell, he managed to peel his hand away.

The room was cold. A chill colder than winter. Absolute cold.

Ice and rime sprang out of the walls, exuding spikes of white crystal, then sublimating as fast as they appeared.

He must be hallucinating. If it was actually that cold, he should be dead.

"Soon."

He tried to look around for the source of the voice. Probably hallucinating, one of those near-death experiences everyone talked about. He tried to speak. Couldn't.

Who are you? he wondered. Actually, he didn't care about that. If it was going to be his last thought, why not instead ask, "Why?" Gradually gathering a lungful, he gurgled out the syllable.

"You are the last," the voice said.

A figure began to materialize, a tall, ghostlike presence. If he didn't know better, he'd claim the apparition was an ancient Fu Manchu imitator. A hologram, obviously. There were a lot of people of Asian descent in L.A., like Violet Rain. He had a brief moment of hope.

"Who?"

38

"I ask the questions here, not you." So, not sent by Vi, then.

"You'll get nothing from me, you... bastard." That was stupid, wasting his breath like that, but he could swear that he heard an annoyed gasp, as though he'd talked back to the teacher in class.

"Take him, Blauw. Get him onto the table," the strange specter commanded. A burly red-haired man hefted him up onto his shoulder, sending waves of pain across Xoan's blackened arm. Dark spots danced across his eyes.

☉

His vision began to clear. He must have blacked out. His face burned in the cold, but surprisingly the rest of him didn't hurt. He still couldn't move, this time because he was tied down. A needle-thin beam of dazzling green light appeared at the foot of the table. Suddenly the beam cut upward between his feet, and moved toward his torso.

All bravery deserting him, he decided to tell them anything they wanted, if only they'd cancel the coming torture. Inexorable, the beam kept moving, piercing his body and kicking up a fine spray of blood. As it burned its way toward his heart, he knew they weren't simply torturing him. He was truly dying. They were utterly fileting him like a steak. Soundlessly, he screamed.

☉

Xoan awoke. He didn't know how much time had passed. He tried blinking, but he didn't seem to have eyelids. He lifted his hand to feel his face, and saw only a metal stub with five small slits.

"Great, you're awake. We can finally begin reeducating you."

Perhaps this was some sort of Sinoese plot. Their ancestors had been unsuccessful in their attempt hundreds of years ago to reeducate the populace to accept a totalitarian regime.

"You are now a subject of the Emperor Calaneris XXIII and his Scientists," the hairy-faced redhead said. Ah, this was something imperial, which was close enough to totalitarian. But what country?

Xoan found he could speak, though not with his own voice. He asked, "Why did you attack our colony?"

"You don't need to worry your pretty little head about that," the man answered. "Besides, we're about to replace it with an even better one." He grinned.

Xoan felt a tug at his neck, followed by a loud snap. His brain felt like it was filled with a hive of angry bees. He reached up again. His stub of a hand was rather crudely rendered against a background grid of faintly phosphorescing lines. This was like a VR chamber that hadn't yet been fully vrekked. His eyes were gone, making him dependent on VR. The realization of being permanently disfigured crept into his consciousness. At least he still had his brain—unless they were going to replace that too.

His dread grew, waiting for him every time he regained consciousness after each new procedure. Bright lights shone in his cybernetic eyes, maxing out his sensors and waking him again from sweet oblivion. His hand had been replaced with an arm bristling with knobby metal fingers. Each finger seemed to be equipped with lethal-looking implements, including an automatic long-range high-velocity shotgun (he discovered that accidentally, by blowing a grapefruit-sized hole in the opposite wall), rotating surgical drill, something resembling an old-fashioned straight-razor, a long switchblade, exploding flechettes (also discovered accidentally), and ammonia spray.

The man with red hair and blue eyes entered the room. "Well, now, you've created quite a mess," he said. "But luckily, you can't hurt your masters. Things are looking quite good." Xoan wished he could cry.

Laughing, the man called Blauw leaned over Xoan, injecting him with still more anesthesia. They were removing his body, one piece at a time. He couldn't imagine why they were turning him into a robot. Why not just build a robot? And the deadly instrumentation did not bode well. They were the kind of weapons used to kill people.

There was nothing for it but to die, take himself out of the game. Yes, it had to be done. He'd never been religious and had argued with his father about it numerous times. He didn't know how to do it, but he'd heard of plenty of people who just up and died unexpectedly, like from grief when a loved one died. He had plenty of grief, although it was for his own self. This would be the final end. He raised his robot arm and stuck a blade into his eye socket. His vision went black. He felt himself rise, taking one last look at the horrendous wreck of his former self below.

"Oh, no you don't," Blauw said. "Here's another mess you've made. No dying allowed, until we say so." Xoan's consciousness crashed back to the ground.

"You're amazingly resilient," Blauw said. "But honestly, it would be easier if you would stop fighting us." *Easier for whom?* "We'll have to beef up your self-preservation circuits," Blauw said. "Might as well beef up your killing instincts as well." Along with his body, they wanted to destroy his humanity. That was an even greater horror.

If he ever escaped, he would take revenge on these barbarians.

"Yes. Revenge. A good instinct to have on hand for the work ahead," Blauw said. Xoan vowed they would never change his soul.

☙

He found himself standing upright for the first time since coming to this prison. A hairy ape looked up at him, showing his disgusting white teeth and jumping around on his spindly legs, babbling incoherently and sticking probes into new outlets on his body.

"The Emperor's going to like you a lot. I think I'm going to call you... No, on second thought, I'm not going to give you a name. You are simply the Emperor's Enforcer, that's all." It dawned that the ape was the Emperor's human lackey, Blauw. He remembered the Emperor, and he remembered Blauw. Blauw wasn't worthy to serve the Emperor.

Enforcer snarled, but no sound issued from his face. He generated waves of hatred toward the ape-man, who seemed totally unaffected. On the other hand, he felt undying love for the Emperor. He would prove it. He felt a thrill of electricity run through him like a freight train, and his accessories all deployed at once. This was great. He could slice, dice, burn, poison, and stab, all at once.

"Down, boy," the ugly Blauw said. "You will be tasked at making sure the last of the interfering humans are eradicated. Does that sound good?"

It sounded divine. He only wished the Emperor would let him kill this ugly ape human too. Maybe if he did a good job, he would be given that privilege.

"Looks as if we need to do some tinkering to give you better control, Mr. Enforcer Sir. You had a little premature ejaculation there." The apelike man showed his ugly teeth again. Enforcer wished he could grind his bones to dust. His hatred and resentment grew, until... blackness.

⟲

Blauw knelt before Calaneris, then rose upon his signal. The emperor commonly assumed a larger-than-life aspect toward the subjects he ruled, and towered over Blauw, even while sitting on an elaborately carved royal throne. Blauw wondered what he really looked like. Probably something too horrible for humans to imagine. He had to admire that. Hovering behind the emperor were several humanoid AIs, who he called his "Scientists." All were dressed as courtiers from ancient Earth. Blauw had been a pirate from 19th century Earth who was drowning in a shipwreck during the Unwinding, when Calaneris swept in and saved his life. He'd been loyal ever since.

"Your Highness, the Enforcer unit is proceeding as well as can be expected, for a human. A former human, I should say. We've removed any loyalty to his species. Or to any other organic species, for that matter. He's loyal only to you. I was originally going to suggest giving him doglike protective circuitry, but you were right to preserve his human aptitude for killing. It will make the unit much more resourceful."

"Can we trust it to do the job? I may be the Emperor, but I report to a higher power myself," Calaneris said. "I've got the Scientists working around the clock to break into the Watchmen's security measures so we can finish off this universe and get the hell out of here."

"I understand, Your Highness. We've run into a snag with removing the twenty-fifth century Earth/Mars timeline. The twenty-first century primitive woman you wanted me to kill, Virginia Sun-Jones, got her hands on a dimensional transceiver. She calls it her "jewel of power" and has been using it to look for her family. She showed up on our doorstep just now. Somebody else sent her to the nineteenth century, and we tried to kill her there, but she managed to jump to the twenty-fifth century, where she was again able to defend herself. It appears someone besides us is after her."

"Is it the Watchmen?" Calaneris asked, a tremor in his voice.

"I don't know yet. I doubt she even knows who the Watchmen are. But somebody managed to put her twenty-fifth century descendant, a Violet Rain, into stasis."

"What? That cursed stasis technology!" Calaneris exclaimed. "We've got to learn how the Watchmen are able to do that. They are standing in the way of the planned demolition of this sorry excuse for a universe."

"Sire, the Scientists have calculated probabilities of the location of Violet Rain, extrapolated over a period from the twenty-first century timeline of Virginia Sun-Jones, to the present. We have a bead on her now. At some time in the past, Violet Rain visited Virginia Sun-Jones in the twenty-first century.

"Violet, Virginia. Why do they all have to have the same names? It's very confusing," Calaneris said.

"I agree," Blauw said. At least, now it will be a simple matter of sending the Enforcer to kill Violet and pinch off her timeline."

"Then, by all means, send it," Calaneris agreed. "I don't need to know the details."

"And, to tie up all loose ends, when she dies, the Enforcer will too. It's from her timeline."

"Well, don't tell the robot that."

"Of course not, Sire," Blauw said. "I'm just trying to explain why we selected this particular person for this task. He was a close friend and former suitor of Violet Rain and should be able to approach her without suspicion once we restore his former appearance."

"Well, get on with it, then," Calaneris said. "And get that fucking jewel off of the Jones woman. It should be mine anyway."

Blauw bowed and scraped his way out of the throne room and left Calaneris's palace in the capital city of Tian Ming Zhing. He paused briefly to admire his own handiwork. The air outside the imperial compound was perfumed with the blooms of rare plants and flowers from across the galaxy, all retrieved personally by Blauw, who had the honorary title of "Imperial Gardener." Colorful festival tents and hidden picnic spots dotted the landscape. A phalanx of Scientists floated a discreet distance away, recording his every activity. Better not to verbalize what he was really thinking:

"If the Emperor, as he likes to call himself, would just listen to my suggestions to use complexity theory to nip off the creation of the universe at the Big Bang, all of this scheming would be unnecessary," he subvocalized. "Oh well, the pay's the same either way." He noticed he was biting his nails past the quick again, a nasty habit. He shoved his hands into his pockets.

After a walk of about a hundred yards through a particularly lush meadow of bluebells, Blauw and the Scientists entered the glass-enclosed pavilion, housing the Emperor's laboratory. A row of arched doorways protected by force fields held the subjects of some of the Emperor's arcane experiments, including the man from Mars.

"I'll handle this," Blauw said. "You wait here."

The Scientists nodded, leaving only one of their number at the entrance, to monitor the force fields and cater to Blauw's orders.

Blauw took out his remote with a kill switch, in case the Enforcer got a little too feisty, took a deep breath, and entered the lab. The cyborg was swinging a large saber around its head, almost too quickly for the eye to see. At best it was just a blur.

"Greetings, Enforcer. The Emperor has a mission for you."

The twirling blade stopped abruptly. "Yes?" The voice was nearly monotone, but there was an unmistakable eagerness.

"You will visit the past and kill a human woman named Violet Rain."

"I will kill all the humans," Enforcer volunteered.

"No, just killing Violet Rain will be sufficient," Blauw said. The other humans would all be superfluous. "Did I mention that you hate her especially, because she betrayed you and allowed you to die on Mars?"

"Many times," the Enforcer agreed. "Consider it done. How do we start?" It took a step toward Blauw.

"Not so fast. You need to look like a human named Xoan-Paulo Hilario. And we need to fill you in on the

45

proper behavior for Earth during that era so you can blend in. You may not even have to use any of the weaponry we've outfitted you with. You could just quietly strangle her, for example. The Scientists will download all the information you will need about where to find her."

"Excellent," Enforcer said. "This Earth woman is as good as dead."

Blauw turned to leave, tossing a "Good luck" over his shoulder. Outside, he began to whistle.

Perhaps the Emperor's scheme wasn't so foolish, after all. Blauw'd built the Enforcer with all the very best components; it was practically indestructible. And it no longer remembered that it was once Xoan-Paulo Hilario. Maybe it could conceivably fall apart all at once at the end of an eon, like the proverbial one-horse shay, but not before it fulfilled its mission to end the Sun-Jones timeline and with it the Earth.

He could hardly wait to have a beer with Violet's newly arrived ancestor, Virginia Sun-Jones and find out how the hell she managed to get here. Time travel was a slippery slidy thing. It would be nice to bed a human woman again. Right before he killed her.

*****~~~~~*****

Chapter 4.

Baby Blue Chasm

As she floated in her tardigrade body through the Hatchery of Universes, Violet gazed in awe. Of course, she didn't actually use eyes here, but the awe was real. She was at least fourteen orders of magnitude smaller than the quadrant of space-time reserved for budding universes. Against such vastness, she felt even tinier. How could she stop these new Unwindings, if she didn't even know for sure that's what they were?

The first Unwinding had been fallout from a dispute between the human-inhabited universe and its nearest neighbor, the Black Universe. Violet's ancestor, Virginia Sun-Jones had proposed the Yin-Yang truce, and *her* daughter Grace and son-in-law Eric had stayed in the Hatchery to administer the peace.

The Hatchery had seemed nothing more than a fanciful concept to humans like Violet. But since the Unwinding, she'd discovered the concept as real as the waterbear body she currently rode in. Invisible to the naked eye but present nonetheless. Drifting in the formless void, Violet recalled Yverra's explanation that the Hatchery consisted of an immense collection of pent-up gravity waves, placed there by the Makers under the supervision of an intelligent baby-sitter entity called Golaeth. Like invisible "eggs," new universes waited to be born while Golaeth stabilized the distribution and creation of matter within them.

47

This would be Violet's first encounter with the fabled Golaeth, since Yverra had conducted all the previous strategic missions by the Watchmen. As insignificant as she was, she'd been spotted trespassing by Golaeth, who had the power to disband universes that either didn't function consistently or caused problems for their sibling universes. Now she was compelled to explain why she'd gone over Yverra's head with what looked like a truce violation. She had a terrifying responsibility, but she was a Watchman now. Violet straightened her bodiless shoulders and prepared to request an audience with Golaeth and Grace.

"Identify yourself, microbe. Failure to do so will result in timeline erasure."

"It's me, Violet, from Earth," she said. "I'm here to see Grace and Eric." She'd overlooked the fact that her personal projector still portrayed her as a tardigrade.

"You Watchmen should work on a better communication protocol. Golaeth just about deleted you." It was Grace. Violet would have expected her to be more diplomatic than that, or at least moderately courteous, but she relaxed a bit. Violet still felt a bit insecure in her role as a Watchman, and her timeslip skills were, to say the least, a bit shaky. Yverra was always saying, "Time is your friend," but she wasn't so sure.

"Sorry, Violet said. "Yverra told me we'd gotten the okay to do whatever was necessary, and I didn't stop to think that there might be a protocol for visits..." Watchman or no, Violet felt like an outsider once more, not even welcomed by her human ancestor. Suddenly she remembered—she didn't look very human at the moment.

"How come you're got up like a bug instead of a person?" Grace asked, again not too tactfully. "Land over here for reassembly."

A large structure materialized, reminding Violet of the empty warehouse she had worked in when she administered her VR channel on Earth. The building, if that's what it was, was lit from within, but there weren't any noticeable light sources, not even stars. Violet felt herself getting bigger, a sensation she was getting familiar with. She turned her head from side to side and was pleased to feel her hair swirling around her. She could even smell her coconut shampoo. She hadn't realized how important her sense of smell was before.

"Thanks a lot, I feel like my old self again, and this place is like a virtual reality channel on steroids," Violet breathed a moment later, stepping off the platform and embracing Grace. Someone had done a very good job with reality here. She glanced around at the homelike surroundings. At any moment, it felt like John-Paul could have given her a shout-out from Mars. She swallowed a lump in her throat and dragged her mind back from the lonely abyss to the present. She was in the Hatchery. With the all-seeing Grace and her new husband Eric. "There, now I'm human. Happy?"

Grace was Violet's umpty-great-aunt, but she was the same age as Violet; they were just from different timelines. They looked like they could be sisters, petite with long, dark hair and big brown eyes. Grace was Virginia's daughter, and even more powerful than her mother. But in reality, they were more like distant cousins. Virginia had adopted Eric's child from a previous affair before he and Grace married. So Violet was Eric's blood relative, but not Virginia and her husband Alan's.

"How about a beer?" Eric asked, opening up a mini-fridge and pulling out a Rolling Rock. He cracked open the green bottle, wiped the condensation off, and handed it to Grace. She *was* a little thirsty, actually. She took a long sip.

The epitome of a Viking warrior, with his blonde quiff and tattooed arms, Eric towered over her. She still wasn't sure Grace's new husband could totally be trusted. He'd betrayed Grace more than once, even if he had managed to save her in the end. Well, Grace loved him, and he was family, if only distantly. Eric took Violet by the shoulders and held her at arm's length.

"You know, you're really good looking. Rad miniskirt. Do you want me and Grace to hook you up?" Eric asked, wiggling his eyebrows. She was at a loss for words, not sure what to say to a grandfather who was acting creepy.

"Leave her alone, Eric," Grace said. "He's only teasing. Just ignore him."

Eric stepped back. "Sorry, kid, I'm just glad to see you." He assumed a sheepish expression, like a puppy who still wasn't quite housebroken.

Violet was happy that Grace had nipped this particular conversation in the bud, but she feared that anyone with two eyes could see that she was lonely. Twenty-nine and not getting any younger. Hanging out with Yverra and the two aliens didn't help, either. Everyone probably wondered whether she was gay. Maybe she was. Some days, anyway. She hadn't seen another human being in ages, just what she could cook up in her imagination. Though she could imagine quite a lot, which was another nice thing about VR. Come to think of it, she had arrived without her personal VR projector, which she'd left behind when she assumed her tardigrade body. Maybe Grace could fix that...

"Um, thanks, Grandfather, but I really came to talk with you guys about the latest incursion. Yverra and I have worked out some time-hacking techniques to enable us to do reconnaissance across the Yin-Yang Boundary, but we still don't understand why new instabilities are occurring. The Unwindings are starting again."

"*Yverra made that clear in her previous visit,*" the voice of Golaeth interjected. "*Why have you returned?*"

Violet exhaled slowly. It would not do to get angry. Golaeth was a gargantuan presence with quantum powers well beyond her understanding, and it acted only in its own interests. Violet swallowed, recalling that

Golaeth had actually been responsible for some of the destructive events of the Unwinding, including probing the humans' universe with high-energy radiation, and wherever it probed, creatures in her universe died. She'd seen the green probes firsthand on Earth. Luckily, her universe had Virginia and Grace to impress upon it the seriousness of the situation. Sometimes bosses were at such a high level that they couldn't truly understand what was happening on the factory floor. Grace would get it, though. She liked living.

"I'm here to ask for diplomatic assistance," Violet said. "So far, our communication attempts have been unsuccessful. We nearly got wiped out ourselves on STS-99 after a recent attack. You may have noticed that I'm in a slightly different dimension than the last time you saw me."

"I thought there was something different about you," Grace said. "Besides the bug body you arrived in, I mean. Let me adjust."

Violet felt a slight shiver as Grace scanned and reset her.

"I've readjusted Yverra and Ben and Ralff, too," she said. "I'll get to Calaneris in due time. No need for you all to have to keep jumping into other dimensions constantly."

"Thanks, Grace." Due to a fluke in her universe, Grace had been born the "Living Cintamani," born with powers quite beyond anything ordinary humans were capable of. Except maybe Grace's mother, Virginia. But even she had to use the Cintamani jewel, a "magical" quantum device, to focus her powers. Grace was the closest thing to a god that Violet could comprehend.

"I guess what I'd like to ask is how the Hatchery manages to stay clear of disasters and disagreements between alternate universes," Violet said. "Like, can you and Golaeth say, 'settle down, you two,' or something like that?"

51

"No, unfortunately," Grace replied. "Golaeth was hard pressed to keep our universe and the Black universe apart before, and was slowly losing control. We were lucky that Virginia and the Watchmen were able to establish the truce."

"Through you, you mean," Violet pointed out. "That's why Golaeth wants to keep you here in the Hatchery, right?"

"It's not keeping me here. *I'm* keeping me here. This is where I want to be, doing inter-universe negotiations and helping to keep the peace. It's what I was made for. Eric and I are very happy here."

"Well, the Watchmen are happy you're here too, but we could use some help in our neck of the woods. Every time an incursion wipes out a timeline in our universe, Poe thrashes around in pain and wreaks even more destruction. Pardon the metaphor." Virginia had given the universe containing humanity the nickname "Poe," after mystery writer Edgar Allen Poe, after following the clues it was giving about the incursions.

"Yes, we see that. I can adjust, but I can't restore what's been deleted," Grace mused. "What do you think, Eric?"

"I think we need to get to the bottom of what is ganging up on Poe. It just sounds too similar to previous occurrences to just be a coincidence."

"Do you think the Black Universe is involved?" Grace asked.

"Maybe not directly, but possibly one of his disgruntled minions."

"Like Emperor Calaneris? He was plotting against us before," Violet said.

"No—" Eric and Grace said simultaneously. Grace continued, "We feel he is totally rehabilitated since the truce. Whoever it is has cloaked itself rather cleverly." Eric nodded in agreement. Grace gazed into the air and spoke. "Golaeth, have you created any new universes that I am unaware of?"

The disembodied entity replied, "***The Makers would end my employment if they deemed my actions anything except neutral. There appears to be a rogue universe, this time not of my making.***"

"Well, he can't stay hidden forever," Eric said. "Sometime he's got to come out in the open to gather the spoils."

"How do you know it's a 'he'?" Violet asked.

"Eric's right," Grace said, ignoring Vi's joke. "I am going to strengthen the dragnet."

"And like I said earlier," Violet said, "we Watchmen have a new reconnaissance method that we're itching to try, as long as it doesn't cause an inter-universal incident."

Golaeth spoke up again. "***Yverra gave us to believe you would avoid violating the truce with the Black Universe at all costs.***"

Violet felt the hairs on her arms rise. "Um, I—uh—"

Grace reassured Golaeth in a soothing tone, "It's all right. There hasn't officially been a breach of the Y-Y Boundary, only an incursion into the human universe." Deftly, she changed the subject. "By the way, Violet, I meant to congratulate you on becoming a Watchman. It's quite an accomplishment."

"Thanks," Violet said. "It's good to have someone to work with. They're almost becoming like family. Almost." Shaking, she was glad Grace was there to handle Golaeth.

"You know," Grace said, "you've still got Mom. I know she's only your grandmother by adoption, but she adores you, she's told me herself many times. We've still got Earth's timelines up to the year 2416, when you were caught in that truly grievous incursion. You could visit anybody in the past."

"Maybe I'll do that sometime," Violet replied. "It'd be amazing to see great-grandmother again and stand on some real ground and see some real sky."

"How about now?" Grace said.

🌀

Violet found herself in front of a modest Craftsman-style house fronted by a substantial porch. Uncertain, she reached to touch the tiny Virtual Projection Assistant she wore under her blouse. The device was still attached, although it was in power conserve mode. Grace must have restored her VPA along with her human body. Violet wondered if it had all of its VR libraries, but decided she'd leave it powered off, to avoid inadvertently creating any more time discrepancies for Grace to have to clean up.

Reassured, Violet looked around. A neatly manicured lawn stretched out at her feet. The sunshine was eye-wateringly bright, instead of the hazy mustard color she was used to in L.A. The smell of warm earth permeated the humid air, quite a contrast to the no-smell of STS-99 and the hydrocarbon tang of L.A. She wasn't sure she'd ever felt real grass before and reached down to touch it. Soft. Deliciously fresh. She wondered if it was edible.

Standing back up, she looked around, wondering where had Grace sent her. To her many-great grandparents? They lived four hundred years before her time, which meant everything she saw was *real*. Virtual reality was just in its infancy. A rounded box mounted on a post displayed a number, 2225 Paonia.

Vi tugged at her miniskirt and tried to stand tall. She hadn't had a chance to talk to Grandmother Sun-Jones since the truce was declared. Homesick after their adventures traipsing around the universe, Virginia and her computer scientist husband Alan had returned home to North Carolina, safe in the past. But what was *she* doing here, in a timeline that wasn't really hers? Well, she had to admit Virginia and Alan were experts on Unwindings. *Just go with the flow, Violet,* she told herself. That's what they did in the 21st century, right?

A faint scratching noise came from behind the house. Taking off her spike heels, she tiptoed through the tender shoots and onto a small flagstone path.

A middle-aged woman in a red bandana and jeans knelt in the dirt, digging with a small trowel and mumbling, "Out, out, damned weed."

"Hello?" Violet said, tentatively.

The woman turned, saying nothing and raising a gloved hand to her face to block the sun.

"Grace? Is that you?" the woman asked. She jumped to her feet and brushed at the front of her pants. "Why didn't you tell me you were coming? I'll tell your dad."

"No," Violet rushed to say. "Grace sends her regards, but it's only me, Violet Rain, I'm afraid." Grace hadn't sent her regards. She didn't realize how lucky she was to still have a mother. Violet swallowed and blinked back moisture that gathered unexpectedly in her eyes.

"Violet! This is wonderful. Whatever are you doing here? I assume this is Grace's doing, or Yverra's..."

"Close, Grandmother Virginia. I'm a Watchman now, but Grace sent me. Sorry for the short notice."

"God, no. I'm thrilled to see you. It's me who should be sorry about mistaking you for Grace. You look so much like her it's scary. Come here and give me a hug."

Hugs. Violet remembered this quaint 21st century custom, of which she'd become quite fond.

"I believe Grace-in-her-infinite-mercy has decided that I am lonely and that it would do me good to visit you."

"Just lonely? Anything else?" Virginia had an uncanny way of cutting to the chase. Grace was her daughter, all right.

"Ginny?" Great-grandfather Alan opened the sliding glass door. "I heard voices."

"Look who's come for a visit, Alan," she said. "We can make up the bed in the guest room. This will be a good excuse to barbecue some ribs and ply her with alcohol until she tells us why she's really here," Virginia said. "Hmm. Not even a toothbrush, I see."

"I didn't have a chance to pack," Vi admitted. Besides, she didn't own a toothbrush. The sonic cleaner in her bathroom on STS-99 took care of all that, plus conducted a complete daily physical.

"Don't worry, we'll go shopping for some clothes for you," Virginia said, her eyes crinkling up. "All the summer sales are going on."

"Oh, don't go to any trouble," Vi said. "I usually just wear this dress."

"It's lovely, dear—the shoes are especially *stylish*—but around here if you wear the same outfit every day, people begin to wonder if you're sleeping around. You know, I kind of miss the days when I was time traveling and got to wish myself up a different get-up every week..." She looked at Alan. "I'm just kidding. I was miserable."

"Are the purple bangs all right?" Violet asked. She considered them her signature look.

"Yes, those are right in style," Virginia said, grinning. "Come on, let's get you settled. You're probably aching for a shower."

☺

"Try the limoncello?" Alan asked, offering the bottle of shockingly yellow liquid.

"Thanks, but I don't drink," Vi responded. "Although I could... My meds would take care of it."

"What kind of meds?" Alan asked. "If you don't mind my asking, that is."

Baby Blue Chasm

"Not at all. They're antenvirals, meant to ward off most of the nasty things in the environment that are out to get you." She held out her arm to show the patch.

"What about your natural immunity?" Virginia asked.

"Those days are long gone—we were hanging on by a thread against all the pollution and biotic changes. Everybody from my time has these updated every few years when they come up with new vaxxes."

"Well, let's hope the environment here isn't too much for your system," Virginia said. "If it is, I'll call Grace to give you a booster shot."

"Booster shot?"

"Nevermind. Tell me more about your work with the Watchmen."

"Yverra has made some breakthroughs in time-hacking, and I'm working on some vehicles for carrying consciousness across dimensions. Like, recently I was using a tardigrade species to slip past the Yin-Yang Boundary." She might as well break it to Grandmother Virginia the real reason she was probably here, although she wasn't entirely sure. Grace could work in mysterious ways.

"Cross the Boundary? Why the hell would you want to do that? The Black Universe isn't very hospitable to our kind."

"We think it's not the Black Universe this time. It's maybe a new one. New to us, at least. And it's causing destruction at the edge. Yverra and I have been trying to monitor it. We went to talk to Grace, and boom, here I am. Not sure why…"

"That does sound alarming," Virginia said. "But if Grace sent you here, she must think there's something that can help you. It isn't anything to do with Calaneris and Blauw, is it? I know they've recanted, but I wouldn't trust Blauw as far as I can throw him, which I did have to do once." She chuckled. "Who wants dessert?"

Violet shook her head, not sure which question to answer.

"I wouldn't pass that up, if I were you," Alan said. "Ginny's a gourmet cook, famous across the universe. We can sort out what's going on over apple pie a la mode."

"Yeah, we're not just all about Kim-Chee around here," Virginia said.

After a brief warmup in the oven, the pie came out hot enough to melt dollops of vanilla ice cream. Digging in enthusiastically, Alan said, "We have a visitor from Silicon Valley in the Computer Science Department who is one of the founders of Canny Divide—maybe you've heard of him? Janus Parker's quite the whiz kid in virtual reality. You could help me show him around, Violet. VR's your field, right?"

"I *would* like to meet him," Violet admitted. "He was one of the pioneers. Everyone studied him in school."

"Let's get these dishes cleaned up," Gin said, rising. "This table looks like Grand Central Station."

ᔛ

"So, you're telling me what you're using are these primitive goggles?" Violet said. She bit her tongue. Too late. She had already pissed off the great Janus Parker. Pulling the headset off, she glanced apologetically at Great-grandfather, who'd gone to the trouble of inviting Parker to his office in the Computer Science Department to meet her.

"Yes, they're bulky, but hardly primitive. They're the latest in wearable display technology. I only recently got the funding to develop better equipment. I've had to develop this in my garage up to now, you know."

"Of course," Violet said. "Sorry." She knew there was rapid progress in overcoming obstacles to making VR an everyday user commodity, mostly thanks to Janus Parker. Getting the displays to actually be realistic instead of cartoon-like, for one thing, and rendering without making the viewer get motion sickness, for another.

"Have you considered holography instead of wearable eyewear?" she asked.

"Yes, of course, but that's still years off, and it's quite compute-intensive. Do you know anybody with deep pockets?"

She didn't. The only rich people she knew were L.A. actors back home, and her college friend, Xoan-Paulo Hilario, on Mars. His Portuguese/Filipino father had bankrolled most of the colony. The thought of John-Paul filled her with sadness. The destruction of the settlement by the Black Universe had been a terrible blow too.

"I've got to prepare for a lecture this afternoon," Alan said. "Why don't you two head over to the Student Union and grab lunch?"

Violet smiled politely. She suspected lunch was Virginia's idea. She was always a matchmaker, and she'd probably grilled Alan for a suitable "friend" to keep Vi occupied during her 21st century visit. Parker was a perfect choice, of course. But maybe she'd already blown it with her stupid goggles remark...

"Sounds good," Janus said. "Do you want to lead the way?"

"Sorry, I don't know where the Student Union is, either," Violet said.

"Well, we can ask directions as we go," he replied, holding the door and waving to Alan. "Professor."

As they walked out onto the quadrangle, Violet stopped to stare up at the gigantic trees filtering the light onto the broad lawn. "Sorry, you were saying?"

"I was just saying," Janus said, "I'm getting a lot of great ideas from Professor Jones. It's like he already knows everything about VR. And he was telling me about some research into quantum computing that could power that holographic idea you were talking about."

"He is a very smart man," Violet agreed. *Maybe too smart, half the time.* Alan probably would have been a good match for Yverra, but he was obviously completely smitten with Grandma Ginny. Violet had to stop herself from following the evil path of the demon matchmaker. It must run in the family...

Entering the cafeteria at the Student Union, Janus pointed her at the trays. She tried not to betray her squeamishness. Plastic had been phased out by her time as toxic to the environment. They slid their trays along a shelf, picking off sandwiches and fruits as they walked.

"How about a drink?" Janus said. "This new tea is becoming popular. I think they call it kombucha."

"Yes!" Violet said, a little too loudly. Finally something familiar in this backward canteen.

"Damn, this stuff is pretty tasty," Janus said, after taking a cautious sip. With his round face, baby blue eyes, and sandy hair trained to defy gravity with liberal amounts of hair product, you could hardly tell him from the students in the room. He wore blue jeans and a hoodie. Both he and Grandpa Alan were unusually pale, strange since the sunshine was so strong here. The cafeteria tables were populated by a mixture of dark- and light-skinned students. It was like L.A. must have been in the old days, as it tried to become more racially diverse. Skin color gradually became more homogeneous and irrelevant, although Violet especially treasured her Hispanic and Asian heritage.

"I agree, this is definitely the drink of the future," she declared, taking another swig of the kombucha.

"How do you know Professor Jones?" Janus asked. "And how do you know so much about virtual reality?"

Violet started to say that Virginia and Alan were her many-great grandparents but remembered that wasn't going to work.

"I was one of his grad students and am stopping by to say hello before I start a new position in L.A," she said. That ought to be far enough away from North Carolina that Janus wouldn't inquire further.

"Los Angeles? I have a lot of friends in California. I'm based in Silicon Valley, you know. San Ramon. So, you majored in Computer Science?"

"Yes." Close enough. Of course there was a lot more to VR Administration than just computers, but you have to walk before you can crawl...

"I'll be going home soon, too," Janus said. "Would you like to give me a call when you get squared away in your new job?" He pulled out a card from his jeans and handed it to her. "Our new secretary, Judith, insisted I get business cards."

"That'd be great," Violet said, fully expecting to never see him again. On the other hand, it would be fun to see what L.A. in the 21st century looked like. She looked at the card. People actually used to carry pieces of paper around. Now that she thought about it, she didn't have any sort of identification "papers," as they used to call them. She'd have to ask Alan what the local customs were.

"I'm sorry I was a little overly sensitive before about my VR work," Janus said. "I just get too passionate about it sometimes."

"No problem. I'm the same way," Violet said, smiling. Janus put her empty wrappers and kombucha bottle on his own tray. "Here, I'll get these."

Violet was already beginning to like this academic, and he'd turned out to be younger than she'd expected. Janus was obviously excited about his work and about the future. She liked his optimism—however ill-placed it might seem in view of the obstacles he would face.

*****~~~~~*****

Chapter 5.

Grounded Fears

Alan looked up from his morning paper, peering over his bifocals.

"How's the visit going?"

"Honestly, I have no idea," Violet replied. "But I really enjoyed meeting Janus Parker today, Grandpa. He's the originator of our whole VR industry."

"Yes, I get that," Alan replied. "Kind of like if I ever got to meet Albert Einstein or Alan Turing."

"Yeah, Alan has a thing for other guys named Al," Virginia chimed in. "I found that out the hard way in 1890s London."

While Violet still didn't have a good idea why Grace had sent her here, she knew it must be for a good reason. It would have been nice if Grace had shared that with her. The only thing she'd done of note while here visiting her grandparents was to meet Janus Parker.

"I have a hunch I'm supposed to maybe work with Janus," she said. "Maybe I should go to California. He said he's setting down roots for his company in Silicon Valley now. He even invited me to visit."

"If you feel drawn in that direction, who am I to disagree?" Virginia said. "The Sun-Jones family always flies by the seat of their pants. Speaking of flying, you'll have to ride a 21st century airplane to get to California. Unless you want to drive, and that takes days and days."

"I've done a lot of flying in VR," Violet said. "Should be no problem."

"This isn't VR," Virginia said. "There's a pilot, and if he crashes, you have no control."

"Don't scare her, Gin," Alan said. "Flying on commercial airliners is perfectly safe. If there's any hazard, I'd say it's from getting claustrophobia, the way they cram everyone into the cabin these days."

"We'd be happy to buy you the ticket, dear," Virginia said. "But since you arrived with no luggage, we'll have to get you something to carry on. Maybe we can get you a few spare outfits too. They say the weather there is always balmy."

"Balmy, like a serious drought, you mean," Alan said. Virginia laughed.

"Let's go shopping first thing and put you on the plane tomorrow," Ginny said. "Do you have a way to get in touch with Janus?"

"He gave me his card," Violet said. "Um, should I have a card?"

"Wouldn't hurt. Your cover is that you're a VR expert, right?"

"I *am* a VR expert," Vi said, sniffing.

"Right. Just kidding. We can stop by one of those quick-print shops in the mall."

⟲

The mall was even larger than the university, spread out across at least a square kilometer, Violet surmised.

Grandma Ginny circled around for what seemed like much too long looking for a better parking space.

"You'll thank me at the end of the day," she said. "By the time we get everything, your feet will be killing you. Especially in those spike heels. I don't know how you can walk fifty feet in them."

"Just used to them, I guess," Vi said. "They make you look taller."

"They also make you look crazy," Virginia said. "Let's start with Brondell's. They have the nicest stuff, all made in America."

The car chirped, indicating it was locked.

Thick glass doors opened onto a brightly lit room filled with merchandise of all sorts.

"This is the Accessories department," Virginia said. "You'll probably want a sun hat. Shoe department, over there. We can get you some sensible shoes. Then over to Luggage."

Violet hadn't heard anything Virginia was saying for the last several minutes. Her attention was riveted to a perfectly fetching beanie, in midnight blue felt.

"I'd like this, please," she murmured.

"Don't you want to try it on first?"

"Oh, can I?"

"Yes, that's the idea. Ah, it looks adorable. That one looks great too. Yes, that one too. Of course, you're young; you'd look good in a trash bag. I'm jealous—I never look good in hats."

Violet came to her senses temporarily. "I think you'd look lovely in a hat, Grandma. Here, try this one."

"Hmm. It's not too bad, is it?" Virginia waved to the clerk. "We'll take these. We'd better get out of here before we buy all of their hats."

"Can we do that?"

"Certainly not, young lady. You can wear whatever you like in VR, but here it costs money."

Violet agreed. In L.A., she had owned practically nothing for that very reason. Things had a cost there, too, so she mostly streamed content to her feed for temporary use.

"I never thought about the 21st century much. Everybody mostly remembers it as the century where the world ignored climate change. I had no idea there were all these interesting foods and fashions. What kind of shoes do you think I should get? I don't want to be overly conspicuous."

"Too late, kid, you already stand out, and there's nothing you can do to hide it. You'll fit in better in California."

They walked through the perfume aisle toward the shoes. A large banner displayed a poster of an Asian American model who commanded attention with her poise and beauty.

"Who's that?" Violet asked.

"That's Lucy Liu," Virginia said. "She is a big Hollywood star, and has her own clothing line now."

"I want to look like that," Violet breathed.

"Don't we all, kid, don't we all. What about these Roman style sandals? The heels aren't too high, and they look comfy..."

☺

"Looks like I'll be paying this off for a long time," Alan said, eyeing the pile of swag that Virginia and Violet had deposited in the living room. "I think Violet is bringing out your maternal instincts."

"What is a great-granddaughter twelve-generations-removed for, if not to spoil?" Virginia replied. "And look, we got you something too." She held up a little bottle of hand sanitizer. "They were giving these away, isn't that great? None of those scary viruses to worry about. Those guys in the quickie print shop looked pretty funky."

"It's getting late, and Violet's got an early start tomorrow," Alan noted. "We'll drop you off at Raleigh-Durham at seven for your eight-thirty flight."

"How long did you say it would take?" Violet asked.

"The L.A. leg will take about five hours," Alan said. "Then, later, if you decide to visit Janus, you can fly to San Jose in only about an hour."

"I'll definitely plan to visit him," Violet said. "I just want to stop in Los Angeles first just to see what it looked like four hundred years ago. Maybe stay overnight." She picked up her new pink carry-on. "I'll pack and see you in the morning?"

"Of course. Well, good night and sleep well," Virginia said, as Violet headed for her bedroom.

"Hand sanitizer, eh?" Alan commented. "Shall I set an alarm for 5:30? Give us time for breakfast and to cram all this stuff into a suitcase—Ginny, what's wrong? Are you crying?"

Virginia wiped her eyes. "I guess the shopping reminded me that she's so much like Grace. Like Grace *used* to be. Before I lost my daughter to the universe."

"I know," Alan said, patting her shoulder. "I'm pretty sure that's partly why Grace sent Violet to us."

"Plus, I get a bad feeling about this plane trip," Gin said.

☺

Sitting aboard the airliner flying to L.A. the next morning, Violet looked around from her assigned seat. The conveyance was spartan, just a long metal tube with seats bolted to the floor. No windows. Not that different from STS-99, really. The ship accommodations she'd given customers in VR were always much nicer, whether it was on land, sea, or space.

After an interminable safety lecture from the flight attendants, the plane took off with a grinding roar and lumbered into the air. She decided to pass the time viewing a 2D movie on the seatback six inches from her face. The presentation was passable, with Greek gods shooting at space monsters, although it seemed silly and highly unlikely. She'd heard they had 3D versions, but those required special projectors not available on this airliner. Why not just do an end run and go straight to VR?

Oh, of course. That VR technology was still years away, once Janus got his act together here in the twenty-first century. She smiled at her own cleverness.

The rotund man across the aisle smiled back. He obviously needed medical attention to restore his body to a healthy condition. Violet noticed that a lot of the passengers on the airliner were in the same state and needed their meds. *Suchiseuleoun.* Disgraceful. She'd point it out to the flight attendants on the way out.

The crackling of the PA system signaled an announcement. Good luck hearing it over this constant roaring noise. She probably could have asked Grace or Eric to pop her over to Los Angeles in a second, but she didn't want to hurt Grandma and Grandpa's feelings.

"Ladies and gentlemen, we're flying near the Grand Canyon, which you can see from the left side of the aircraft. This week they're releasing a high volume of water from the Glen Canyon Dam, so that's what all that foamy white stuff you see is, not beer." Laughter.

Necks craned to that side of the plane. Just her luck to be on the right. Wait a minute. There were no windows on this plane, so she wondered how people could see the Grand Canyon. Did they have virtual reality after all? No, a view was being projected along the walls of the cabin. Not even the real thing, probably, just a recording. She was still getting used to the inconveniences of the 21st century.

"Attendants secure for landing," the PA announced. The plane began to drop like a stone. She'd be glad when they were finally on the ground. This reminded her of the time she'd landed on Mars, only it felt more dangerous.

Violet waited impatiently as her fellow portly passengers hauled luggage out of the overhead bins and shuffled toward the exit. Finally, she reached the gangway, practically running onto the concourse.

Grounded Fears

Violet gazed out two-story window. The view was mostly blocked by airplanes, but through the smoggy distance she could see the San Gabriel Mountains in the distance.

She was home!

But home was quite different in this time, in spite of the scenery. The majority of people in the airport looked to be of northern European extraction, rather than the more Asian population she was used to. Immigration patterns would change a lot over the centuries. But one thing wouldn't change. This was Hollywood Land.

Violet remembered that she was supposed to call the grandparents when she arrived, to let them know she'd gotten there safely. Not a bad precaution. She'd noted a number of maintenance issues on the airliner—none terribly serious—but still an indication of primitive monitoring technology and practically nonexistent compute power. She pressed the call button on her borrowed portable communication device.

"Hello, Grandma?" Buzzing noises. Oh, she had to wait until they accepted the call.

"Violet, is that you, sweetheart?" She missed Grandma already. "Glad you got there in one piece."

"Yes, I got here, and it's really beautiful. I'm heading toward the ground transportation now. I'll let you know when I reach the hotel. Bye, Grandma." Violet pushed the red button, eager to get going.

The device beeped, ending the call.

Violet wheeled her pink bag to the exit. A blast of warm air met her as she stepped outside. Hundreds of cars circled the area, some painted yellow to indicate they were for hire.

One pulled up to the curb in front of her.

"Taxi, ma'am?"

"Yes, I'm going to a place called... " She reached into her matching pink courier bag. "The Airport Homeplace Suites, if you don't mind."

"Sure, hop in."

She started to walk around to the passenger side, but the driver jumped out and opened the rear door. Oh yes, Grandma had told her to get in the back seat. "And watch the meter. Don't let them drive you around the long way. Some of those guys are crooks!" she'd said. Luckily, this driver wasn't a guy. An odd-smelling paper pine tree flapped in fron the the air conditioner vent.

Besides, how would she know? She had no idea where the hotel was located. Back home, you always got to your destination in the shortest possible time. The VR administration guaranteed it.

The taxi pulled out into traffic and left the aircraft facility. Violet rarely had to travel physically back home. The number of cars on the highway was amazing—all driven by people. Quite dangerous and inefficient. The driver made eye contact via the rear-view mirror.

"Coming home, or just visiting?" she asked.

"A little of both," Violet said. "I grew up here."

"Really? I'm originally from here too, but I went to college in New York. I missed the climate, so I ended up back here."

"Is this the best job you could get with a college education?" Violet asked. The car swerved a bit, then sped up.

"Times are tough," the driver replied. "And I don't have your looks."

Uh, oh, she'd obviously offended somehow. Twenty-first century "Amerishock" strikes again. *"What's looks got to do with it?"* she wanted to say. At home, people were valued for their brains and talent, not their accidental heredity. Anyone could look any way they pleased.

"I'm sure you'll find something soon," Violet said. They entered the freeway and drove in silence.

Violet opened her pink courier bag to look for Janus's card. She'd call him when she got to the hotel. The cab lurched suddenly, brakes squealing.

"Oh, my God!" the driver yelled. Violet's world turned upside down in slow motion. After that, everything was black.

Violet awoke. Her head hurt. The cab was on its side, halfway off the roadway. Smoke and steam filled the air, rising off the hot pavement. She scrambled to her feet against the side window and pushed on the door handle at her shoulder. The door swung open, and she climbed out. She limped around and looked through the front windshield. The poor girl was still there, trapped by a large balloon against the seat. Blood dripped from her mouth.

Violet bent to see if she could help the driver, when a missile, narrowly missed her head and hit the hood with a thwack. She flattened herself on the ground. Perhaps a piece of metal had exploded from the smashed car. No, that didn't make sense. Another shot, piercing the windshield, striking the driver in the forehead.

Horrified, Violet turned away. Using the cab for temporary cover, she crawled a few feet, then jumped up and ran. Some sort of mucker, she surmised. They had those back in the 21st century, angry people who would go insane for no good reason and start killing innocent bystanders using high-velocity weapons. They didn't have VR monitoring to see when people were going off the rails or needed help.

Looking behind her as she fled, she saw that traffic had ground to a halt and people were getting out of their cars, clutching communications devices tightly to their ears to summon assistance. A larger explosion pounded the taxi, and the car burst into flames, pushing the crowd back. Violet realized this wasn't a case of bystander collateral damage—someone was targeting the cab. Targeting *her*. She'd done enough VR war dramatizations to know that.

A grove of bushes divided the highway. She pushed her way in and scanned the scene. Screams and shouts and the sound of approaching sirens pierced the air, but the assailant remained hidden. No one with large weapons. No grenade launchers or the like. No obvious muzzle flashes. Then she saw him. About thirty feet away, a slim, dark-haired young man walked from car to car, looking inside windows, and moving along. He appeared to be unarmed, and he smiled and waved at people, as if reassuring them that things were all right. He looked familiar.

With a shock of recognition, Violet knew who he was. John-Paul! What was her ex doing here, 400 years in the past? Was this Grace's doing? Or Grandma Virginia's? Hadn't John-Paul died on Mars? Grateful that her friend was still alive, she stepped out of the thicket. A bolt of green flame poured out of Xoan-Paulo Hilario's hand and ignited the bush beside her.

"Wha-haat?" she muttered. She didn't understand. Not at all. The rational part of her brain turned off, replaced by panic.

Violet cursed, her mind coming up blank for the dimensional shift technique Yverra had taught her. Yverra had noted that shifting to the fourth dimension was a good way to escape danger, from the point of view of a third dimension creature. "It's essentially time travel," she said. Now, what was it Yverra had said? "Slide, slide, just a little..."

Violet blinked. The accident scene had vanished, along with John-Paul. She patted her side, relieved that she still had her bag across her body, which partially shielded her from the flames. She had to get out of here. Her friend was trying to kill her. The time to ask why was "later."

Setting off cross-country, she spotted the exit ramp descending from the highway. The cabbie had said that was their exit, number 2A. But the poor girl had never made it. The hotel was only a quarter of a mile off the exit. She could see the sign from here and ran for it. Her minuscule time slip was disintegrating, so she would be back in real time any second.

She plunged into the wet, tall grass alongside the road, still glimmering with early morning dew. Her boots sank into the soft ground, slowing her down. Soon, she was out of breath, gasping for the next lungful of air. Her legs were fairly strong from cycling in her VR world, but she had never liked running. Too hard to balance the oxygen demands. Plus, she hadn't taken her meds. Grandma Ginny had sent her off with a hearty breakfast of scrambled eggs and bacon, but it didn't make up for years of indolence, exacerbated by sitting at a screen most of the time. Her chest began to burn, and she slowed to a walk, stumbling and looking over her shoulder. She felt exposed, surrounded by open space and undisturbed ground cover, rolling prairie, and scrub brush. She would keep her head down and stay in the low areas between hillocks. Her weariness subsided a bit, and she picked up the pace. The hotel was only a few hundred feet away now. Potted palms flanked the driveway in front of the hotel. She glanced over her shoulder. It looked clear.

Violet stepped inside the lobby, accidentally sending the swinging glass door slamming against the wall. The man at the counter stared at her.

"Um, sorry," she said. "I believe I have a reservation. It's for Rain. R-A-I-N."

Sweat began to trickle down her armpits as the man frowned at the screen for what seemed like an eternity. Muffled music drifted through the air from tinny speakers not very cleverly hidden in the ceiling.

"Right. Here it is. Violet Rain for two nights, checking out on Thursday?"

"Yes."

"Says here you're all set. You're in room 217, second floor at the end of the corridor to your left. There's an elevator if you need help with your bags." Her suitcase was back in the burning cab, along with her new clothes.

"Thanks, I just have my courier bag. Uh, do I need a key?"

"No, just open the hotel app and swipe it at the door."

No time to wait for an elevator. John-Paul might come looking for her. What was his deal, anyway? She ran up the stairwell, yanked open the door marked "2," and sprinted down the hall.

It was a good thing Grandpa had given her his comm device. She held it to her face and whispered. "Open hotel door."

The device responded, "I don't understand that command. Do you want me to open a hotel app?"

"Yes!"

"May I use your location?"

"Yes!"

"Opening the Homeplace Suites app."

Thank God. She waved the device at the door and heard the bolt slide. She entered the room, and quickly closed the door behind her.

Time for a change of plans. She lifted the comm device and said, "Call Janus." For once, the device obeyed her order properly.

"Hello?"

"Janus?"

"Speaking—is this Violet? I was expecting you to call soon. Did you have a good flight?"

"Hi, yes, it was fine. But I'm kind of anxious to see more of your VR company. Would you mind if I came up tonight? I know it's a day early."

"Sure, that would be great. Let me know when you get here, and I'll pick you up at the airport."

"Thanks, Janus. It's really nice of you. I'm finding things a bit... stranger than I was expecting." Violet couldn't hide the slight tremble in her voice.

"That's L.A. for you," he said. "Strange Days, am I right?"

☺

Violet slipped out the back of the hotel and headed toward another large building. The ugly concrete pile turned out to be an apartment block, but at least it would offer temporary shelter. Stepping into the entryway, she scanned the names on the wall, each with a button one could push to gain entrance. It was probably better not to get yet another innocent bystander involved.

She spoke to Grandpa's device. "Get me a cab, will you?"

"Do you want me to call a cab to this location?" it replied.

Violet sighed. "Yes, that's what I just said." She left off, "you moronic program."

A few moments later, one of those yellow vehicles pulled up. She dashed out the front door and hopped in the back. She was beginning to understand the customs now.

"The airport." The cabbie pushed the fare register and pulled away from the curb.

Violet breathed a sigh of relief when they made it to the airport in one piece. She hadn't said a word to this cabbie, finding it best not to get too attached. Just in case. She fished in her case for the ticket north and headed for the airline counter to check in.

"You'll be able to exchange this, but it'll cost extra," the clerk said.

After the plane lifted off, she turned Grandpa's device back on, as the loudspeaker suggested. She'd gotten a seat next to the wall this time, but no views were showing at present. She began playing a game to pass the time.

"Ladies and gentlemen, we'll be landing in San Jose in about thirty minutes, so please turn off all laptops, electronic games, and phones."

"Make up your mind," Vi muttered, and stuffed the phone back in her pocket.

The wall lit up, showing a panoramic view of a sprawling metropolitan area. It was beautiful, full of trees, grass, and tiny blue pools of water. As she leaned in to take a better look, a dark shape zoomed by the wing of the aircraft. A flock of birds? They were still flying rather high up; she hoped they weren't killing birds. Birds were mostly extinct back home. Violet always added them to her scenarios whenever she could. Luckily, she had a large library of bird songs to choose from.

Zoom. There it was again. Then a boom. The plane shuddered. She looked up toward the aisle where the attendant stood trying to sell consumer goods to the passengers. The woman ran to the front of the cabin and pulled a microphone off the wall, stretching the coiled cord until it was close to her mouth.

"We may be encountering some turbulence. Please keep your seatbelts buckled." She dropped the microphone and tapped on the cockpit door.

Violet feared it wasn't turbulence. Another boom. Passengers began to scream. It felt like her stomach was heading toward her mouth. This plane ride was much more thrilling than the first one. The wall viewscreen turned off abruptly. Claustrophobia inside a falling canister. She'd complain when they landed. *If* they landed. She remembered Grandpa Alan's reminder that these planes had real pilots.

The plane rocked from side to side, but then slammed to the ground, bouncing a few times before braking hard. All the other passengers were gripping their armrests.

Violet hurriedly unbuckled and jumped to her feet, eager to get out and away from the airplane. Trapped against the wall, she would be one of the last to reach the stairs to deplane.

Tearing metal screeched as the roof ripped off, flooding the cabin with bright light. Violet squinted as her pupils shrank into focus. A man flew overhead, pointing some sort of weapon. She swore. John-Paul had tracked her down. She shouldn't have turned on the comm device. She'd ask later how he was flying like that. Not really interested right now. She ducked down, pulled her new hoodie up over her head, and leaped to the ground. More of those annoying siren sounds filled the runway. She took a zigzag path away from the terminal.

John-Paul pursued, touching down to the ground and running after her. A beam of green light shot by her head. Thank God he had a lousy aim. The green reminded her of something. Probably a laser. She was thankful for the lightweight hiking boots Grandma Ginny had made her buy, but he was gaining on her. Time for another dimensional switcheroo. He'd caught her off-guard in L.A., but she'd had time to remember her lessons since then.

She crouched into a bundle, making as small a target as possible, and concentrated. She could picture Yverra coaching her.

Slide, slide, just a little...

Violet stood up and turned back toward the terminal. The plane was sitting on the tarmac, all in one piece. Nothing had pounded on it and sliced it in half. Passengers were disembarking and talking. Not screaming.

Though it was quieter now, Violet could hardly keep herself from crying. She had a moment to catch her breath, but it was pretty hard to do that right now. Her old boyfriend, a man she had trusted and—let's just admit still had feelings for—was trying to kill her.

The pain and guilt of their breakup came crashing down on her. John-Paul had followed her around like a puppy dog and carried a rather fiery torch for her, which at the time she had told herself was kind of embarrassing. She'd really fooled herself. She hadn't been embarrassed. She'd been scared of making a commitment. And when he reached out to her, she ran away. Just like now.

Only this time, Violet could go anywhere and anytime. Except back. She knew the betrayal was connected somehow to the last call John-Paul had made when Mars was destroyed during the Unwinding. Unbidden, tears ran down her cheeks and onto the bag Virginia had bought her.

Yverra said these dimensional transfers were only good for a couple of minutes at most, so she had better get moving. Violet jumped into a luggage trolley and pulled bags over herself. Soon enough, she could again hear sirens and smell smoke.

*****~~~~~*****

Chapter 6.

Native Cuisine

"I'm thinking of changing the name of the company to 'Sensorial Ink,' you know, with I-N-K rather than I-N-C. Canny Divide seems to repel new backers off right off the bat," Janus said. He buttered a large wedge of pastry and stuffed it in his mouth. Violet had pled starvation due to having nothing on the plane—not to mention hours of running and hiding—and they were in the divine-smelling Claudette's Crêperie sampling the *clafouti*.

"I kind of like Canny Divide. I think it will have staying power," Violet said. "Um, are you sure that food is good for you?"

"Has anyone ever told you you're kind of judgmental?" Janus replied.

"Umm..." Violet didn't think so. Janus was just a shade overweight, so she was doing him a favor to nip those budding health problems in the bud.

"Clafouti's just pancakes, with plums cooked right in. So, you've got your bread group, your fruit group, and your laxative all in one."

Violet laughed. She *was* ravenous, after all. She tried a bite of the unhealthy monstrosity.

The tang of the plums blended perfectly with the sweetness of the cake. Suddenly she felt much better. "Pass the butter," she said.

"That's why they call it comfort food," Janus said, smiling. "It's good to get away for a little while with you, Violet. My pals would be shocked if they saw me out with a good-looking girl. They think I'm obsessed with this VR stuff, while holography and 3D video seem to be plenty fine with them. To me, that's just *augmented* reality."

"What *is* your obsession, exactly?" Violet asked, quenching her thirst with a refill of the deliciously bitter French Roast. She'd get it straight from the horse's mouth.

"Well, you might think this sounds kind of crazy, but I've always had the idea that people and machines were going to get together in a way that's bigger than both."

"A lot of people would argue with you on that," Violet observed. "Like that guy who thinks computers will take over, or that they will become so smart that they'll leave humanity behind." She was quoting from the history books.

"Yeah, the supposed Singularity. I know. But it's a big universe. With all the great distances involved, I think humans are special. And any other species that becomes sentient, even if they're what we'd call machines, are in the same boat. We've got to work together if we want to survive. I also think maybe the universe itself is sentient."

Violet was amazed at Janus's foresight, although it seemed to be based on no hard evidence whatsoever. Her "Grandmas" Ginny and Grace had actually *met* universes. No doubt they were alive. And there were more than one of them. But Janus couldn't know that.

"What about the possibility of intelligent species being hostile? Say we found one, or our computers became superbeings. What if they decided they didn't like us, or they'd be better off by themselves? Straight survival as the prime directive."

"I just don't see that as logical," Janus said. "Look at evolution. It could easily just be survival of the fittest, but it doesn't work that way. There's always altruism and cooperation built into a species' behavior, and it almost always benefits its survival."

"Sure, I get it. But evolution is slow. Where does your virtual reality come in?"

"I think it'll prepare us, teach us to roll with the punches."

"Like, make us more creative?"

"Absolutely. For our own protection."

In Violet's time, VR had definitely made her and everyone else exercise the hell out of their imaginations. But the computers were just there to serve human whims. They hadn't made any sort of intellectual jump of the sort Janus was envisioning. But they would.

In fact, it had taken a human from the past, Grandma Ginny, to architect the Yin-Yang, teaming up with an advanced AI. She shivered a little. Right now, *in the future,* the Black Universe was up to no good. Sometimes it helped to think in terms of cycles. First things went south for a while with the rampage of the Black Universe, then things were on the upswing with the creation of the Yin-Yang, and now it was looking bad again for our universe. Was it just that entropy always tore down whatever you built up? She was finding it a little difficult to keep up this facade of optimism about the ultimate fate of the universe.

"Hello?" Janus said. "Violet? I think we lost you for a minute. What were you thinking?"

"Oh, I was just thinking about all the possibilities that VR could bring in the future," she said. "If for nothing else, it could be great for virtual travel. I just took two rather unpleasant plane trips that I could have avoided."

"But then you wouldn't have arrived here physically, and I wouldn't have gotten to get out of the office to dine with you in this charming establishment. It's not the same as a conference call."

"No, not yet," she agreed. She didn't mention having to crawl out from below a pile of suitcases and hide for several hours in the women's restroom at the airport. Afraid to use her cell phone, she finally got the nerve to ask the woman at the next sink to borrow hers. Then she'd hailed a yellow car to meet Janus at this restaurant.

Janus hadn't seemed surprised when she asked to sit as far from the window as possible. He was something of a celebrity around here himself and had offered to order while she sat in a dim corner contemplating the flags on the wall.

"What does that one stand for?" She pointed to the one with the bear, and the legend, "California Republic," which was especially pretty.

"You like grizzly bears, eh? That's the California State Flag, of course."

She'd forgotten her history. Such flags had ceased to exist, except as decoration, since the VR channels had replaced national and state boundaries.

"Can I get you something else?" he offered.

"No, that was great. I suppose you need to get back to the office."

"Not at all. I had Judith block off my whole day. I'm at your complete disposal. What would you like to see first?"

"I've never been to Northern California." Even in her dreams. "What do you recommend?"

"I see you like to hike. What about the Redwoods?"

"Redwoods?" She didn't know what those were, but she was fairly certain she didn't like to hike. Oh, *the boots.* They still had mud on them.

"Yes, the tallest trees in the world, the sequoias."

"Oh, right."

"Or, if that sounds boring, there's Monterey Bay Aquarium. You can pet the fish."

Violet laughed again. Where she came from, no one was allowed near the fish farms. Too great a chance of poaching. Or sabotage. Or contamination.

"Perfect."

"Good, I'll call Judith to book us a couple of rooms at Asilomar. It's worth staying overnight there."

"Rooms? You're quite the gentleman."

"That sounds like the prudent way to be. Professor Jones would have me killed if you came to any harm here."

"Oh, I'm sure he wouldn't do any such thing," Violet laughed.

"He could get me blackballed from the computer science funding scene, and that would be the same as ending me."

"Don't worry about him," Violet said. "Alan Jones is the least of your problems."

"What do you mean by that?"

"Oh, nothing, just that you can trust him."

☙

"The trees are amazingly twisted," Violet observed as they walked along the sandy soil on the beach near Asilomar. The squat pine trees barely moved, hulking menacingly against the backdrop of the choppy sea.

"The wind stunts their growth," Janus replied, his cheeks growing even pinker. His close-cropped hair didn't move, but her long ponytail threatened to lash her to death. They'd had the beach all to themselves all morning, which Janus swore was highly unusual, but now a slim figure was approaching down the strand. It was approaching fast. Faster than a person would walk. Maybe it was about to fly. Violet's pulse quickened.

"Um, Janus, this wind is getting to me. How about we move along?" She grabbed his hand. He glanced down, looking pleased.

"Of course. Would you like to do a whale watching excursion instead?" Not answering, Violet began to run, nearly pulling Janus off his feet.

Seeing one of the great leviathans in person would be wonderful, she thought, but there wasn't going to be time today. Violet gave Janus a small tug, just as a sharp bit of seashell whizzed by their heads.

"What— what the hell was that?" Janus asked.

"Don't look now," Violet answered. "Things are about to get real."

Slide, slide, just a little…

"What's going on?" Janus asked. "Did you push me?"

"We have to get out of here," she said.

"I said all right," he protested. "What's the big hurry?"

"Haven't you got some movie where the character says, 'come with me if you want to live?' Well, do that."

"Listen, I do want to live, obviously, but I don't see any danger."

"I don't know if you've noticed, but you're bleeding. That man was going to kill us. Or rather, me, and you as well if you got in the way. Which you did, incidentally. You've been shot."

"My God. I didn't even feel it. What man?"

She loosened the bandana she'd tied around her neck to keep the sun off and wrapped it around his bicep. "It just looks like a graze… Come on, I'll explain later." She only hoped she would be able to.

☺

Violet herded Janus back into the cavernous Asilomar entrance hall. Its tall rock fireplace and chairs made of leather and wood were obviously designed to express a "rustic" feel to its guests. Unconsciously, she started to make a mental note to correct some of her VR modules, but then caught herself. She didn't have that job any more. Some of her richer customers had been sticklers for absolute accuracy, though. It was a hard habit to break.

She went to the innkeeper and asked if there was a public phone.

"Why?" Janus asked. "Would you like to borrow my cell?"

84

She pushed his phone away.

"No, he'll be watching yours too, now."

The clerk ushered them into the back office and pointed to the ancient landline. A coiled wire connected the receiver to an ancient keyboard, arrayed with mechanical buttons.

"Dial 9 to get out. We can charge the call to your room."

"Thanks," Violet said, making no move toward the phone.

"Oh, you probably want privacy. I'll just leave you alone, then," the desk clerk said.

Violet began pushing buttons to call Grandpa Jones. Nothing was happening.

"Here," Janus offered, lifting up the handset. "Hold this to your ear. I don't think this one has speaker."

"Right," she said. A series of beeps and buzzes indicated that the call was connecting.

"Hello, Grandpa? This is Violet. I'm in Northern California. Yes, fine, it's been a fun trip. But I'm calling to tell that we're going to be out of communication for a bit. Something's come up. We? I mean me and Janus. He's been with me, showing me around for a couple of days. Yes, he's been very helpful... No, no need to call her yet... Thanks, Grandpa. I'll tell him."

The buzzing resumed in her ear. Call ended.

"What did he say?" Janus asked.

"Um, he said they've got a lead on an interested party to invest in your company," Violet improvised

"Oh, I thought I heard you talking about a woman...I'd better call Alan back, then," Janus said, pulling his cell out of his pocket.

"No, that wouldn't be a good idea right now," she said, snatching the cell from his hand and throwing it on the ground. The glass on the front broke with a tinkling sound.

"Hey, you broke my phone. What's the idea?"

"How do you feel about Las Vegas?" She'd always wanted to visit the fabled city, long paved over with solar collectors by her time.

"That's at least a nine-hour drive! But I suppose we could catch a redeye flight there..."

"No more airplanes," Violet said firmly. "Besides, it'll give me a chance to make something up—er, get you patched up and talk about why I'm really here."

"Somehow I knew you weren't a tourist," Janus said. "I have to say this is the most exciting thing to happen to me in a long time. Someone's after us, right? But why Vegas? This isn't just an excuse to wear those high heels I saw in your bag, is it?"

"Funny, as usual," Violet said. "Just keep your head down. I wouldn't want anything to happen to it."

"I'll do the driving." Janus assumed a conspiratorial expression. "Lucy, you've got some 'splainin' to do."

They left without ever looking back. A real shame they'd miss out on going whale watching, though.

*****~~~~~*****

Chapter 7.

The Drive

After stopping at a drugstore to pick up some bandages and adhesive tape, they began the long drive.

"At least there will be some great food along the way, right?" Violet said.

"You haven't told me why someone is after you," Janus grumbled, cradling his injured arm.

"I'm really sorry," Violet said. But she still wanted to know the answer to that question herself.

Janus showed where his favorite stations could be heard on the radio, but within a few hours they had passed out of range.

"Keep pressing the right-arrow button," Janus said. "It'll stop when a new station comes in strong."

The car accelerated briskly, and at first the tires seemed to hum along with the music. But the narrow northern California roads gradually fell into disrepair, and the jolts of rocks and gravel hitting the bumper made Violet jump repeatedly with each nerve-wracking mile.

To stave off boredom, they stopped every few hours for hamburgers, sandwiches, wraps, and fried vegetables. Even so, they would be there before dark, if they didn't stop too often.

"I think we should go via Yosemite," Janus said.

"Is that the fastest route?" Vi asked.

"Well, no, but it's the most scenic."

"I'd very much like to see all the wonderful scenery in 21st century America, but I think it's best we get to Las Vegas as soon as possible," Vi said.

"Via San Mateo, it is," Janus replied. "At least we'll get to be on 101 part of the way. That's pretty scenic, even if it's only for half an hour."

They drove to Gilroy, turning east toward Pacheco Pass.

"There's a great little Japanese restaurant here where we can get some more of that comfort food," Janus said. They then headed south down I-5 to Bakersfield, passing acre after acre of farmland. Great. She was starving again. Fortified, they drove on.

As they stepped out of the car to stretch their legs near Barstow, they were met with a blast furnace of hot air. "I'm not sure this is the greatest idea. It's the middle of summer. I hope the air holds out." He mumbled something about Death Valley, which Violet didn't quite catch. She'd heard of that place in the VR westerns. She was beginning to think Janus had been right about this route not being the best. But at least it was obscure. As long as they stayed off the radar, she hoped they'd make it.

"Violet, I know you're impatient to get to Vegas, but can I show you one more place? It's just a short detour."

A short detour indeed. They cut across the tip of Nevada and bypassed Las Vegas by about 30 miles, into Arizona. Violet did appreciate natural scenery, but this was ridiculous. A sign read, "Boulder City, Hoover Dam Exit."

"Let's turn in here," Janus said. "It's pretty impressive, and it's where all of Las Vegas's water comes from. The water gets collected into Lake Mead."

Dams. Violet remembered now. Massive concrete dams were how people saved water back in this century. Quite an engineering feat, really, like the dikes in the Netherlands and the photo-biocollectors in Saudi Arabia. But reservoirs weren't enough to keep up with the demand of thirsty desert cities like Vegas and Los Angeles. Microscale resolution models now calculated needed responses to the air and sea-surface data flowing in from all over the world, and the coastal nuclear generators would make it rain only when and where needed. Of course, people could be inconvenienced occasionally, but it was much better than the constant weather and climate disasters the world had been experiencing during the previous couple of centuries.

Passing a row of winged statues, they paused atop the dam's wall. Their gaze plunged down seventy stories to the base of the concave, shield-shaped structure, where cascading water was channeled through giant hydroelectric generators. Too bad wonders of the world such as this had been gradually "liquidated," so to speak.

"I'm glad we came, Janus," Violet said. "Now, can we please go?"

*****〜〜〜*****

Chapter 8.

Playground

Violet noted that Janus seemed to be an ancient music fan, from the era where heavy drums and poetic exposition seemed to dominate. The rhythm of the drumming *did* seem to make the miles move by faster. Most of this music had been lost to oblivion, and she felt that was unfair. So many talented people, now consigned to oblivion. If she got the chance, she'd come back and record some of it for posterity. Maybe she was meant to be a historian instead of a VR administrator. Actually, the two went well together. VR allowed everyone to work and play at the same time.

But the momentary lift this gave her feelings soon deflated. There was no timeline after the 25th century, when she'd first met Virginia Sun-Jones, and ultimately been stuffed into stasis.

Unbidden, the memory started on playback. It began as just an ordinary day at Skywriter Ranch. Virginia rode in on a big old Korean dragon. At first, Violet had assumed it was VR like everything else, but this creature was real, and gigantic, so big it took up most of the VR hangar. A woman climbed out of the saddle and said, "Who's in charge, here? I'd like a word, if possible."

Violet's mouth had fallen open.

"Wow, that was quick, the way you whisked me away from that castle," the woman said. "Where are we now?"

"Um, you're in the same place," Violet answered.

"The same place?"

"Everything is VR here." The woman looked confused. "You know—virtual reality?"

"So I was never actually hanging from a cliff or flying through the air?" the woman asked.

"No." In retrospect, Violet realized Virginia probably *had* dangled off a cliff and flown in. That dragon was not just a figment of compute cycles. "You have to park that beast outside," she said. The beast growled at her. "Not very friendly, is he?" She decided to drop it.

"You just travel anywhere and be anything you want? Sweet."

"That is physically impossible," Violet said.

"Where am I, exactly?"

"This is Los Angeles."

"I mean, *when* am I?" Grandma Gin had asked.

"It's June 14, 2416."

"L.A. used to be a big city."

"This is VR Channel 16747," Violet said. "Millions are tuned in to different channels, although only a few show up at the actual projection points, like you."

"I— I was expecting to meet some people here," Virginia said. "Have you seen a young couple and a man more my age?"

"Everyone assumes the visage they desire here," Violet had replied, again not too helpfully.

"Visage? You mean I might not recognize them if I saw them?"

"Not unless they chose to reveal themselves."

"Pardon my manners. I'm Virginia Jones. And you are?"

"Violet Rain."

"Perfectly named, I see. I love your purple bangs. You remind me a little of my daughter. Her name is Grace. I'm looking for her—and my husband. Is there some way I can let them know I'm here? I didn't really make an appointment."

"We'd be happy to take a message," Violet had said. What a dummy she was then.

"I'm looking for Alan Jones, Gracie Magnusson, and Eric Magnusson. Anybody by that name show up here recently?"

"Almost no one uses their real names in VR," Violet said, explaining that she was the channel manager and offering to have her avatar assist.

"Well, you mentioned messages. Are there any for me? It could be under Sun-Jones, Virginia. Gin or Ginny for short."

"None that have come through this channel. Do you want me to check the others?"

"How many are there? Will it take long?"

"There are about 100,000, and they are adding channels every day. It shouldn't take long, though, perhaps a week."

Violet was justly proud of her compute resources.

"I'll wait," Ginny said. "And could you broadcast that I am here and am looking for those people?"

"Certainly."

"What's there to do around here while I wait?"

It was short notice, but there was nothing wrong with pushing this nice lady to the front of the queue. "Do you like cyclocross?" Violet asked. An open outdoor park appeared, with a quarter-mile track coursing up and down small hills. It might be fun to time-slice a bit and get some exercise at the same time.

But the woman's family hadn't turned up after a week.

"How's the search going, Violet?"

"I'm sorry, Ginny, there haven't been any responses to your broadcast.

"Well, are there any other human habitations besides here on Earth, a space colony, perhaps?" An odd question. Everybody knew about Mars.

"It is funny that you should ask that, Ginny. We have just gotten news of the destruction of our colony on Mars. It has wreaked havoc on our communications throughout the solar system."

"Can you show me?"

They stood on a rubble-strewn plain. A dark sky brooded over the scene. A bubble dome nearby flapped almost imperceptibly, a large rent in its side.

"You didn't have to transport me there, just show me," Virginia said.

"VR feels quite real," Violet noted. "I don't think you would have found your friends here. Mars is close enough that they would have responded to your message long ago. Before the destruction, that is."

"So there are other colonies besides Mars?"

"Yes— Oh my God."

"Violet? What is it?" Mars melted away, and they were back in the big empty VR hangar.

A blinding beam of green light cut into the ceiling from above. They heard screams.

Another beam struck near the first, then another. They continued to strike, systematically heading toward them in a straight line. Puffs of concrete flew into the air as the floor of the hangar disintegrated.

"All citizens are advised to return to reality and take shelter. All citizens are advised to return to reality." The broadcast repeated over and over.

The floor shuddered. Violet scrambled to regain her balance. The VR room was gone, replaced by a scene of devastation. Miles of urban habitation stretched into the distance. Huge plumes of smoke rose, punctuated with the sounds of small explosions. The green beams seemed real enough, though, and they were continuing to approach. Huge cloud-to-cloud lightning strikes crossed the sky.

"Violet, can you hear me?" Ginny shouted.

"Yes, Ginny?"

"I have to go now. I'm really sorry. I'll try to come back with help."

"Where are you going? Ginny, I was going to wait to tell you, but you know how you said I reminded you of your daughter? I've done some research and discovered we are related. The Magnussons, they—" More screams.

That's when her many-great aunt Ginny disappeared and Violet blinked out of existence as far as the universe was concerned.

More amazing architectural constructs came into view as Violet and Janus finally neared Las Vegas. Towering buildings rose along the main thoroughfare, signs flashing even though it was only late afternoon. There was a replica of the ancient Tour Eiffel in France, and another of an Egyptian pyramid. Violet realized it was one big amusement park. Janus selected one of the hotels, where they turned over the car to a parking valet and were given a room with a view overlooking the glittering avenue. The boulevard crawled with people who appeared the size of ants far below. It was a good thing Vi wasn't afraid of heights. Off in the distance, a row of fountains danced and waved fronds of water in the air. No wonder there had been a water shortage. Most of it was being evaporated into the air. Still, viewing the past in person was a unique opportunity for a VR expert.

"So, you didn't say much on the trip here," Janus said. "Are you going to tell me what this is all about now?"

"Absolutely," Vi agreed. "But first, can we just look for something to eat? I'm famished."

"I don't know how you stay so skinny the way you eat," Janus said. "There's a Cheesecake Factory in the lobby downstairs. If that doesn't fatten you up, nothing will."

"Cheesecake? I've never had that..."

"Then maybe I'd better not take you there. It's addictive."

"Really?" She'd heard about the many addictive substances people used in this century. That behavior needed to stop if you wanted to survive beyond age 30. Illicit drugs were replaced with antenvirals that kept the body running efficiently and removed dangerous toxins. And a healthy body was a happy body, for the most part.

"Just give me a minute to jump in the shower," Janus said. "Driving always makes me sweaty."

Reluctantly, Violet agreed to wait. It seemed like these people were obsessed with taking showers.

"Man, look at this bathroom," Janus said, stripping off his shirt and stepping in. The sound of running water could be heard through the closed door. *Tremendously wasteful*, Violet thought.

Violet peeked into the adjoining room. It bore little resemblance to her grandparents' small grooming room. An expanse of shiny white marble (a probable falling hazard in these heels) stretched to the door of a glass shower enclosure, and gold-veined mirrors lined the walls.

"What's this?" she asked, pointing to a little table and tufted seat.

"The vanity? You sit here in front of the mirror and primp all day," Janus said.

She chuckled. *Vanity.* Appropriately named, for sure.

᭸

Immobile, the Enforcer stood before Blauw and Emperor Calaneris, while they discussed what to do with him next. He'd been recalled after several failed attempts on Violet Rain's life.

"I am quite disappointed, Blauw," the Emperor said.

"I wasn't sure what was going wrong at first," Blauw replied. "But I did have a chance to talk with the other Earth woman Virginia Jones when she showed up.

Playground

The Scientists at the STS-99 space station said she was particularly interested in the Big Bang, which is where we've seen this strange species, the Watchmen, hanging about, albeit in a dimension we've been unable to reach so far. Jones has disappeared—"

"What? She's disappeared?"

"—and I think she has somehow joined the Watchmen. As you know, they've perfected a technique that allows one to shift between dimensions for short bursts of time. I'm almost positive that's how Violet Rain has been escaping the Enforcer, although I'm puzzled as to how she has learned to use the technique. I was about to interrogate Jones, when she jumped away. So, while I theorize that it's possible Jones learned the technique from the Watchmen, I don't understand how she could have taught it to Violet Rain. Virginia Jones once met Violet Rain, but that was in Earth's 25th century. I'm positive Rain didn't know the technique at that time. It's a perplexing paradox. Of course, anything's possible with complexity theory in play."

"You said, 'at first,'" Calaneris said. "Do you know how to dispatch Violet Rain now, or not?"

"Yes, my lord. If you'll just give us another chance, I know it will work this time."

"What sort of chance?"

"We'll simply return the Enforcer to the 21st century to finish what he was designed to do."

"Why would we do that?"

"I managed to deduce the dimensional shift secret, right after Jones disappeared," Blauw said. "Her son-in-law Eric helped me with it. He's rich and good-looking but incredibly simple-minded. I've programmed the Enforcer to track and follow now. Violet Rain won't escape this time."

"See that she doesn't. I want results. Any more mess-ups, and I assure you that you'll be erased along with the Earth's 25th century timeline."

97

"Yes, sire, of course."

ꙮ

Fortified with a broccoli and chicken stir-fry and cherry cheesecake, Violet and Janus strolled out of the Cheesecake Factory and onto the casino floor.

"Care to play a game of chance?" Janus said, raising his eyebrows.

"Based on what I've heard about gambling, there is very little left to chance," Violet said.

"My treat," Janus said, pulling out several twenties. "Get some chips from the booth over there."

Violet looked at the odd greenish pieces of 21st century paper currency, which featured the portrait of a fluffy haired white man with bushy eyebrows. She walked up to the cashier window and put the money on the counter.

"Hey, cool purple bangs," the woman behind the window said. She pushed a tray containing a stack of chips out toward Violet.

"Thank you. What do you recommend?" Always best to ask the natives.

"Um, maybe roulette. You have almost a 50-50 chance if you stick with red or black. Give it a whirl."

"Where is this roulette game?" Vi asked Janus.

"They have them strategically placed on tables at intervals all over the room," Janus said. "And, of course, there is the Big Jackpot machine up on the wall there. Not much chance of hitting on that one, though the lights are pretty."

"Hitting, as you quaintly put it, should be no problem," Violet said.

"Really. Well, you are about to find out the hard way."

Violet placed a bet and watched as the wheel spun, bright lights marching around the circumference of the wall display until it slowly came to a stop.

"No winners," the attendant announced. Violet glanced around. She was the only person betting.

"Let's try again," she said.

Bells clanged raucously, and a voice announced over the public address, "We have a winner on the Big Jackpot."

"Beginner's luck," Janus mumbled. "Congratulations."

Violet spun again. And won again. A small crowd began to gather.

"This is fun," she said, spinning once more. This time, the top line on the Big Jackpot lit up. All action in the casino stopped, drowned out by the honking clarions and ringing carillons of the Big Jackpot. The unthinkable had happened. Everyone had seen a big winner. Luckily, no one had seen her slip forward in time to see the winning number each time.

The manager of the casino and an employee armed with an SLR camera marched up and took Violet's picture. The manager pointed her to the cashier, mentioning something about "tax withholding."

Violet approached the cashier's booth. The woman greeted her with a big smile. "Super, a big winner! Congratulations! Here's your voucher for the winnings. I can keep it here for you if you want to keep gambling, but if it was me, I'd get away while the getting was good."

Suddenly Violet remembered that she *should* get away. Winning big had simply taken her worries away for a brief period and probably drawn too much attention. "Thanks, I'll leave the money here until we check out," she said.

"I wondered when you would come to your senses," Janus said. "What part of laying low don't you understand?" As they turned to leave the casino, a young man ran up to them.

"I'm from the local paper. We'd like to put your picture in as a big winner," he said. "And I can send the news to your home town, too, if you want."

"No, thank you," Janus said, taking Violet's arm and steering her out of the casino.

ⓢ

The sheets were crisp and the bed was comfortable, but Violet still couldn't sleep. Her feet throbbed. She and Janus had spent the rest of the evening marching up and down the Strip, looking but not gambling. Janus had the room near the end of the hall next door, and she hadn't heard a peep since the toilet flush around 2 a.m. She closed her eyes and tried to coax sleep to come. Tossing down intoxicating turquoise-colored "dranks" had been fun at first, then soporific, but now that she sat in bed, she felt dehydrated, and she couldn't stay asleep. She'd missed her antenvirals. She punched her pillow and lay back down.

A slight scratching noise came from the vicinity of her door. Someone putting a door card in the wrong room? Like her and Janus, everyone in Las Vegas seemed to be consuming way too many mind-altering toxins.

She sat up. A shadow partially blocked the light shining under the door.

"Hello?" As soon as she said it, she knew it was a mistake. The counterfeit Xoan was all too familiar with her voice and was probably going from room to room, looking for her.

The shadow moved away. Violet touched one bare foot onto the floor and then the other and crept toward the door. Taking a deep breath, she yanked the door open. No one there. She looked down the long hallway, deserted except for the soft humming of a vending machine near the elevator. She jumped as a cube dropped in the ice machine.

Violet told herself she was just being silly, but she couldn't shake the feeling that whoever had been there was probably coming back. Grabbing her kimono, she padded next door, the heavy wool-like carpet aggravating her sore feet.

She knocked. "Janus?" she whispered. She knocked again, a little harder.

The door opened a crack. "Violet? What time is it?"

Violet slipped in and closed the door behind her.

"We have to go again."

"Can it wait until morning?" Janus asked. "This is all quite exciting, but my arm hurts, and I need to get back to work."

"I have something to show you." Violet opened her short robe. The *hanfu* was the last souvenir she had of her home, given to her by her grandmother. Janus's eyes widened.

"Relax, it's not what you think," Violet said, and pulled a small wad of what looked like modeler's putty out of a packet in the underarm of the robe.

"What is it?" Janus asked, his interest evaporating.

"Try to concentrate, Janus. This is my VPA." When he looked blank, she added, "—Virtual Projection Assistant. To do VR right you need a supercomputer. But some of that compute power is distributed. So, everyone gets one of these little jobbers to communicate with their VR channel. But each one also has a pretty powerful little brain all its own. Because I was VR Administrator for Los Angeles, mine is more powerful than all of the compute power on Earth right now."

"That's ridiculous. You'd need millions of processors."

"Yes. Your point being? Anyway, I think it's about time I let you know—"

"—you're from the future," Janus interrupted. He rolled his eyes, the universal signal of skepticism. "I've guessed something like that for some time, and I actually believe you. The question is: Why would you bother to come back to a more primitive time, unless..."

"Unless some serious shit was about to go down. Yes. And I think that somehow you are one of the keys to heading that off. Or at least postponing it."

Janus raised his sandy eyebrows. Ah, she'd gotten his attention, after all.

"Me? Why me?"

"I don't know. You've got to work with what you've got. Plus, you're the father of VR."

"What... I am? That's really cool."

"It's especially cool, because it means you will live through this—whatever it is."

"Tell me everything."

"Soon, but I'm not kidding when I say, 'serious.'" She squeezed gently on her VPA, which began to glow a warm, soft yellow.

Violet grew about a foot in height and became a man wearing a backwards-facing baseball cap, Lakers jersey, and baggy pants. A spray of stubble crossed his lip and chin.

Janus gasped in astonishment.

"Who do you want to be?" Violet continued. "May I suggest a hip-hop dancer? That way we won't look unusual when we leave the hotel. Just a couple of entertainers. The shoes are ugly, but it can't be helped."

"I wouldn't mind looking like a basketball fan too. But will I suddenly be able to dribble and dunk?"

"Of course not. A VPA just projects an image, it doesn't change the person underneath. Still, your brain may *believe* you're a basketball player, so it'll be no big deal to learn to dribble and dunk. With VR, we can do anything we can imagine."

Janus shrugged. "We have a saying, 'Any sufficiently advanced technology is indistinguishable from magic.'"

"We have that saying, too," Violet said, smiling.

"Hit me with your finest illusion, then. Um, could you also add a gun? Even if it's not real, it might help scare someone away."

She again squeezed the VPA. Janus's skin darkened, and he wore a jersey similar to Violet's, except with many gold necklaces. Elaborate blue tattoos traced his arms. He pulled up his shirt to reveal a handgun tucked into the athletic pants.

"Hmm, looks real enough. Say, did this have anything to do with you winning the Big Jackpot?" She shrugged.

Violet opened the door a crack and peered out. "Let's go. And stop grinning like that."

⟲

A little after two in the morning, the lizard man strode up to the front desk of the hotel. He wore a steampunk outfit with leather breeches and a bowler hat, and his skin had been painted with green scales, like a reptile. The desk clerk yawned.

"Finish your show at Circus-Circus?" he asked.

"I'm looking for a guest named Violet Rain," YDorian said. "She won the Big Jackpot earlier tonight."

"We can't give out information about our guests," the clerk said. "Those yellow contacts with the slit pupils are really creepy, man. You look just like a snake."

"And you look just like a human," the man replied.

"Thanks. I think."

YDorian spotted the sign pointing to the parking garage and entered. Yes, Violet Rain had been here, but there was no lingering timeslip trail. She'd probably shifted dimensions to make the jump.

Certainly, YDorian had had disagreements with Yverra about investigating the Unwindings. She was headstrong and went ahead anyway, though he warned her about the possibility of disaster. They argued, and he'd left in anger, exiling himself a few hundred years in the past on this backward planet, where he expected that no one would ever come looking for him.

He'd been shocked to see a human exhibiting Watchman time-hacking capabilities in the casino. Was it a coincidence, or had Yverra sent Violet Rain after him? Either way, it was undesirable.

☉

"What the hell?" Janus said. "How did we get to the parking garage so fast?"

"Dimensional shift," Violet replied tersely. She gestured toward their rental car. "Hurry. You drive."

They left the garage, driving out onto the Strip, still gaudily flashing lights to attract more customers, although it was almost three in the morning. Violet was going to miss the free breakfast she'd heard so much about.

Once they headed out into the desert, the only lights were the occasional pair of headlights, temporarily blinding them against the pitch darkness. Janus began singing a song called "Home on the Range." Janus was intelligent, friendly, and funny, but Violet couldn't afford to become too attached. She remembered the poor cab driver she'd gotten killed a week earlier, and she didn't want to repeat that mistake. But it was becoming hard to keep her stories straight.

"You said you wanted to know everything," Violet said. "Are you sure? Or do you want to 'get back to work,' as you put it?"

"You said I was the father of VR," Janus replied. "Of course, I want to know more. I'm obviously more than just your Uber driver."

"You're right," Violet replied. "We think you must be important in the scheme of things. I know that sounds vague. And the truth is, I know a lot about virtual reality, but I'm new at dimensional shifting as a form of time travel." *Here it comes,* Violet thought. The inevitable flood of questions.

104

"Can everyone shift dimensions in the future? This isn't just VR projection..."

"No, not everyone can do it."

"So you're some sort of time raider agent?"

Oh, hell, truth was always the best policy.

"I'm a Watchman, yes. There are only four of us. The rest are dead." Violet sighed, knowing she was the only *human* Watchman.

"Very sorry to hear that. Sounds dangerous. Heading off time disasters must keep you pretty busy."

"More than you know."

"Do you always run around in these disguises?"

Violet shrugged. "Sometimes it makes things simpler."

"What's your favorite one?"

"Well, I was a tardigrade recently."

"Gross. Isn't that one of those tiny bugs that can survive in the Arctic?"

"Yes, they're very tough creatures, unlike humans." *Unlike me*, she thought.

"That would be weird. May I say that I'm glad *you* don't look like a tardigrade. Hard to find a girlfriend, I would think."

Violet flushed, growing irritated. "They're hermaphroditic. In this case, I used it to cross universes without instantly dying."

Janus whistled. "'Universes,' plural. So there *are* more than one, like the scientists think. But tardigrades— Who would make up something that unbelievable?"

"I'd appreciate it if you'd quit babbling about things you know nothing about," Violet said, looking daggers his way.

Janus slumped over the wheel. "Sure, sorry." He leaned back and stole surreptitious glances at the amazingly real-looking rings on his fingers as they gripped the steering wheel.

"Don't tell anyone about this," Violet said, interpreting the expression on his face. He shook his head.

"Or else you'll have to kill me, I get it."

A thin line of red light crossed the horizon in front of them. The sun would be rising soon.

They headed northeast, thinking to cross Utah and take I70 through Colorado. Having cooled off, Violet wondered if she had been too harsh with Janus. She'd seen from his reaction and silence that she'd said something wrong. Again. She'd probably been just as bad with John-Paul, rarely stopping to think about how her actions might have affected others, including her family. Her mom was still alive before the Unwinding. Maybe Violet could see her again, someone who actually loved her unqualifiedly. Too dangerous. She decided against it.

After an hour Janus was talking again, complaining that it was too difficult driving into the sun. Violet agreed. Besides, it is harder to spot a maniac killer coming at you that way, so they decided to stop in St. George.

"What's the specialty of Utah?" Violet asked.

"You mean the Mormon religion?"

"No, for breakfast."

"Honestly, Violet, are you just going to eat your way across America?"

"I think better on a full stomach," she replied.

A sudden, high-pitched wail interrupted their conversation. Janus frowned at the rear-view mirror.

"Uh, oh, looks like the CHIPS are after us."

"CHIPS?"

"Well, the Utah version, anyway. Cops." He slowed and pulled over.

"Wait... " Vi said, reaching toward the wheel.

A tap sounded on the driver's side window. Janus rolled it down a crack.

"Do you know how fast you were going?" the cop asked.

"Um, sorry officer. We were just—"

"Let's see ID and registration."

Violet swallowed. Janus did not look *at all* like the photo on the driver's license in his pocket. She groaned loudly. Janus and the cop looked over to see a visibly pregnant woman in the probable throes of labor. "I think she's coming, dear," she said in a quivering voice. She started to pant.

"You're still a mile from the St. George hospital, ma'am," the cop said, recoiling in alarm. "You two'd best be on your way. Want me to escort you?"

"That's not necessary, but thanks anyway." She waved as Janus pulled away.

"What was *that* about?" Janus asked. "You aren't really, um, expecting, are you?"

"That cop could have been Xoan," Violet said. "Besides, you still look like a Black basketball player, you know."

"My God, I'd forgotten," Janus said, chuckling. "Well, maybe we ought to change the way we look a bit, so we won't stand out so much. There are a lot of mountain biker tourists around here. Everyone expects them to look hungry."

"That's great!" Violet exclaimed. "I have just the clothes for us. I had a track on the Ranch at home." She resumed her normal aspect and was now wearing elbow and knee pads. Her long hair was done in a braid which hung down behind her helmet.

"Um, that looks pretty good," Janus said. "You did your homework."

"I even rode an expensive cross bike back home," Violet added. "All VR, of course. It was just an antique junker underneath. Ooh, here's a café."

The waitress at the pancake house delivered little glasses of orange juice while they waited for their order of pancakes, scrambled eggs with spinach, and hash browns. Violet quickly tossed hers back.

"What? Running is thirsty work," she said.

Janus shook his head and resumed the grilling.

"If you don't mind my asking, if you are so powerful that you can jump through dimensions and space, why don't you just jump us to our final destination. Speaking of which, what is our final destination?"

Violet was loathe to put down her tumbler of orange juice, but she forced herself to do it. "We're heading to North Carolina," she said after one last slurp.

"Your grandparents, right? Do they have superpowers too?"

"Alan and Virginia are not technically my grandparents. But they *do* have a direct line to the powers that be."

Janus cocked his head. "You mean there are more powerful beings than Watchmen?"

Violet thought it'd take too long to explain about Grace and Golaeth.

"Of course, silly. I'm just an ordinary girl."

"Why don't you call them to ask the powers that be to whisk us to North Carolina?"

"One, I think Xoan is back, and he's looking for us, so no Earth-based communications, and two, the pulse of Hawking radiation released to get us to North Carolina would definitely be noticed by the natives, primitive as they are, not to mention Xoan."

"Xoan is the guy who tried to kill us back in Monterey?"

"Yes, or at least he used to be a guy."

"What is he? Some sort of killer android?"

"It's complicated. He was my boyfriend."

Mercifully, the questions stopped there. They checked into a motel to rest for a few hours before hitting the road again.

Violet's throat felt urgently dry, desiccated even. Feeling oddly out of sorts, she closed the bathroom door and stared at the sallow face in the mirror. It'd been a long week; she decided she must be dehydrated. She picked up a glass from the sink, ripped off the wrapper, filled it with water, and gulped the contents down. Relieved, she felt a little better.

Well, Janus was going along for the full ride. She told herself that was good. That, plus a bit of fear at the thought of being alone again. Huh, she wasn't actually dead inside after all.

And Janus's question about the powers that be was a good one, Violet thought. Come to think of it, Yverra had a theory that the Watchmen—the real, original ones— were still alive somewhere, if not this planet. If she could figure out a way to talk to Grace, maybe she could go to the Watchman instead of her grandmother's. Grace had been dubbed "the Living Cintamani," and could do pretty much anything from her post in the Hatchery of the Universes.

Violet put the glass down and opened the bathroom door to see Janus softly snoring on one of the beds.

*****~~~~~*****

Chapter 9.

Flight

Violet knew she was wasting time by driving. Stalling. She was supposed to come to the twenty-first century, probably to meet up with Janus Parker—and do what? Earth had already been destroyed in the twenty-fifth century. She couldn't tell Janus that. It would be devastating. In fact, she was still devastated herself, along with her other friends, Ben, Ralff, and Yverra. Their worlds had been devastated too, a real bonding experience. Her eyes burned.

Janus reached over to change the radio station as they passed out of yet another FM reception area. "FM is line-of-sight," he said matter-of-factly. So, the signal reaches farther on the plains. Once we reach the mountains, we can kiss reception goodbye."

Violet wondered if there were similar limitations of communication among universes. Probably. Might explain the little misunderstanding that had led to Earth's demise.

They climbed into the Rockies, crossing through a long, FM-free tunnel of silence. As the car barreled downward from the Continental Divide, myriad radio stations announced their presence, bursting through a haze of static.

"We're getting close to Denver," Janus said. "This is where I grew up, but I haven't been back in a while. Queen City of the Plains, they call it. I usually fly straight between the East and West Coasts, and all this land just looks blank. Of course, that's because there aren't any windows in the new planes..."

Violet smiled, pulling her sweater closer. She'd be glad to get to a lower altitude where it would be warmer.

"Is this the Badlands?" she asked. "I had orders for Badlands simulations almost every week. People liked Westerns."

"'Fraid not," Janus said. "Whole different state. Plus, the days of horses and rustlers are long gone. But you can put on a cowgirl outfit if you want. I won't object."

Though it was warmer in Denver, they didn't stop to admire the skyscrapers sprouting from its downtown. The gray, concrete strip that was the Interstate stretched off eastward into the distance. Seventeen hundred miles to go. Still so far. They periodically left the Interstate, taking connector spurs where possible to throw off their trail from the horrible thing that looked like Xoan. She felt certain in her heart that John-Paul had died on Mars, and this was a killer robot duded up to look like him to get to her. Unregulated virtual reality could be a real pain sometimes. She shivered and wondered briefly if it would have been a better idea to take one of those flying deathtraps to North Carolina. She dismissed the idea again just as quickly.

They passed through a number of states that Violet had forgotten existed since the VR channels had taken the place of most political boundaries. Eventually they turned off I70 in West Virginia and headed south toward North Carolina. She wasn't sure what she was going to tell Virginia and Alan, but at least they could contact the Hatchery in relative safety and perhaps get Grace and Eric's advice.

"Where are we going, again, exactly?" Janus asked.

"They live in Raleigh," Violet replied, "but to be safer I think we should head for the Outer Banks. They drove over to the coast, passing a number of lighthouses.

"Let's stop for a bit," Violet said. "Stretch our legs before calling."

"I get it. It's not polite to just drop in out of the blue with an uninvited guest in tow," Janus replied.

"It's not that. It's not polite to drop in with a *dangerous* uninvited guest right behind you," she corrected.

They took off their shoes and walked along the sandy beach, inhaling real salt air. Lovely. And not so windy as it had been in California. The water was warmer, too.

"Well, I guess we should take a chance and try calling them," Violet said. "Do you still have your phone?"

"Yep, and I've kept it in airplane mode the whole time," Janus said, handing it to her.

"I won't even ask what that is," Violet said. Almost yelling, she ordered, "Call Grandma."

Janus chuckled. "That's not going to work. What's her number? Here, I'll make the call." As if an invisible hand had ripped it away, the phone flew out of his hand.

"What the—" He bent down to pick it up, but it cartwheeled down the beach, propelled by hurricane-force blasts.

"Violet, are you doing this? It's not funny." He started to chase the wayward phone, but Violet stepped in front of him.

"I think he's coming. I'm sorry, Jan. I thought we'd be safe here, but this is where we part ways. I've got to make myself scarce for a bit. Why don't you go to my grandparents, and I'll join you there later." She pulled out a pen. "Give me your arm."

Janus held out his palm, and Violet hastily scribbled a number.

"I promise I won't wash it off until I get there."

The wind grew wilder, and the calm gray waters began to grow whitecaps. A bolt of greenish lightning struck on the horizon. Violet's vision blurred, as if she was looking through a sheet of wax paper. She realized she was crying.

With a little scream, Violet vanished abruptly. The calm weather resumed, as if nothing had happened.

Janus pushed up at his blond high-top, which was now flattened and sticking out sideways. He heard the rumble of a car engine.

"Violet?"

"Janus!" It was Alan Jones. "Get in."

๑

"We were together, and then Violet just disappeared," Janus said. "She said she'd join us here later." He sat on the Jones's overstuffed tweed couch, nursing a scalding hot cup of tea Virginia had pressed into his hands. He checked his palm. He still hadn't washed his hands. No need now. He had tried to explain it to Professor Jones during the 200-mile drive from the coast, leaving out the part about how he'd fallen in love with Violet.

"Hmm," Alan said. "If that were true, we'd have seen her by now. She can travel time and dimensions like a pro. She's a Watchman now."

"I don't know what to tell you, except that there was this guy following us all the way from California. "

"Yes, the one she mentioned in the phone call a few days ago," Alan said.

Janus squirmed uncomfortably in his seat. "I think *something* bad thrust itself into our world, something unnatural. And maybe it took Violet with it when it left. She said it *used* to be her boyfriend."

"The thing that puzzles me is the storm and the green lightning," Virginia said with a worried look. "That's the signature of an Unwinding. Every time such a storm happened around me, I got whisked away to Poe's stasis point—it looks a lot like the beach at Nag's Head, you know."

"You think she's at the Beach, Poe's nexus?" Alan mused.

"If she is, there's no way we or anyone else can get to her. Poe has it locked down. It's his panic room."

Janus vowed to himself to never again ridicule those scifi TV shows where part of the population simply vanishes with no scientific explanation.

☙

Shocked, Violet stared into the eyes of a humanoid alien, covered in scales and blinking at her with large golden eyes that had slitted pupils.

"Yverra! How did I get here?"

"I'm not Yverra. How do you know her?" the person asked, though presumably a female Watchman like Yverra. The wasp-waisted creature wore a coat and breeches made out of the skin of some other scaly creature. By now, Violet was used to her Watchman friend's total lack of fashion sense. This was good news. Perhaps unwittingly, she'd gotten pulled into her Plan B—to enlist the pre-Unwinding Watchmen in helping to fight Xoan.

"Um, my name is Violet Rain. I'm guessing that we are still somewhere in my past, but I'm not sure how I got here. Where is here, exactly?"

The Watchman pointed. A dozen hazy figures gathered about a brightly shining orb perched on a pedestal within what looked like a cathedral. Congregants murmured incantations and reached into the fog, pulling out one person at a time. None were people Violet knew.

"I pulled you out of your predicament, of course," the Watchman responded. "YDorian told us to keep an eye out for humans like you bouncing around in time and space between Unwindings. Sure enough, there you were, so I grabbed you."

"What about my companion?"

"What about him?"

"Nevermind." Best to leave Janus out of this for now.

"Would it be possible to speak with Yverra?"

"She has been preoccupied with retrieving an Earthling ally like you, who is currently investigating the Big Bang along with the Emperor Calaneris and his Scientists. This is a dangerous enterprise, and many of us feel she is foolish to get involved at all. However, based on our extrapolations, we believe she can help us achieve success in curtailing the destructive incursions reverberating through the universe."

Realizing she had jumped into the midst of the Unwinding, Violet laughed, a sour taste in her mouth. They hadn't managed to save very many people from the Unwinding, had they?

"Yverra is with Virginia Sun-Jones?"

The Watchman nodded. "They've been working together for some time, and have discovered that these disturbances are actually probes by the Hatchery intended to repair anomalies accidentally introduced by your universe. Your ancestor has traveled to the Emperor's planet to meet her daughter, Grace."

"Something told me I wasn't in Kansas any more. Now I remember. Grace is the Living Cintamani, and she went to help settle the dispute between universes, but something went wrong. The Emperor imprisoned Grace…"

A slight shimmer appeared in the air to the left of the Watchman. The false Xoan stepped out, already shooting. A hole appeared in the Watchman's face; red blood spurted onto Violet's dress as the woman fell.

Violet screamed, and regretted it instantly. Xoan turned toward her, a smile on his face that was definitely not John-Paul's smile. The air shimmered again. Violet's stomach lurched, as she and the mortally wounded Watchman shifted dimensions to escape the onslaught.

Flight

Violet opened her mouth to shout, but there was no air for her lungs. She and the Watchman were floating in interstellar space, their life expectancy about thirty seconds, hers perhaps shorter. Before them, a water planet loomed. The Watchman had tried to take them home with a dimensional shift, but that was no longer a possibility. A brilliant green beam of radiation marched across the continental surface, piercing the crust and unleashing volcanic eruptions from the planet's core. The Watchmen's home world was being torn into pieces, red lava tracing a path of total destruction and boiling the dark oceans. Violet imagined she could feel the heat of the holocaust and prepared to die with her new friend when the shock wave reached them.

Violet's mind shouted out her grief for the Watchmen, Yverra's—and now her—people. This was their end, and she had been powerless to help them, too overwhelmed to even try her new skills.

She felt herself shift again. The Watchman had moved her again, thrown her free. She hadn't even had time to learn the woman's name. Violet found herself on STS-99, in her lab. She gasped, gulping in great lungfuls of air. The unknown Watchman had saved her. She was safe. *No.* The air sparkled. Not-Xoan flung a blade at her, cutting her side and taking with it a slice of her hair. Ducking, she searched frantically for a place to hide. She spotted the container of microscopic tardigrades and *jumped* into the next available dimension. That was the last thing she remembered.

*****〜〜〜*****

Chapter 10.

The Search

They were all looking at her, as if she had the answer. Virginia turned the strange story over and over in her mind.

The storm that Janus talked about was almost certainly an Unwinding, but was it just a coincidence that he and Violet had been there to witness it? There were lots of witnesses to the other Unwindings that Gin had seen, but most of those witnesses were dead. Rips in space-time tended to be hard on human beings. She'd survived several Unwindings herself by wielding the Cintamani, a powerful quantum dimensional transporter loaned to her by the universe, whom she'd nicknamed Poe for its mysterious and intermittently sentient behavior. The Cintamani, a small, pearl-like jewel, translated some of Poe's desires into language she could understand.

The Cintamani also seemed to ensure her safety, often returning her to a quiet beach, a stasis point in the midst of chaos. The Beach was the universe's heart, and it was the white dot in the black side of the new Yin-Yang universe.

Could Violet be there? Gin could easily picture Poe thinking of Violet as one of Gin's prized offspring and reaching out a tendril to preserve her. Poe's usual behavior was to never communicate, so unless Gin could find a translator, she wouldn't be able to ask Poe about it. The only possible translator she knew personally was her daughter Grace. She sighed. She felt a little sorry she'd given up the Cintamani and returned to the everyday life of a normal housewife, but one adventure like the

Unwinding was enough for a lifetime. She didn't want to bother Grace, but... oh, what the hell. Grace would take a call from her mother, surely.

"Hi, Mom. I could feel you reaching out to me," Grace said, a nonverbal voice in Gin's head. "You know, I can always feel it when you're in pain or in trouble. What's wrong?"

"It's Violet," Virginia said. "We can't find her. I know we promised to look out for her during her visit to the 21st century, but she seems to have vanished. We've been frantic."

"Hmm. Offhand, I can't sense her either. You don't think she's dead, do you?"

"I'm hoping not. The last time we saw her, she was at Nag's Head. A storm came up, and she vanished. Sounds uncomfortably like an Unwinding, don't you think? Is it possible you could ask Poe if she's at his Beach?"

"I'm doing that now... No, she's not at the Yang stasis point. Poe says she was on the STS-99 station for about five-and-a-half seconds, but now is back on Earth."

"Transported to another time, perhaps? That's what always happened to me after Unwindings."

"No, she's now but somewhere in America, I think. Do you want me to notify the other Watchmen? I think they would be the best at initiating a search."

"Yes, thanks, Grace. Again, I'm really sorry about messing up Violet's visit."

"Oh, stop it, Mother. You're always apologizing for things that aren't your fault."

Virginia choked back a sob. She missed Grace so much. "Right, of course."

"And one more thing, Mom."

"Yes?"

"The man that is chasing her was sent by Emperor Calaneris and Blauw. I'm pretty sure it's a construct sent to kill her to cut off her timeline forever."

"What? But she's alive in the future, so they mustn't have succeeded, right?"

"Only if we manage to prevent them somehow."

"Can't the Hatchery or Poe help?"

"We can't control everything due to the uncertainty principle. And I think the universe only had an interest when it thought it was under attack. Your Yin-Yang solution took away that danger. Or, at least it will, if we make it to that future."

"But Violet and Yverra said the Unwindings seem to be starting up again. Isn't that enough of a danger to warrant intervention?"

"Apparently they don't think so. But let me work on them. I'll get back to you."

☺

A haze of cigarette smoke hung in the air of the cavernous casino, softening the glaring light flashing from the many gambling machines.

"The clanging bells and colored lights are quite stimulating, don't you think?" Ben asked. "Quite the contrast from back home on Jandalat, where there was little to do but contemplate the cosmos. Ooh, and I can feel low-frequency rhythmic throbbing, indicating live music."

"Yes, but they are mere diversions meant to distract the unwary from the fact that they are giving up their money," Ralff said.

The Watchmen had decided to track Violet's travel from Las Vegas, the point where Janus and she had decided to "disappear."

"But we didn't mean that literally," Janus had reported. "We just meant to drive to North Carolina. We were almost there, when the guy showed up, and Violet really *did* vanish."

The two tall aliens strode across the expansive casino floor, checking sensors that would be able to detect the presence (or absence) of Violet Rain. None of the gamblers showed any interest in the unusually tall visitors. Hooded caftans were an everyday sight, with the growing popularity of the casinos with Middle Eastern and Asian guests with money to burn.

"Perhaps people will think we're in the band," Ben said, looking hopeful.

"Ah, here is the Wheel of Fortune Janus spoke of," Ralff said. "It shows she has been here, but is not here now."

"This seems like a rather arduous way to look for her, don't you think? There was no sign of her in San Jose, Asilomar, or the Hoover Dam, all places Janus thinks she had some familiarity with. She could have hidden there."

"We're looking for an intersection of places she lingered and made an impression on the timeline, her "essence" you might say, but narrowing it down to only those places where the assassin was able to find her. Strange, isn't it? It's behaving like a Watchman itself. Presumably at some point it learned dimensional shifting and was able to start following her. We need that trail to be able to find where she has ended up."

"If she's still alive," Ben said.

"If she's still alive," Ralff agreed.

Ben and Ralff stood by the lighthouse at Nag's Head with Virginia, Alan, and Janus.

"We've come up empty," Benrus said. "Her trace seems to have simply vanished at this point."

"But Grace said Poe said Violet is somewhere on Earth," Ginny protested.

"It is a contradiction, certainly," Ralff said.

"Perhaps there is some fact we have been overlooking," Ben added. "She's here yet not here."

"Sounds like one of those tough riddles," Alan said. "You know, ones like, 'A man and not a man saw and did not see a bird and not a bird perched on a branch and not a branch and hit him and did not hit him with a rock and not a rock.'"

"Well, what was the answer?" Ginny asked, looking dubious.

"It was a eunuch, I think," her husband said, scratching his head.

"Oh, good grief," Virginia said. "But I see what you mean about a riddle. But if we can't find her, probably that assassin can't either."

Janus pursed his lips. "I'm sorry to have to say this, but I need to go home. I've already taken too much time touring the country with Violet, so to speak—though I like her tremendously, you understand—"

"Of course," Alan responded. "You've got a business to run."

"I'm grateful you introduced me to Vi," Janus said. "She's given me a lot of good ideas for how to make some important breakthroughs in virtual reality."

Virginia gave Janus a hug.

"You did your best. Go home. We'll find her."

"I'm truly sorry," Janus repeated.

"No need to keep apologizing," Alan said. "This family has its issues, and this is just something we have to deal with on our own."

"You'll call me when you hear something?" Janus asked.

"Of course."

࿊

Yverra walked into the lab aboard STS-99. "What's that noise?" she asked.

"It's Earth music," Ben said. "Isn't it marvelous? The rhythm is so catchy. It's a band called 'Scotch Scorpion,' who were playing in their settlement called Las Vegas. I understand the band is named after an especially spicy vegetable the natives grow. Our food on Jandalat is so bland, don't you agree, Ralff? Virginia didn't complain about it—she was too polite—but I could tell she could hardly swallow it, although she badly needed the nourishment."

Yverra responded, "Some Earth food may be edible, but to me the music is positively terrible. Turn it off."

Ben rose and scrambled to press a button on the console.

"That's much better. Now, let's go over it one more time. We need theories for solving the enigma as to why Violet can't be detected by any known method, yet the universe is positive she's alive and somewhere on Earth in the 21st century. We're at a distinct disadvantage here, as we are all logical creatures, rather poor at crafting outlandish-but-possible scenarios. Violet is by far the most talented in that respect. Benrus, any new ideas?"

"You're right, Yverra," Ben said. "I recall Virginia saying that our universe really liked creating mysteries and leaving her to set about solving them. We followed the trace she and her companion left from her arrival in the United States, all the way to her disappearance on the opposite coast. Poe said she was here on the space station for five-and-a half seconds before vanishing entirely."

Yverra closed her golden eyes, deep in thought. When she opened them, her gaze fell on the projector Violet had been experimenting with to transfer her virtual consciousness to those microscopic creatures called tardigrades. Yverra had even helped name the new species Violet had engineered, *angelensis.* If Violet had come to STS-99 in the present, she could have jumped into a tardigrade body.

But there were no tardigrades on STS-99 in the 21st century. Violet hadn't begun her experiments until recently. In fact, the space station was mostly a derelict hulk, floating empty for eons, until the Watchmen had decided to colonize it. Emperor Calaneris had forced Virginia's daughter Grace to build it at the dawn of the Big Bang billions of years ago so they could study the birth of the universe for anomalies that could explain the Unwindings.

"Tardigrades," Yverra said aloud. "Unlikely, but that's the only explanation I can think of. What do you think of the idea of her putting some tardigrades on the station back in the 21st century? I got the impression from Violet that they are very sturdy creatures. They could easily go dormant until reawakened with water, or food became available."

"That's brilliant!" Ben declared.

"So you think Violet could be in a tardigrade body again?" Ralff said. "It's a leap, but there's no other explanation. We *must* have put some of the little creatures on the station 400 years ago."

"Before we act too fast, there's the little matter of the projector," Yverra said. "Violet's the one who developed the technique for sending her mind into the creature, while leaving her body behind, safe and sound here at the station. We can transport the projector along with the tardigrades, but it's one of a kind. Once we leave it behind, we can't be sure we'll ever see it again. It certainly wasn't here when we got here a year ago. So, if we did move it, and if Violet used it, what happened to it? And what happened to her body?"

"Another riddle," Ralff said. "All of the possibilities sound impossible."

"Let's do it anyway," Ben said. "We can't use the projector without proper training anyway, and if it has a chance of recovering Violet, I vote for setting up her lab here in the 21st century. Just because we didn't see it when we got here doesn't necessarily mean it was destroyed."

"Although that is the most logical explanation," Yverra observed.

The Watchmen carefully documented the exact placement and inventory of Violet's laboratory. None of them voiced the disturbing possibility that if Violet had somehow jumped into a VR body, her human body and the whereabouts of the VR projector would never be discovered.

"Ready?" Yverra said. Although the time hack was not a very large one, it had to be done right. The consequences of a mistake would probably cost Violet her life. The three, the last remaining Watchmen, joined hands and did the closest thing they knew to praying: they held their breath and jumped.

⟳

Janus stared at the fake porthole to his left, which displayed an ersatz view of the sky outside, occasionally swiping to an ersatz 2D view of the ground far below. He sighed and looked back down at the paperback thriller he'd bought at the airport. But he couldn't concentrate. His eyes hurt. They wanted to look far off into the distance, to stretch their muscles. He'd looked it up once. There were these ciliary muscles, forming a ring around each eyeball, that helped focus the lens, and they could get tired if they couldn't relax. Of course, his vision hadn't been 20-20 since he was twelve; that's the price you pay to be a nerd who knows a lot more than all the other kids.

He noticed that one of the other passengers wore a clip-on augmented reality device on his eyeglasses. He admired the inventor, who had the goal of bringing the world of knowledge within easy reach without the need to carry a computer. But now he knew that even with big advances in computation, that goal would never quite be reached—at least not without breakthroughs in deep learning. Violet had showed him that when she opened that kimono thing and took out a tiny supercomputer. She called it her personal projector.

He sighed again. He felt bad that he had constantly quibbled with Vi, even when she had revealed that she was here to save the world. Probably he just wasn't cut out to be a sidekick... On the other hand, wasn't that what sidekicks do—bring the superheroes back to reality when their grand schemes aren't working out?

The Search

What was Violet's grand scheme, anyway? He wasn't quite sure. She had singled him out when visiting the past, that was clear. He suspected the invitation from Alan Jones was just a subterfuge. She'd said Janus was the father of virtual reality... He resolved that he would do his best to live up to that moniker. He was no Shakespeare, but this would be his chance to gain immortality of a sort.

On the third hand, he missed Violet. For a moment, he felt he'd rather be an obscure inventor, toiling in the background of history, if she could be there with him. He realized he was a little in love with her, the way her slender hands moved constantly, whether she talked expressively or attacked a smothered burrito. She refused to talk about boyfriends from the past, though. Or was it girlfriends? She did seem rather friendly with that cashier in the casino, leaving her a lavishly excessive tip. Maybe it was just nerd love he was falling into. But he had to admit, Vi was his platonic ideal. Beautiful and smart, in equal doses. But looking at it rationally, there hadn't been a real spark, had there?

Violet was on a mission, that was all. Plus, he didn't really have time for a relationship. But if Alan and Virginia ever found her, he'd be back like a shot. He wanted another chance. There was always a chance, right?

He looked around at his fellow passengers, none of whom appeared to be enjoying the ride. One thing was for sure. Virtual reality had a long way to go.

*****~~~~~*****

Chapter 11.

The Devil's Circle

"This is where she's supposed to be," Yverra said. "When we set the projector with our best guess, it seemed that somewhere near Alan and Virginia, yet secluded, would be best. And this is the right time. But I can't see her. She's usually easy to spot with her high infrared. Rather a waste of energy, but that's human physiology for you."

"Well, as you pointed out, she may not be a human at the moment," Benrus said.

"She's always a human," Ralff demurred. "But I can't sense her. Maybe she's just unconscious."

The three Watchmen had arrived at a swampy area inland from the beach at Nag's Head. A sign read, "Nature Conservancy Wildlife Preserve."

"I certainly hope Violet's life is being preserved, even if we can't see her. Oh, look alive, some humans are approaching," Ralff said, pulling his cowl up so as to not shock the locals. They stepped further into the bushes.

A man, a woman, and a smaller human entered the clearing. The smallest immediately headed for a puddle of water and began stomping it, splashing most of the contents into a ring of mud.

"Bobby. Stop that!" one of the larger humans said. "You'll disturb the animals. Remember, we're supposed to be visiting the forest primeval. Be on the lookout for carnivorous plants."

129

"Not to mention the alligators," the other human said.

"Seriously? There aren't really alligators around, are there?" the first replied. She grabbed the small human's hand, and they hurried on across the clearing.

"What's wrong with alligators?" Yverra whispered. "One of the more attractive species on this planet."

"Well, I for one would prefer not to meet one in person," Ben said. "Let's set up a recorder that will transmit any activity remotely."

Yverra agreed, and after one more in-person sweep they vanished.

☉

At the end of the day, the human family returned the way they had come. As they again entered the clearing, the boy stopped, cocking his head to the side.

"What is it, Bobby? Do you hear one of the birds on our list? A whistling duck, maybe?" his father said.

"No, it's talking to me."

"That's silly," his mother said. "Wild birds can't talk."

"It's not a bird," Bobby protested. "It's someone in the ground."

"It's been a long day," his mother said, putting her hand across Bobby's forehead.

"It wants a drink," Bobby said.

"I think you're just dehydrated," she responded. "Let's get to the car. I have some Gatorade drink there."

"Ha, Gatorade," the father said. "Told you."

☉

"Where am I?" She wasn't quite sure how to interpret the signals she was getting. She was awake, so there must be food and water nearby. She had a vague recollection of having been in much worse circumstances. And she was pregnant. If she could just get to some of that water, she could reproduce and start swimming about. She tried to wiggle, but she was stuck.

130

"Hello?" She could speak, at least. She would call for help. "A little help here? I need some water."

There was no answer. She was already growing drowsy. If she didn't get help soon, she knew she'd go dormant. Dormant was all well and good, but she wanted to live right now. For some reason, that seemed important. She redoubled her efforts.

"Hello, help me, need water!"

It was no use. Perhaps after a little nap, she'd feel stronger. She rolled up into a ball and went to sleep.

Later, she didn't know how much, she felt a welcome spritz of water, awakening her. She tried to speak, but she wasn't fully reconstituted yet. She was getting there, though. At last, she was able to call out.

But again, there was no response. The warm rays of the sun were waning, and she felt the pull of morpheus yet again. Wait, the ground was vibrating. She felt the approach of large creatures.

"Water! Please help me. I need water..."

The ground vibrated again, but the pulsations began to gradually die out. The creatures were leaving.

"No, come back. Help me." She had been patient, but this was growing frustrating. She'd try again tomorrow.

�◎

"Hmm. Look at this," Ben said. "There's still no sign of Violet, but something's definitely going on at the projector site."

"What have you seen?" Yverra said.

"This location was previously deserted, but the activity of humans passing nearby has increased exponentially. The first day it was three people, nothing the next five days, then another group of humans. See here? They pause, like they see or hear something, then move on through."

"Yes, so? It's probably just a weekend," Ralff said. "I noticed that in Las Vegas the humans seemed to swarm every five to seven days. They called it the 'weekend.'"

"Perhaps. It is definitely periodic," Ben conceded. "But look at the next weekend: there are twice as many humans passing through as before. And it doubles again..."

Yverra stopped him. "You've definitely identified a pattern. We must return and investigate. Besides, I look forward to the chance of getting my feet wet again. The lack of humidity on STS-99 is terribly uncomfortable. Half the time I can't even sleep at night."

☺

The three stood at the Nag's Head Wildlife Refuge sign, each wearing hoodies, boots, and gloves over their customary outfits. The raucous sound of approaching humans assaulted their ears.

"Best to stay out of sight as best we can," Yverra said, withdrawing from the trail.

"This is where you can hear it," a human was saying.

"Oh, come on, you can't tell me you believe in the Devil's Circle? That's an old superstition."

"I definitely heard a voice," the human declared. "Here, stand here. Maybe it will speak again."

The skeptical human tramped over to the spot he pointed to, his boots kicking up clods of mud in the soggy ground.

"Help me! I need water! Please don't leave like the others. Help me!"

Obviously startled, the human jumped back.

"What the hell? Let's get out of here."

"I told you. Voices are coming from the ground. And someone said they saw a walking alligator man round here. Or—maybe this is an old Indian Burial Ground and we're trespassing."

"I'm not an Indian," the voice said. "Water. I need water."

The two men looked at each other and ran away.

"Well, I certainly didn't see anything out of the ordinary," Yverra whispered. "But those humans were definitely interested in something, and it appears they were frightened away. "Let's get closer."

Ben lifted up the hem of his caftan and tiptoed to the place the men had stood. He sniffed the air, his large flat nostrils flaring. "No, nothing."

"Really? You don't smell anything? This place is full of biological activity." Yverra frowned, or what Ben took to be a frown, and stepped forward. She hit a patch of greenish mud and skidded a few feet before pitching headlong. She landed with an especially resounding thud.

"Hello? I need water. Can you help me?"

"Violet? Is that you?" Ben exclaimed, helping Yverra to her feet.

"Where?" Yverra said.

"I'm here," a disembodied voice said. "I don't mean to be a nuisance, but I'm lost, and I ..."

"Just keep talking," Yverra interrupted. "The projector must be picking up her communication commands... Tell me if I'm getting closer."

"Well, then, shouldn't *you* keep talking?" the voice asked.

"It's Violet, all right," Yverra muttered. "She must be in the soil, and is probably no larger than a speck of dust. Dig up the top 10 centimeters, and we'll take it back to the lab for analysis."

"Allow me," Ralff said, pulling out a small black cylinder. "Stand back." His laser cutter traced a circle around the clearing and lifted out a horizontal slice under it. The dirt hovered just above the ground, ready for transport.

"Hey, what are you doing?" a man in a ranger uniform asked. This is a wildlife refuge. You're not allowed to take any of the plants or vegetation as souvenirs. I'm going to have to write you a ticket..."

"Terribly sorry, officer. We're just leaving." The three suspects began to fade, along with their booty.

"Fleeing the scene is a federal offense," the ranger warned.

They were gone, although he heard a faint voice say, "Don't forget the monitor."

The ranger gazed around the forest. What could they want with a bunch of mud, anyway?

ᯤ

The Watchmen unloaded their sodden cargo in Violet's lab on STS-99 and began scanning the soil they had lifted from 21st century Earth.

"We'll have to return this to Earth as soon as we're finished with it, or it will cause a lot of unnecessary ripples in the timeline," Yverra noted. "Any tardigrades we find excepted, of course. It will speed things up if we moisten the mineral and organic matter, assuming we're dealing with a tardigrade body."

After thinly spreading the swamp dirt into a wide circle, Ben applied a light mist with a spray bottle. The moist aroma of *geosmin* filled the room, yielding up its essence of dying bacteria and creation.

"Hello?"

"There she is, that's her," Yverra said. "Violet, can you hear me? It's Yverra. You're here with us on STS-99."

"I— I don't know who that is," the voice said.

"Eureka," Ralff said. "She's in this cubic centimeter. No movement, however. She's become a slow stepper, all right."

Yverra continued, "Don't you know us, Violet? We rescued you from Earth. You were attacked, remember?"

"I don't remember anything," Violet said.

"That is going to be a problem," Yverra responded. "We don't know what you've done with your body or the

VR projector, although we assume they're together somewhere in the universe."

"Can I have more of that delicious water?" the creature formerly known as Violet said. "I'm carrying about a hundred babies, you know."

"Don't worry, we'll take good care of you," Ralff said.

The Watchmen huddled in conference.

"If we can't locate her body and projector, that at least means the assassin can't find it either," Ben pointed out. "Any ideas where she might have put them, Yverra? We used to be expert dimensional shifters, but after spending almost 800 years cooped up in stasis, we probably aren't up on the latest techniques."

"I'm at a loss as well," Yverra said. "Wait, I have a thought. You mentioned stasis. What if her body is in stasis somewhere?" She blinked. "That is a very dangerous gambit. If no one knows its location, she could be there until the end of the universe."

"What about asking Poe? Could they be at the Beach?"

"We already asked Poe and were told she was on Earth."

"Poe was telling the truth. Violet's consciousness was indeed on the Earth," Yverra said. "But perhaps it would be prudent to rephrase the question. If Violet's body is on Poe's Yin-Yang stasis point, this would indicate that Poe has been dissembling somewhat."

"You mean he might have lied to us?"

"Not exactly. Poe may be concealing his true motives. As the Hatchery has said before, it's up to us to take any action we find appropriate to get to the bottom of the latest Unwindings. Maybe that's all Poe is doing too."

The Watchmen stepped back toward the table where the cubic centimeter of soil containing Violet rested.

"Hold on, Violet, we may have a clue about your body's whereabouts," Yverra said.

"My body is right here," the voice responded. "And I'd like to be called Cheon-Sa, if you don't mind. I'm not this Violet you keep talking about, or at least I can't remember it. I could hear everything you were saying, by the way. I have quite acute vibration senses. Perhaps I could meet this Poe person. He sounds like a very interesting character. I'd like to live on a beach. Lots of water there."

"Cheon-Sa," Ben mused. "That's encouraging. It's Korean for 'Angel.' Violet speaks French, Korean, and English, so maybe she's still in there somewhere."

"What could have caused Violet to suffer such a complete break and lose her memory like this?" Yverra asked.

"It must have been something quite traumatic," Ralff said.

"Sometimes I miss the obvious," Ben said. "You've always been the sensitive one."

Janus emerged from the jetway onto the concourse at Mineta Airport in San Jose. He carried Violet's courier bag, which had fallen to the ground when she disappeared. He supposed he should have mentioned that to Alan and Virginia—and he still might—but first he wanted to study its contents, if only to clean out any snacks Violet had neglected to inhale. He smiled and lifted the bag across his body. It was good to be back in Silicon Valley.

But things didn't look the same to him since his little adventure with Vi. People seemed to look at him a little too long. Complete strangers he would ordinarily ignore looked suspicious. He tried to shake these feelings off as baseless paranoia, but now he knew they weren't totally baseless. Maybe that's how it would be from now on...

The Devil's Circle

The drive home was uneventful, but when he got there his phone wouldn't open the door. Fighting a feeling of unease, he punched in the combination on the keypad and entered. The place was obviously empty, looking neat and tidy from the weekly visit by his housecleaner, Markita. Finding nothing amiss, he brewed a cup of coffee. He relaxed a bit as the aroma filled his kitchen, and sat down at the workstation in his study. The latest prototype VR headset lay on the desk. He blew off a light coat of dust. Markita never touched anything in his study. He kept the room unfurnished except for his workstation, which was inset into the wall, so he could walk around with the headset on without tripping over anything or injuring himself. He slipped on the opaque goggles and selected a program, "The National Parks Tour."

The rendered world, a panorama of mountains, lakes, and waterfalls, was beautiful, a product of the best 3D graphic art money could buy, but it still looked painfully unrealistic. Avatars dressed as hikers came upon a barren circle in the middle of the forest subtitled, "The Devil's Tramping Ground." This place was alleged to be haunted by the Devil so that nothing grew there. Janus wasn't impressed. At best the avatars were like expertly painted cartoon characters. Kind of creepy, actually. Critics called it the "uncanny divide" with good reason. His new company name played off that, implying it would soon overcome that limitation.

The key was miniaturization, right? He remembered Violet's personal projector, an amazingly powerful supercomputer about the size of a quarter. It had no buttons. There was no need for a headset. But he still had no clue how it worked. He felt like a character from that old movie, "The Gods Must Be Crazy," the South African bushman encountering a soda bottle for the first time. Except that glass soda bottles had been quickly replaced by aluminum cans and biodegradable plastic pouches. New ideas quickened, leapfrogging other previously promising avenues in ways that were seemingly unpredictable. It was crazy indeed. It was clear he needed to take the leap, but where to? In Violet's world, it was nothing to cross the abyss stretching below him, but in this world it would get you killed if you stepped outside of your study. What would it take to turn his work into a true technology disruptor and avoid being just another engineering has-been like the Sony BetaMax?

Frustrated, he pulled off the headset, accidentally knocking over his coffee. *Shit.*

He tossed the soaked dishtowel in the laundry for Markita to attend to. Time to get some supper and hit the hay. He sometimes had his best ideas while dreaming about impossible things.

☺

The trail had gone cold. The Enforcer had jumped a split second after Violet left the space station, but his tracking technique had failed somehow, and he ended up at the end of one of the many wormholes ringing Calaneris's STS-99 station. The stupid red-haired human had probably entered one of the quantum equations wrong in his programming, and now was returning the Enforcer to Earth on the orders of the Emperor. Blauw was unworthy to serve the Emperor. He would kill the human at his earliest opportunity.

He would begin the search back at the 21st century. He could not go back to the Emperor again unless he could report success.

The Enforcer had the gnawing feeling, some might call it intuition, that Violet would seek out friends and relatives and hide among them. His natural inclination was to kill all of Violet's friends and relatives, one by one, for all the trouble she had caused him. But his programming also specified that he was to make as little impact on the timeline as possible, save for the removal of her from it. He had made a serious error in attacking her outright, when Blauw had given him instructions to insinuate himself as her former friend, "Xoan." In his enthusiasm for killing humans, he had pushed that heuristic down the stack. Now that it had popped back to the top, his analysis showed it had been rather practical. At first. Until Violet had decided to avoid her old friend for some reason.

But when he returned to Earth, Violet Rain was nowhere in evidence, even with repeated biometric scans. He scanned her relatives, the great-grandmother and grandfather, and ascertained to his satisfaction that she was not there. Backtracking, he recalled Violet Rain's journey with a male companion, the ineffectual Janus Parker. She was most likely hiding with him somehow. That was where he would begin.

*****~~~~~*****

Chapter 12.

Competition Is Good For You

Janus entered the convention hall, wearing a cross-body courier bag and hiking boots, his new uniform. He hadn't let the bag out of his sight since it had fallen to the ground upon Violet's disappearance. He'd searched it several times, but had found no clues either to her virtual reality secrets or to her abrupt departure. There was only that funny little silk bathrobe. He pulled his earbuds out, pausing the old Chris Cornell tune that had become one of his favorites. The singer had "nearly forgotten" a broken heart.

A temporary sign pointed to Hall A, where the annual graphics conference would be convening its opening ceremony. A table sat out front, laden with coffee and danish. He helped himself and entered the hall, where three large projection screens offered closeups of the five men sitting on the dais. He scanned the room. A few dozen attendees were scattered around the ballroom, most sitting by themselves, head down, probably reading email or sifting through the multi-tracked schedule to find something of interest. Nobody threatening.

Glad he'd gotten there early, Janus headed to the front, climbed the short stairway to the stage, and took the sixth seat.

"You should try out your mic before we get under way," the man next to him said. "This place is notorious for having lousy A/V. Ironic, isn't it? You gave your visuals to the ready room, right?"

Janus nodded. He was far from being a newbie at professional conferences, although this was the first time he'd been invited to give the keynote address. The hall was filling rapidly.

After Deneb Vohra, president of the Southwestern Graphics Society, and several of the officers had thanked the many sponsors, the loudspeakers blared a bootlegged version of the theme to a popular science fiction movie.

"Ladies and gentlemen," the president said, "we are on the verge of some very exciting breakthroughs in three-D visualization, as I'm sure you'll agree when you hear from our keynoter, Janus Parker." The president tried to summarize Janus's vita, but was quickly drowned out by the cheering crowd.

"Thank you, Deneb," Janus said. "It's an honor to be here, something I've been working toward my whole life. Receiving the Roland D. Robertson Innovation Award is a special thrill." The audience cheered again.

"As you know, humans are strongly visual creatures, and that's why the field of graphics has been so important in helping people make sense of scientific data. Graphics have become an indispensable part of entertainment and everyday life as well.

"But however useful and attractive visual graphics can be, we all know it is only part of the perfect sensory experience that we as humans hunger for." The room grew silent. Janus licked his lips, his mouth suddenly dry.

"You've probably heard rumors about what we're working on at Canny Divide. Those rumors are true. We are developing virtual reality environments that you can taste, touch, and hear, not just see."

The keynote ended with more music, as the attendees filed out, presumably inspired to attend more sessions and take home his message.

"Good stuff, Janus," Deneb said, shaking his hand. "I look forward to seeing your demos tonight at the gala."

Janus had a hard time stifling a yawn. The demos would be state-of-the-art, of course, but inwardly he felt ashamed that he would not really deliver as promised in the keynote. Couldn't be helped.

☉

Janus took a swig of his vitamin water beverage, grimaced, and quickly set it down on his desk at work. He stared at the label: "Grape flavored." Ugh, far from it. He picked up the newspapers and trade journals that his assistant Judith had stacked neatly on his desk.

Grafix Today had a nice spread on the conference. He scanned the narrow columns, looking for a mention of his name. Ah, here was something. A frown creased his forehead as he read. The report said, "Canny Divide CEO Janus Parker announced a breakthrough in quantum methods that will increase compute power at least a hundredfold, enabling much more realistic simulations— and most excitingly—manipulation of environmental resources. It looks as though the days of the replicator are here at last."

Janus stopped and re-read that last bit. He'd said no such thing. He turned back to the start of the article, checking the byline. How was the reporter able to get away with just making crap like this up? Of course, it was the press, and the press couldn't be trusted. He turned to the table of contents, and the author bios for the magazine. No, this guy wasn't a journalist. He was a scientist. A computer scientist. A computer scientist with Berkeley credentials. This must be some sort of a joke. He remembered the time someone on his staff had written an April Fool's spoof memo announcing his retirement at the age of 30. He got up and walked out to his assistant's desk.

"Judy, would you find out more about the guy who wrote this article?" He handed her the magazine, where he'd circled the author's bio in red. Since she'd been promoted to personal assistant from secretary, she might as well start pulling her weight.

"Sure, Janus. Hmm... He claims some fancy degrees in his bio. Are you interested in hiring him?"

"We'll see," Janus said. That's just what he needed. Another faker with a fancy degree. Just like himself.

A few minutes later, Judith knocked on the door, rousing Janus from his reverie.

"I got a number for Dr. J. P. Hilario from *Grafix Today*," she said. "Want me to call him and set up an interview?"

"Yes, let's call him. But it'll just be a phone conversation for now."

"Check."

Janus busied himself checking last night's test runs, his eye straying occasionally to the magazine on his desk. Sprinkled among the results were a number with the notation, "FAIL." He sighed. They had their work cut out for them. A shadow fell across his desk.

"Yes?"

"I have Dr. Hilario on the line."

"Okay, thanks, put him through." It was time to get to the bottom of this.

"Hello, Dr. Hilario. This is Janus Parker. Thanks for taking my call. I wanted to contact you after reading your article in *Grafix Today*. Good job, by the way."

"Thank you. I do my best," the voice at the other end responded. Formal, but a not unpleasant baritone. Slight accent, unplaceable.

"There were a few details you got wrong, however," Janus said.

"Really? What would those be?"

"Well, some of the quotes were not what I actually said, for example," Janus said, a little too loudly.

"But there were no errors of fact, were there?" Hilario asked.

"No. Well, maybe not." Janus didn't want to give up the upper hand in this conversation, but on the other hand, the article contained assertions about VR developments that he wasn't sure about. They could be true—and he devoutly hoped they were—but he didn't have any first-hand knowledge. Only the fact that a woman named Violet Rain had predicted that they would come to pass.

"Um, your resume is quite impressive. I was wondering if you might be interested in working with Canny Divide?"

"You're offering me a position with your company?"

"Yes, that is, if it works out."

"I should be very pleased to work with you. Directly, of course."

This guy had balls, that was for sure. Most people would be excited to get any kind of job here, much less demand a high-level post.

"You'd report directly to me," Janus said, trying not to show his annoyance. "When can you start?"

"I'll be there tomorrow. I look forward to trying some of your Jamaican Blue Mountain coffee."

How did he know Canny Divide had only the finest coffee in its cafeteria? The guy wanted to work here all along, and he'd obviously done his homework.

"Welcome aboard, Dr. Hilario. Oh, by the way, we go on a first-name basis here. What does the J. P. stand for?"

"You may call me John Paul.

As he hung up the phone, Janus noted the man's accent again. He'd pronounced his name something like "Zhwan Paul." Close enough.

⌖

The Enforcer's eyes opened after spending the night standing on sentry mode. He rented a cheap one-room efficiency apartment to give the appearance of having a permanent address. It had been no problem duplicating the plastic card that the humans called a "driver's license," which they seemed to use for almost any purpose other than driving automobiles. He checked his skin coating and garments, which were all in good condition, and stepped outside. A human in the hallway waved to him. The creature presented little threat, probably just a neighboring occupant.

His neighbor said, "Hey buddy, be sure to lock your door. This isn't exactly the best part of town, you know."

"Thank you," John Paul the Enforcer said. There was really no need to apply security to a totally empty enclosure, but he fashioned a key in his coat pocket, pulled it out, and made a show of locking up.

He scanned the area to make sure no one surveilled him. Negative. The humans in this era were woefully lacking in security measures. He descended to the foyer, which was deserted. The wind chuffed, rattling the glass doors and making a hissing sound. He wrestled his way out onto the still-dark rain-slicked street. At least the rain had stopped, if only temporarily. He decided he'd walk to work instead of driving, to take a more detailed reconnaissance of the route, including closed circuit television cameras. The sidewalks outside his apartment building were cracked and broken. Obviously no maintenance drones had visited in a long time. As he passed out of the "bad neighborhood," his neighbor had warned him about, video cameras became more numerous, spaced at more frequent intervals. All were primitive, and some of them weren't even turned on. He approached a plastic roofed shelter displaying a San Francisco transit map and schedules.

A lone human woman sat on a bench, apparently engrossed in reading from an electronic device. She glanced up at him and returned to her feed. He felt a slight buzzing sensation in his arm, as he noted the woman had long, dark hair and wore a purple jacket and hat. He made as if to stumble, catching himself with one hand on the bench and brushing the woman's face lightly with the other.

146

"Ouch," she cried, jumping to her feet. "Watch where you're going, would you?" She touched her cheek, then stared at the drop of blood on her fingertips.

"Sorry," he mumbled, setting off at a brisk pace and knocking over a bottle of kombucha she had been drinking. Picking a sheltered spot out of sight of the bus shelter, he examined the results of the DNA sample he'd taken. It was not Violet Rain, although the woman did share some genetic heritage with his target. It would be good when this timeline ended, taking with it all of the Violet Rains of the universe.

The mounting sun burned through the low fog on the street, and as rush-hour traffic picked up, the wind died down and the atmosphere filled with the fumes of incomplete carbon combustion. Suddenly anxious to get to work, the Enforcer broke into a run. He arrived at Canny Divide and fumbled with cold fingers for his false id. Janus Parker stood in the reception area, chatting with the receptionist. Her orangish hair and large white teeth were slightly disconcerting, although the Enforcer lacked data as to why. Parker strode forward, hand out, to greet him.

"Have a good night, John Paul?" Janus asked.

He supposed it must have been a good night. He could remember nothing when in sentry mode, unless some sort of emergency were to come up requiring him to wake up and destroy things. He didn't require rest, but his regulated heartbeat did require a small amount of energy.

Janus grabbed his hand and shook it, briefly. "Chilly, ain't it? That's northern California for you. You know the old Mark Twain saying, 'the coldest winter I ever spent was a summer in San Francisco.' Let's get some of that Jamaican coffee into you."

The Enforcer adjusted his skin to a slightly warmer temperature and nodded. His energy levels had dipped slightly.

As if reading his mind, Janus said, "And maybe some breakfast? You can sample that coffee or any

147

caffeine-containing beverage of choice. We're all caffeine junkies around here."

"You must have been starving, the way you put away the eggs and bacon," Janus said a little later. "I'm a little envious. I'm on a diet, so even if the food here's an employee benefit, I need to show a little self-restraint." Truth be told, he also envied John Paul's slim physique and bespoke suit. He sighed and set aside his empty container of granola and yogurt.

"I received your proposal for a new project this morning by special courier, but I haven't had time to review it completely. Or at all, actually. What did you have in mind?"

"We will need a couple of 90,000-square-foot sound stages, painted completely black…"

"Sound stages? What for?" Janus asked. "Our virtual worlds just *look* big, they aren't actually any bigger than the user's imagination."

"For it to function properly, you will need both space and compute power."

"It?"

"A proper VR channel such as I described in the article."

"You wouldn't happen to know someone named Violet, would you?" Janus asked.

This Parker human might link him to Violet Rain if he weren't more careful. "I haven't had the pleasure," John Paul said. "Perhaps sometime you could introduce us."

"Sorry, but she's someone who you remind me of, but we lost touch a while ago."

⑨

Janus sat in darkness, except for a pool of yellowish light from a desk lamp lighting his keyboard. His knuckles reflected the bluish glare of the monitor. The project John Paul had proposed was brilliant. Excited, Janus had green-lit a crash program to bring the new virtual reality project to fruition as quickly as possible, even contributing many of his own ideas along the way, including the name—"the Jeweled Cave." Although Janus was used to working long days, John Paul had proved a demanding partner, and this was the first chance he'd had to be alone in days.

He'd built the first sound stage John Paul had demanded, at a long-term cost of six million dollars. It would take him five years to pay off the mini-perm setup loan, assuming he didn't go bankrupt first. He'd been skeptical about whether such a facility was needed, but if they were going to manipulate matter like John Paul claimed, it was better it be done in a remote building, far from prying eyes. He still wasn't sure how to link reality with imagination, a seemingly impossible order. Even with unlimited compute power, the human brain was too slow to process unlimited data input.

A sudden idea jerked him into razor sharp consciousness. Time-slicing, of course, but combined with shortcuts that the human brain would mistake for reality. That would make it possible to both serve many users and save compute cycles at the same time. He would call it QVR – Quick Virtual Reality. It could be used as a speed-learning device by police, firefighters, and military who needed to instantly "understand a situation," as if seeing it through their own eyes.

Janus scanned the nightly test results. Every single damn one of them said PASS. That was a first.

The Jeweled Cave simulation was fantastic. Not just fantastic or pretty, but *big*. It filled the entire warehouse. Paths of sparkling minerals led off in various directions, beckoning the user to explore. Multicolored semiprecious stones lined the walls: rhodochrosite, amethyst, sapphire, and emerald. A touch on the gaudy side, but guaranteed to bedazzle even the most jaded connoisseur. Was jade a gemstone? He made a note to look it up and add it tomorrow.

Part of the expense of building the sound stage had been the addition of solar panels. They covered a fraction of the electricity needed to run the simulations, but it was going to be worth it. He had to be cautious, though, and not over-promise. There was still a long way to go before the claims in the article could be accomplished, possibly not in his lifetime.

John Paul had come along at just the right time, that was certain.

☺

Before going into sentry mode the previous night, the Enforcer again wondered about Janus's statement that he reminded him of Violet Rain. It was insulting to be compared to a filthy human. But he needed to be patient. Janus was obviously hiding something, hopefully Violet's whereabouts. He would just have to wait for the opportunity to discuss Violet Rain, and only if Janus brought her up, seemingly as his own idea. The Enforcer had put too much effort into ingratiating himself with the oafish brute to lose the trail now. Something about his blond hair and pink skin was especially repellent. And Janus's staff of bootlicking idiots was not much better.

John Paul Hilario straightened his tie and walked into the sound stage. A group of Canny Divide employees was gathered around the single workstation in the far corner, chatting.

"Hi, John Paul," one of them said. Raymie, as he recalled. This was one of the more tolerable employees, with dark brown skin and eyes. But he was no smarter than his employer, unfortunately.

"Good morning. You may address me as Dr. Hilario. We are not going to make our schedule standing around engaged in pointless socializing," John-Paul replied. The group broke up, two heading for the exit to ramp up the generators, and the other two to tune the solar arrays to capture the maximum amount of energy. They'd scrimped on the cost of automated seasonal adjustments.

Still, it wasn't enough power. Raymie remained, seated at the workstation.

"Begin the first test," John Paul said.

Raymie opened the test application and selected the sensory suite. The program would simulate various sensory experiences, including heat, cold, and wind. Other experiences, such as sound and light, could simply be projected as needed.

A black pedestal about three feet high and a foot in diameter appeared to rise from the floor, a green light indicating readiness. A spotlight traced a circle around the pedestal to demark the test site boundary.

"Nice projection," Raymie murmured.

John Paul didn't comment. "Raise the temperature of the air in the cylinder."

"How high should I make the cylinder?" Raymie said. "The amount of energy we need will be dependent on the volume of air we're simulating."

"A height of eight feet should be sufficient," John Paul said.

"Raising the temperature. The default is one degree C per minute. Do you want to modify that?"

"Yes. Make that 10 degrees per minute for 10 minutes, then go all the way up to 1400."

"Okey doke, the parameters are entered. What are we expecting to see here?"

"We're expecting to see the pedestal turn red hot and then melt."

"Sounds fun. That's the kind of thing customers would like. They could surf around in molten lava and the like, without getting burned. The beauty of virtual reality."

Twelve minutes later, the pedestal had indeed begun to glow. The green light winked out, and the black box started to quiver.

"Nice! This new QVR technology that Janus invented is so realistic I can almost feel the heat the thing's putting out," Raymie said.

Abruptly the metal probe collapsed, forming a liquid that rapidly seeped to the edges of the test enclosure. Some of the liquid steel splashed into the air as it encountered the boundary.

"Good thing we're keeping this stuff corralled," Raymie said. "Someone could get hurt," he joked.

"Conclude the test and mark it as a PASS," John Paul said. "I have left instructions for the rest of today's test for you to complete. Let me know of any problems." He walked briskly to the exit. Daylight briefly poked into the all-black room, until the door again closed.

Raymie shut down the test and sat back in his chair. He stretched and looked at the puddle of molten metal, which was slowly congealing back to a gray-black color. He got up from the workstation and walked over to the test enclosure.

"It's still radiating heat," he said. "Wait a minute. This is just supposed to be a visual simulation." He reached his hand into the enclosure. His shirtsleeve burst into flame. He screamed.

☺

"This is unacceptable, John Paul. You didn't follow proper safety procedures, and you never informed me or the staff that you were introducing hazardous aspects into the test simulations. This is supposed to be virtual reality, for chrissakes."

"The primitive simulations you have been producing cannot rightly be called virtual reality," John Paul retorted. "In order to reproduce the full human sensory experience, you must be able to manipulate both graphical representation *and* matter."

"Well, I agree, but you can't do it by killing our employees with real burning steel and laser beams. Why don't you keep it simple, like producing a cup of coffee, you know, like the replicator on that star travel show."

"It's far from simple, either way. In fact, a laser beam is much easier than a cup of coffee."

152

"I don't care. There will be no more staff injuries, do you understand?"

John Paul's eyes narrowed. "Perfectly."

"I've sent some flowers to Raymie's hospital room, with our apologies. Luckily our employees sign an agreement not to sue us in the event of unavoidable accidents." Janus turned to the papers on his desk. "Oh, and before you go, I want a more detailed report of how you were able to excite these air molecules with no external application of radiation."

"If you will look at the report before you, you will see that a small amount of the podium's mass was all that was required. You can't get something from nothing, of course."

As the door closed behind the elegantly attired John Paul Hilario, Janus stared blindly into space without blinking.

"What kind of energy equation are we talking about here? Neither the podium nor the air were moving when the test began. The amount of energy in the test enclosure should have remained constant, right? Sure, rest-mass has energy, but changing it, getting access to it, or doing anything useful with it is incredibly difficult. What changed?"

He reached for the intercom.

"Judy, get me a list of the high-energy physicists at UC Santa Cruz."

The Enforcer realized his investment in this ruse was yielding diminishing returns. He had given the human friend of Violet Rain numerous hints on how to get from graphic simulation to full virtual reality, and had been criticized at every turn.

All of the employees hated him, and he hated them in return. Janus had even threatened to fire him.

He wondered briefly how he had gained so much knowledge of virtual reality. The torturer Blauw must

153

have done an unusually thorough job in programming him in that discipline. He had to give him credit for that. But he would still kill Blauw for his insolence, as soon as the Emperor would allow it. Meanwhile, he must not forget what he was here to do.

He inserted a very small change in the test suite. A change that would have a rather big effect.

It was time to shake things up a bit.

*****~~~~~*****

Chapter 13.

Not Feeling Myself Today

Every little nondisclosure hides a lie, Janus thought, double-checking the NDAs on his desk. The alpha testers were so eager to try the next new thing that they would sign away any right to talk about what they'd seen.

Janus was fairly certain that what they were about to see would be disappointing, and he didn't want that to get out to the public until well after the holiday buying season. He felt a little guilty and took to heart the accusations that Silicon Valley was out to addict people to their products. But only a little guilty. Some designers who had helped create addictive technologies like cell phones and social media were even cutting themselves off from their devices. That seemed like an overreaction. And so far, it mostly wasn't founders or CEOs like himself.

John Paul's revelation about matter transcription was revolutionary, of course. But it was far too early to release the technique to the great unwashed. Too early and too dangerous. The guy was a visionary, but he seemed reckless, possibly self-destructive even. Janus wished Violet was here to tell him whether this was the right path. He'd received a terse note from Alan Jones that there had been some progress in finding her.

He crossed the corporate campus and entered the vast windowless soundstage. Several employees were talking animatedly to the latest set of guinea pigs. He had to remember to call them the "focus group." John Paul was there too, but he was the perfect definition of "standoffish."

"Welcome, everyone. Thank you for agreeing to give us your valuable opinions about our upcoming product, which we've given the code name, "Interregnum." It's a big word that means the suspension of the normal, and that's what we believe our new technology will achieve."

The testers smiled, none appearing uncertain. They were all fans of Canny Divide.

"Let me present to you—the Jeweled Cave," Janus said, signaling to Mike Liu, the DJ for the day since Raymie's injury. The pulsation of a throbbing samba beat and echoing shouts filled the big room, and the cave shimmered into existence.

"Explore at your leisure, folks. We welcome any comments you might have."

"Don't we need headsets or glasses?" a stocky young man asked. "I've always—"

"No, the cave will generate all the images in three dimensions," John Paul interrupted. "Everything will be rendered in real time, but without the lag that causes some people to feel queasy."

Janus already regretted letting John Paul comment on the user interface. Developers weren't supposed to lead the focus group, just note their reactions. "Just feel free to walk around, folks," he said. He smiled toward a woman with sun-bleached streaks in her brown hair.

She reached out to touch the wall. "Oh, I felt a little shock," she said.

"Yes, you're right. That's our first attempt to add tactile sensation to the simulation," Janus said. "Perfectly harmless, of course."

"Of course," she said, looking down at her hand, then rubbing it on her skinny jeans. She lifted her hand and glanced at her palm. Giving a little cry, she began shaking her hand as though she was trying to shake something loose. Maybe shocks weren't such a good idea. Janus looked over her shoulder to get a closer look at what she was seeing. Her hand seemed to have grown a mouth. The mouth opened into a grin, showing a set of pointed white teeth. She shrieked.

The music—Mike called it "trance"—grew louder, well above the decibel level considered good for human ears.

"Could you turn it down a bit, Mike," Janus said. Mike didn't seem to hear him.

"Mike!" he yelled. Another snafu. He was well used to things developing glitches during demos, but this virtual reality was rapidly becoming unreal. Jewels—or were they stalactites?—began dropping from the ceiling, one narrowly missing his head but shooting out a spark of static electricity as it passed. His ears felt like hot pokers were piercing them. He fell to his knees, covering his ears. A drop of blood seeped out of the woman's nose. She was screaming, but Janus couldn't hear it. He scrambled to his feet and ran toward the rear of the cave.

A red fireball mushroomed to fill half the soundstage, reflecting prettily off the jeweled surfaces of the dissolving cave and nearly knocking Janus to the floor. He turned to see a person step into it, seemingly untouched by the fire.

John Paul?

John Paul's clothes caught fire and burned off, along with his skin, revealing a metallic body underneath. A static discharge flashed across John-Paul's face, which was replaced by a terrible but familiar visage with lidless glowing red eyes. Janus recalled a demon character from one of the many fantasy tales he'd read, where victims were sliced with long, bloody cuts... But this was just fiction, right? Or was this the new virtual reality? How had the Jeweled Cave VR projected Janus's suspicion that John Paul was the killer robot that had pursued him and Violet?

That was the last thing Janus witnessed, before he too was enveloped by flames.

157

Alan folded his newspaper. He still stubbornly refused to get his news online, even though the news in the paper was often a day late.

"Look at this, Gin! There was a big fire at Canny Divide yesterday, and Janus Parker was apparently killed. It's strange. I texted him about finding a clue about Violet only a couple of days ago."

"My God!" Virginia replied, setting down the coffee carafe. "What happened?"

"They were trying out a demo of the newest VR program, when a fire broke out in the computer lab projection equipment. They had just finished building the special facility. Six people were believed killed, including Janus and his COO, a man named John Paul Hilario, but they're still sifting through the site looking for bodies. No one in the headquarters was injured, but one employee has been arrested. He claimed he was injured in an earlier experiment and was fired. He's threatening to sue. But they consider him a person of interest, one of those "disgruntled ex-employees" who could have gone on the rampage. Two hundred people are now wondering whether they still have jobs."

"That's lucky more weren't injured, I guess. What are we going to tell Violet, if we do find her? They'd grown so close..."

"Well, I guess she already knew Janus would be considered the father of VR, and I'm guessing she gave him some help in that direction before he died. Then there were all those fancy claims in *Grafix Today* that Janus was on the right track."

"We may never know," Virginia said. "I hope any information she gave Janus didn't get him killed."

"I know what you mean. The big fire seemed to be an uncomfortable coincidence with Violet's disappearance. She and Janus were being chased by some sort of monster from the future before Vi just vanished."

"I'm going to call Grace again," Virginia said. "I need to hear her voice, just to make sure she's all right. Who knows if this was really an accident?"

"I'm sure she's fine," Alan said. "She's helping Golaeth run the Hatchery of Universes. What could be safer than that?"

☍

Yverra stood in Violet's lab on STS-99. The attempt to contact Poe had been unsuccessful.

"Not accepting any callers, do you think?" Ralff asked.

"He will take my call," Yverra asserted. "It just may be necessary to go knock on his door."

"That's impossible," Benrus pointed out. "The Yang stasis point is practically in the center of the Yin universe. That was the whole point of the stasis exchange, that neither universe could get at the heart of the other."

"You're forgetting that Violet crossed the Yin-Yang Boundary in the body of a tardigrade. I propose doing the same."

"How? Her projector is missing."

"We'll build another one. Violet kept careful records, so I think we can do it if we put our heads together. If that doesn't work, we can steal one from someone in the 25th century right before the Unwinding. They won't be needing it any more."

"Assuming we succeed, how would you know where to look for Poe's stasis point?" Ralff asked.

"And even if you find it, how would you get in? It's impregnable from the outside," Ben pointed out.

"One step at a time," Yverra said. "It's a shame we can't send Violet. She's already in the tardigrade body, but her intellect is compromised."

"Or her memory, at least," Ben agreed.

"I do have an idea of how it might be possible to enter Poe's stasis point," Yverra said. You get started building a projector from Violet's notes. I'm going to go talk with Virginia Jones."

⟳

Virginia placed her foot on the shovel and stabbed at the weeds encroaching on her garden. When she'd encountered Blauw and Emperor Calaneris, she'd had nightmares about an evil force murdering her beautifully kept garden on Earth. She glanced at the rowan tree to reassure herself. The little mountain ash was fine, perfectly healthy, putting on a fall show with its shiny red berries. Still, it had been hard to forget what they'd put her through trying to find her family during the Unwindings.

She began to hum a tune called "Sally in the Garden." Though it was in a minor key, it always cheered her up. Finishing off the last of the plantago, she rose and brushed the dirt off her cutoff jean shorts.

A woman with vaguely reptilian gold eyes regarded her solemnly.

"Oh!" Gin said. "It's Yverra, isn't it? Sorry, you startled me a bit."

"My apologies, Virginia. May I have a word?"

"Of course, come inside. What would you like to drink?"

"Violet recently introduced me to a beverage made of steeped plant materials and flowers."

"I'm sure I can cobble up something on that order," Gin said. "Have you heard from Violet? I hope that's why you're here. Have you found her?"

"Not exactly. We found her consciousness projected inside a small, insectlike Earth creature. The details are rather complex, but I and the other Watchmen have a theory that her actual body may be sheltered in Poe's stasis point, and you might be able to help us retrieve it."

"Hmm. I'm not sure I understand. Violet's now an insect?"

160

"I'd like to ask about a device Poe gave you. I believe you called it 'the Cintamani.'"

"Yes, but I gave it back to Poe, along with my Korean dragon, Hangul."

"So you believe Poe still has possession of these artifacts?"

"I assume so."

"Do you think Violet could wield them if they were in her possession?"

"Maybe. The Cintamani did seem to be keyed to me only, though. When Calaneris tried to take it from me, it didn't work. But if there's anything inheritable coded into it, Poe might be willing to give it to Violet. Or, it's possible he would find me and Violet to simply be interchangeable human females. But I don't know how you could get it from Poe if he's hidden it in his heart."

"Do you think you could ask him for it back?" Yverra suggested.

"Whoa, the Cintamani is powerful and unpredictable. You know the old saying, 'Be careful, you might get what you wish for.'"

"I'm not familiar with that saying," Yverra said. "I would promise to be careful with it."

"That's not what I mean," Virginia said. "Let me think about it and get back to you."

☯

Grace's normally brown eyes pulsed a brilliant blue briefly, indicating a prophylactic burst of gamma radiation along the exterior boundary of the Yin-Yang universe. Word had raced around the Hatchery that Violet Rain had breached the interior border somehow, and Golaeth had demanded that border security be beefed up. Poe and the Black Universe had a past tendency to settle disputes violently, ignoring other universes that got in the way. This was just to further insure that the truce would continue.

She sensed her mother was about to call and hoped it wasn't about this latest breach. Grace was in enough trouble as it was, just being related to Virginia Jones and her progeny. She had to hand it to Violet, though. She was a lot like Gin. She smiled.

"Yo, Mom. What's up?"

"How're things in the grand hall of mirrors?"

"Fine I guess. It's been pretty quiet lately. Except maybe in your vicinity…"

"Grace, you remember how I turned in my Cintamani, along with Hangul?"

"Yes, you said you wanted to go home, instead of gallivanting all over the universe."

"Well, I wonder if it would be possible to get them back."

"What?"

"It's not for me. It's for Violet."

I knew it, Grace thought. Gin thought of Violet as her successor. Oh, well, it wasn't totally unexpected.

"Hmm."

"It's not what you think, Grace. It's actually for Yverra. She just visited me."

"Yverra—why?"

"She thinks she can use it to get to Poe's stasis point inside the Yin universe and see if Violet is there."

"I thought we'd already established that Violet was on Earth, somewhere near you."

"You failed to mention she was near *me*, Grace," Gin said.

"My bad," Grace said.

"I forgive you. But at any rate, she isn't on Earth any more. The Watchmen picked her up, but she was in a tardigrade body. They're back on STS-99. Yverra wants the Cintamani to see if Poe has her human body. Oh, I should mention that Violet has totally lost her memory and can't help. So, Yverra wants to cross the Yin-Yang

Boundary in a tardigrade body herself and use the Cintamani to enter Poe's heart."

Grace considered Yverra's plan for a millisecond. The Cintamani was useless in hands other than her mother's. It might not work. Plus, it was quite big, about the size of pearl. Tardigrades were not well known for carrying cargo other than babies.

"It's a pretty radical plan, and it has some flaws," Grace said. "But, I might be willing to help out, just this once."

"That would be wonderful, dear. You *are* the Living Cintamani, after all."

"Don't remind me," Grace replied. "On one condition. I want to go along. Besides, I still owe the Watchmen for not being there to stop Calaneris when… Tell Yverra to call me when she's ready to go."

"I feel so much better knowing you're willing to help."

"You know, you're still the consummate Wizard, Mom. I can't believe I taught you gaming strategy."

"Beginner's luck?" Virginia asked.

"Right."

⟲

The Enforcer pondered his next steps. He marched in a widening circle, kicking up red dust, until he could no longer see the sky. As a matter of pride, he couldn't go home and admit to the Emperor that he had failed in his mission. He realized he hadn't gone very far away after destroying Janus Parker's VR channel. He'd found himself translated to a nearby planet, one with geology as ancient as Earth's, but which had no water—and no coffee. Was it possible he was beginning to miss those backward humans or had this been programmed into him by the torturer Blauw? But thinking about Violet Rain, the human he was supposed to kill, caused a slight sensation of—call it discomfort. More faulty programming by that bastard, he supposed.

Oddly, the barren landscape felt familiar, like he'd been there before. He pictured a man visiting the home he'd grown up in as a child and finding everything changed from the way he remembered it. Damn. He was identifying with humans again. His discomfiture returned. The humans had a word for it: *nostalgia*. Pain of the past. Maybe it was something toxic on this blasted planet. The feeling grew, an irritation seeping into his whole being. He shut down into Sentry mode.

☉

"Welcome back. Any luck?" Ralff asked.

"I think so," Yverra replied. "But we aren't going to need the projector."

"What? I spent days reconstructing one, and it's almost finished," Benrus protested.

"I'll be getting a free ride into the heart of the universe," Yverra said.

"What do you mean? No knock at the door of the stasis point?"

"That is correct. And that wouldn't have worked anyway. Nothing can get in or out of Yang's stasis point. At least, nothing from our universe. Much to my surprise, the Living Cintamani has offered to get me inside and demand an audience.

"So, she knows our requests for information are being ignored?"

"I'm not certain. Virginia Jones intervened on our behalf to see if Grace could help find Violet's body and probably told her of our theory."

"Why's Grace doing this? Doesn't she work for Golaeth and the Hatchery now and isn't supposed to play favorites?" Ralff asked.

"I got the distinct impression from Virginia that Grace had some ulterior motive—although I find it hard to imagine that presiding over interactions between multiple universes could ever be boring."

"What a break! This is wonderful news, indeed," Ben said. "Maybe the Watchmen will all be back together soon."

"I am hopeful," Yverra said. "I'll go explain this to Violet, although I suspect she won't understand a word of what I'm saying until she's regained her memory."

"I hope it will be easier to convince her who she is once she's back in her real body," Ben said.

⟲

The Living Cintamani and Yverra heard the music first. It was beautiful music, the kind you'd imagine was being played in Heaven, if there was such a thing.

Grace concentrated, forming the matter of her own body and that of Yverra from stray quark gluon plasmas.

Yverra blinked. "Where are we exactly?"

"A place no one has ever been," Grace said reverently. "Except maybe my mother."

Yverra looked around. There was little to be seen. A gray fog filled the air.

"Are we inside?"

"Yes, I believe so, but Poe is still considering whether or not to show himself. Wait, do you feel that? We're standing on solid ground."

"It feels a little like interdimensional shifting," Yverra observed.

"That's right. I'd forgotten that you're an experienced traveler."

"We call it hacking," Yverra said.

"Well, now might be a good time to synchronize," Grace said.

"Done," Yverra said.

The fog vanished instantly, though the sky remained gray. They were standing on a beach, waves lapping gently at their feet. Grace bent down and put her fingers in the water. It was warm.

"This is how she described it," she said. "We're at Mom's Beach, Poe's heart." She exhaled.

"It is odd that the universe has this scene at its heart," Yverra said. "I wonder what induced Poe to take such an interest in Earth."

"I think this is just an illusion for my mom's and my benefit," Grace said. "It feels really good to be in my body, I have to say."

The music continued to play, but more softly. Grace wasn't sure, but she thought she heard a voice, a voice filled with longing.

"We're coming," Grace said. "Let's go Yverra, someone's calling us."

"Is it Violet?" Yverra asked.

"I don't know yet. It's just something I feel—that we should go in the water."

"It'd be my pleasure," Yverra said. "Are we to swim?"

"I guess so," Grace said. "No—here's a rowboat. It's like you just wish for what you want here. It really is like Heaven."

Yverra lifted an oar. "Heaven. A place on Earth, I suppose. Which way?"

"Straight on," Grace said. "I think the voice is growing louder."

They climbed aboard and rowed for what seemed like hours, until the beach was no longer visible. At last, in the distance a small island appeared.

"I was beginning to worry that we were on a wild goose chase," Grace said.

"Wild goose?" Yverra asked.

"Just an expression."

"You humans have a lot of expressions. You should just say what you mean."

They pulled up alongside the island, which seemed to be ringed by a jagged reef. They traced the circumference of the island, and didn't see any sort of opening.

"How do we land?" Yverra asked. "This reef would make short work of the boat. I can lend you some of my leather armor if you want to chance swimming it."

"There's something interesting," Grace said, pointing. "It's Violet."

A young woman lay on the sand, her hair spread in a dark nimbus around her head and shoulders.

"It's Violet's body all right, right down to the bright purple bangs. She seems asleep or unconscious. How was she able to call us?"

"If we could wake her up, perhaps she could show us a safe passage," Yverra said.

"Hey, Sleeping Beauty!" Grace yelled. Their calls did nothing to rouse Violet.

"If she thinks we're leaving without her, she's mistaken," Grace said. "Now I wish I had brought armor like you."

Yverra stripped off both of her arm guards and handed them to Grace. Her arms were quite leathery themselves, formidable protection even without armor.

"I'll carry you across the reef," Yverra volunteered. "But if I should trip, at least you will have some protection to break your fall. Climb onto my shoulders."

Forming a tall, wobbly totem pole, the pair began wading across the waist-high water. The reef proved to be slippery as well as sharp, forcing them to pick their way in a zigzag pattern.

"This is going to take forever," Grace observed. "I know this is cheating, but let's just fly." She levitated into the air and held out a hand for Yverra."

"Sorry to hurry this along, but I need to get—" Grace started to say.

A water monster with glistening scales rose from the waves to a height of over ten feet, splashing them both and wetting them from head to toe.

"Agh," Grace said, shaking her head and spraying water on her companion. "It's Hangul."

Grace backed toward the boat cautiously, keeping a respectful distance from the formidable-looking creature.

Yverra stared in awe. "Ah, Virginia Jones's Korean dragon. I always admired her chosen mode of transportation. Until now... "

"You're here for us, right, boy?" Grace said.

Hangul bowed, lowering his head until his whiskers were close enough for Grace to touch.

"Can you take us to Violet?" Grace asked. "Come, Yverra, let's climb aboard."

But instead of allowing them to mount, Hangul charged at them with a roar. Grace and Yverra shot into the air, barely escaping being rammed. Hangul leapt out of the water in pursuit, his claws stretched out in front. Lightning played over the serpent's hide, threatening to burn Grace and Yverra. Dark clouds filled the sky, and sheets of rain began to pummel them.

After several minutes of terrifying violence, Grace said, "Hangul's guarding her. Poe's not going to let us take Violet's body. When I was at the top of our little totem pole, I noticed Violet's dress was covered in blood. Maybe she was mortally wounded."

As if to emphasize her point, a ray of green lightning struck the comatose Violet, turning her into a log-shaped pile of burning ash.

"—And if we stay here any longer, we're going to die, too."

"Indeed, it appears that our mission has failed," Yverra said. "I will miss our new Watchman greatly…"

They crash-landed onto the floor of the lab on STS-99, dripping wet and exhausted.

"Well, that was almost a disaster," Grace said. "I would have thought Hangul would have been our friend. Maybe if I'd had the pearl…"

Benrus and Ralff rushed over to help her and Yverra to their feet.

168

"What happened?" Ben asked.

"Everything that could go wrong, did," Grace said. "Poe destroyed Violet's body."

"It appears that Hangul only obeys his own Cintamani," Yverra said.

"I must go back to the Hatchery and see what can be done about that," Grace said. "I have a mind to confiscate Poe's Cintamani and take his pet dragon away from him."

"Now, let's not be hasty," Ralff said. "I'm sure there's a civilized way to approach this."

"Well, at least I got Violet's projector before Hangul turned her into a charcoal briquette." She reached into her pocket, pulled out the small supercomputer, and tossed it onto the laboratory table. Grace's irises turned a blinding shade of blue, and she vanished.

*****~~~~~*****

Chapter 14.

An Orphan of the Storm

Now that they had recovered Violet's mind but her body was destroyed, Benrus wondered whether it might be worth the effort to try to retrace her steps from the space station. Of course it was worth it. He was a scientist, after all, and he wanted to know how Violet had managed her escape feat, with a dimension-shifting killing machine hot on her trail. Rather than simply projecting her consciousness into the tardigrade, she had split herself into two halves, the physical portion of which traveled instantly to Poe's stasis point. Obviously it was some sort of quantum entanglement, but it had gone wrong somehow. Violet's human body had traveled to one destination but her tardigrade body and mind to another. The quantum teleportation had failed, and the body at the other end had probably arrived a mindless shell. He and Ralff continued their research aboard STS-99, hoping that would turn out to have been a minor setback.

Yverra had been unusually grumpy, even for herself, since the ill-fated trip to Poe's stasis point. She entered the lab and frowned.

"What's this new decor?" she asked. "Another souvenir from your Earth visit?"

"It's a Christmas tree," Ben said. "Primitive light-emitting diodes are used to accentuate the branches. Ralff installed it."

"What is it for?" Yverra asked. "Attracting insects?"

"It's just to add a little cheer to this otherwise sterile laboratory," Ralff sniffed. "The natives use it to ward off the cold and darkness of winter. I think it's pretty."

Luckily, Yverra changed the subject before Ben's partner could get further miffed. "How is the Violet reclamation project going?" she asked.

"This little field trip of Violet's to the 21st century wasn't such a good idea," Ben reported. "She's still hanging on, but confused about who she really is. And the disruptions along the Yin-Yang Boundary are still occurring."

"It's quite discouraging," Ralff said.

"Don't become discouraged just yet," Benrus said. "Maybe we can reconstruct her body from a cell or two left here in the lab."

"I suppose so," Yverra agreed. "Grace is on our side, and I think she feels guilty for suggesting the trip in the first place. If we can reconstruct Violet, we might get back on track."

"It's not Grace's fault, really. Poe wasn't exactly forthcoming with information about Violet, and the whole cremation thing must have been a shock," Ralff added. "Best of all, Violet's amnesia seems to be gradually receding."

"No need to talk about me in the third person. I can still hear you," Violet said. "Oh, all right, I'm willing to concede that I'm this person Violet you keep on about, but only because I'm getting visions—or are they memories?—of a boy I used to know."

"That's wonderful, Violet," Ben said. "What sort of memories? Who is this boy? Was he by any chance named Janus?"

"No, that's not it," the voice from the invisible tardigrade said. "It's Xoan, I think. Does that ring a bell with any of you?"

"Not me," they all chorused. "Juan, you say?"

"No. It's a Philippine name, spelled X-O-A-N."

"You must have had a strong bond, however," Yverra said. "We'll research people named Xoan who may have played a part in your past. It might help you to remember more."

"Here it is," Ralff said. "Xoan-Paulo Hilario. Violet served with him on Mars. He was killed in the 2416 Martian incursion by the Black Universe, slightly before the Earth's destruction."

"And close in time to the destruction of the rest of the Watchmen's home planets, as well," Yverra added.

"Am I being too paranoid, or do you think there might be a connection to Emperor Calaneris?"

"I doubt whether you could be too paranoid in his regard," Yverra said. "But I think it warrants closer inspection."

"If these are memories, they're scary ones," Violet said. "You mentioned Janus…"

"Yes?"

"Now I remember him too. I seem to recall we were on the run."

"Yes, that's right."

"We were being chased."

"By a killer assassin, right."

"No!" Violet shouted. "By Xoan."

"You're confused, dear," Yverra said. "This was a military robot equipped with time-hacking capability, not a human. We're still trying to track it down and deactivate it."

"No, he knew me. He knew where I would go."

"Yes, he knew how to use hacking to track you."

"He knew me." A slight sob. "Why— Why was he trying to kill me?"

⑨

The Enforcer winked into consciousness for a microsecond, to check his circuits and the status of his internal daemons. They were all running nominally in the background. It seemed unusual that he had gone so long without a system reboot. Racking up too much system time could lead to disastrous glitches, necessitating hard reboots, lost memory, and unanticipated downtime. But he didn't have time for prophylactic maintenance. Besides, he felt fine.

What the hell. He'd take another few microseconds to check his memory. His scan moved methodically across quadrants, revealing nothing corrupted. He paused to take a closer look. He walked along a warm, sandy beach. Ocean waves lapped quietly, their susurration a calming song. A woman walked toward him. A beautiful young woman with long, straight dark hair topped by a purple fringe. Her eyes were large and dark, and her mouth was tiny, her lips shiny and red. She was naked, except for a necklace of rare golden pearls. He would call her Anghel.

When she smiled at him in welcome, he registered a serious voltage spike. She was the human target, doubtless, and he should have dispatched her instantly, but he was momentarily paralyzed by the realization that the pearls came from the bay outside his childhood home in Manila. Stunned, he tried to raise his weapon, but her beauty stayed his hand. The compartmentalized data that Blauw had not seen fit to clean up exploded across his consciousness, completely fragmenting his cybernetic control system. A flood of log data scrolled across his vision, indicating a memory fault. He couldn't move, and he didn't want to. He only wanted one thing: to see Anghel again.

☺

Yverra mulled over Violet's statement about her friend trying to kill her. The whole idea of making an assassin robot that looked like a past lover reeked of Calaneris. She too had once quarreled with a lover, which she also laid at the scheming feet of the former Emperor. The three lids covering the pupils of her slitted eyes snapped closed as she lost herself in thought. YDorian had warned her not to get involved with the Unwindings, pleading with her to steer clear of the dispute over the boundary between the two universes. He'd been right, of course. Now, with the Watchmen gone, there was nothing to be done; she would never see him again. But in spite of their worst arguments, YDorian had never tried to kill her. He had simply left. Her eyes slid open again. She blinked, a new thought forming.

He'd left. So, he wasn't there when Calaneris destroyed the Watchman home planet. Could he still be alive? Was it just coincidence that Grace had suggested Violet make the field trip to visit Virginia in the twenty-first century? She didn't think so. Grace could make all sorts of connections and extrapolations.

But if YDorian were still alive, shouldn't she have noticed his presence when she visited Virginia to ask for the loan of the Cintamani? Assuming Grace knew he was in the same time and dimension. Being across the North American continent would be no impediment. Of course, she could be wrong. She knew she should concentrate on Violet and Xoan, but this new thread pulled her too strongly. Maybe she wasn't the last Watchman…

"All right, boys," Yverra announced. "I've discovered some unfinished business in the past. I'm going back to retrace Violet's route." For the moment, she wouldn't mention her new mission.

"I was going to suggest that myself," Ben said. "I thought there must have been something we overlooked. I just hadn't got round to it yet."

"Isn't that dangerous?" Ralff said. "That robot may still be wandering around."

"Yes, I think it's another one of Calaneris's loose ends," Yverra said. "And when I find it, I'm going to terminate it, Violet's old lover or not. Feel free to keep studying the entanglement idea."

Violet/Cheon-Sa felt dry.

"Ralff, is it? Can you spritz me?"

A fine mist floated into her enclosure, delicious.

"Is that better?"

"Much. I think it helps me remember, too. If I get too desiccated, I seem to just shut down."

"Probably a survival mechanism," Ralff said. "It takes energy to move around—and to think."

"You're a physicist, right? Grandmother Ginny told me about you."

"Um, yes, and we've been through a lot since then. You were like a sister to us. I mean, you *are* like a sister. You're one of the Watchmen now."

"I still don't remember that, but I'm trying."

"You do seem to be remembering your earlier life. It's probably imprinted on your personality most strongly. Why don't you tell me more about your life—the part you remember, I mean. Maybe it will help you recover the newer memories too."

"Well, I remember being human. A woman. I lived in a big city. Los Angeles."

"On Earth. Yes."

"I didn't stay on Earth all the time, though. I traveled to another planet, Mars. I was smart. And my boyfriend said I was pretty."

"What did you do on Mars?"

"I— I made life bearable for the other people living there. I was in charge of virtual reality. We'd established a new VR channel for the new colony."

"What do you mean by making life bearable?"

"Well, it was a really barren planet. No water to speak of, except some ice that was frozen into the soil. I could get by on that now, but as a human, it was too bleak. I set up all of the supercomputing processors and tailored programs for the colonists on request."

"That sounds like a lot of work."

"Yes, it was a position with a lot of responsibility." Violet paused.

176

"Violet?"

"Yes, I was just thinking. I was really busy filling requests for all the colonists, but I was lonely too. That's when I met John-Paul."

"Ah, he became your lover, right?"

"Yes, how did you know that?"

"I've had enough time to become acquainted with your human mating rituals, quaint as they are. Of course, now you're a tardigrade."

"Quaint. That's a good description. As you point out, I don't need to mate with a male any more, so I can reproduce any time conditions are right. But I can get lonely. John-Paul was lonely too. And homesick. He asked me to create a VR environment for him that was like his home on Earth. It was tropical, with a beautiful ocean nearby. It wasn't that different from where I came from, so I felt comfortable existing in his world. He even gave me a necklace of freshwater pearls to show his commitment. They weren't real, of course. But we were fine. Then I got called back to Earth. I couldn't pass up the opportunity to head up the VR channel for one of the biggest cities on Earth."

"So you parted ways?"

"Yes, I told him distance would only make the heart grow fonder. He claimed he'd be heading back to Earth in a year, himself. I said that seemed unlikely. He looked so grim when I left... scowling and clenching his hands into fists. It was a little scary."

"Do you remember the Unwinding?"

"The Unwinding?"

"Earth and Mars were destroyed."

"And Xoan? Was he killed? I seem to remember that."

"We thought so, until recently. We think he might be alive, inside the robot that was pursuing you."

"Why do you think that?"

"You told us yourself. Since you became a Watchman, you can sense the presence of consciousness, even across dimensions. Actually, that's kind of how you're able to talk to me, even though you're in a tardigrade body."

"I want out of this body."

"We're working on it. We're cloning you a new one."

"What happened to my human body?"

"The robot had something to do with it, we're not quite sure what."

"He tried to kill me," Violet said. "Xoan tried to kill me."

"There you go again, referring to the robot as Xoan. We think they must be one and the same."

"Can you go away and leave me alone for a bit, Ralff? I need time to think."

Vibrations told Violet the entity known as Ralff had physically moved himself a short distance away. Good enough.

Memories came back in a torrent. She'd been a deadly hunter in search of bloody food, she'd been the wily creature being hunted, she'd been the pilot of a starship fighting a valiant battle, she'd been a princess with armies at her hand, she'd raced a bicycle with her grandmother through a park in Los Angeles, she'd lived in a forest where the trees talked, she'd walked the cold red sands of Mars, she'd been a human woman who made love to a man on the beach. She'd been all of these things, and many more. And now she was a Watchman.

*****~~~~~*****

Chapter 15.

Lay Your Money Down

Yverra had followed an anxious, tedious trail, retracing Violet and Janus Parker's route across the American continent. Contrary to what Ben and Ralff had said, it wasn't that difficult following the two, who left obvious signs as they wandered through the twenty-first century. But she'd seen no sign of YDorian. If he was around, he'd been much better at hiding his trace.

The vicious machine did shift in and out several times, but Yverra knew Violet had managed to escape it on each of those occasions. Where was it now? Why couldn't she sense it? Her worry increased as she considered the increasing possibility that the "new" universe incursions would mean another disaster for her own.

She stood in the casino of the Lucky 7 Resort Hotel, where Ben and Ralff had last verified that Violet was still human. She couldn't really blame them for not being thorough enough. They were just neophyte Watchmen. She scanned the room, sensing nothing new besides the awful noise the humans called music.

"Hello, it's good to see you again," a human said to her.

"You've seen me before?"

The young man laughed. "You Circus Circus people really stay in character, don't you? The green skin is wicked cool, and the steampunk outfit too. I wouldn't take it off, either."

Yverra cocked her head, listening for a dimension shift or a time hack. Yes, there had been one recently.

She'd nearly found what she'd come for.

"Could you remind me where you saw me last?" Yverra said.

"Parking lot, dude. You really ought to go home and get some rest."

"I'll do that, thank you," Yverra said.

She strode to the sign marked "Hotel Parking" and followed a ramp leading to the cavernous underground building. Yes, Violet had dimension hacked right here. But that wasn't the interesting thing. They'd been seen by another witness. A Watchman. Her people communicated via pheromones, but only within a dimension or close range. It was a male. She shifted rapidly back and forth, becoming invisible to the humans who might wander into the garage. A feeling, almost of exhilaration, warmed her blood.

"YDorian? Are you here?"

The creature, almost her twin, stepped forward from behind a concrete column. She'd nearly forgotten how her people looked. Used to look. She checked her time. Still in the same approximate timeline.

"Hello, Yverra. I didn't think I'd see you again. How did you escape the Unwinding?"

"It's a long story, and I would ask you the same thing, except that I knew you ran." She was falling into her old accusatory pattern. That was wrong of her, she knew. "Please accept my apology. I meant to say that it's good to see you. Also, that I need your help." She would try to make amends and apply the tips she had painfully learned from Violet for making and keeping friends and allies. "I regret our earlier disagreements," she added.

"No offense taken. We were young. I decided to strike out on my own to visit Virginia Jones's home to gain further information about her civilization and its relation to the Unwinding. I lost my nerve and never spoke to her. I meant to return, really I did. But then, as I moved forward in time, I saw the Unwinding unfolding, destroying this timeline. I felt marooned."

"You were merely being prudent," Yverra observed. "I have just made a similar pilgrimage to Virginia Jones's home. While it is indeed true that this timeline will end abruptly in three centuries, we now have a dimensional workaround to preserve what's left of the Watchmen."

"You mean you saved the Watchmen? I can go home?"

"Yes and no. You are correct that our home was destroyed by the Unwinding. But we only have shelter on a space station at the future edge of the universe."

"There are Watchmen there?"

"Yes, but I am the only one from our old race. The others are human and Ranstalat. They are a young and naive group, but full of energy and hope. I am training them in our ways. You apparently encountered one of them, I think. The human is Violet Rain."

"There was a second human with her. Is he now a Watchman as well?"

"No, he is a contemporary human. Unfortunately, they are going to be separated soon."

"Yes, that would be wise. They were being pursued by a cybernetic human hybrid. But what about the Unwinding?"

"It was resolved temporarily by a truce proposed by Virginia Jones, but it seems to be unraveling. That's why when I found out you might still be alive, I came to ask for your help."

"I must say it is an honor to once again see the most beautiful Watchman. I would give much to leave this backward civilization."

"Really? I have begun to appreciate some of its finer points. Particularly in the area of survival against all odds."

"All I've seen of this civilization is the tendency to overeat, and your two human examples are no exception. However, there must be some truth to your words if you are here before me now. What do you want me to do?"

"First, let's get out of this dank garage." They blinked.

☺

"We found Violet here, her consciousness trapped in the body of a small creature called a tardigrade," Yverra said, gesturing toward the forested area. They had decided to take a direct route to North Carolina.

"This is a lovely area," YDorian observed. "Water and forests, much like our aboriginal home. I hope they are taking steps to preserve it."

"Take care not to be seen. The local inhabitants are not as sophisticated as the ones in the West about people who look different than they do."

"The robot is not here," YDorian said. "I was halfway expecting that."

"I agree. But where could it have gone after the attack at the space station?"

"We've proven it was never in this forest. May I advance a new theory?"

"Of course."

"Perhaps it returned to the home area of the other human, to lie in wait for Violet."

"But she wasn't planning to visit Janus again."

"You said he was the father of virtual reality technology in Earth. You also said the robot has hacking capability. Perhaps the robot's strategy was to interfere with Janus's history."

"And that might attract Violet. She would try to coax the timeline to stay on track, at least until the 25th century."

"What was the name of Janus's company? Let's stop by."

"I'm beginning to understand the true meaning of Grace Magnusson's expression about chasing wild geese. California, here we come."

"Indeed."

"The robot hybrid's been here. But he's not here now," YDorian said, surveying the wreckage of the Canny Divide warehouse. Since it was hunting Violet, and Janus was the father of virtual reality, my theory that it'd show up here turned out to be correct. But Janus Parker is dead. This assassin's more slippery than a time squirt."

Yverra looked at the handsome Watchman. His scales were practically glowing with the heat of his exertions in bringing them all the way across the continent again. The thought of the robot as Violet's lover wormed its way back into Yverra's head.

"Humans are exceptionally passionate. Sabotage of VR certainly helps explain the destruction that the robot brought down on Janus Parker, but what if it had more to do with its anger at not being able to find Violet. What if it went to a place where it and Violet were lovers, even if only in virtual reality?"

"I hadn't thought of that, although it seems logical."

"I think I know where he is now," Yverra said. "Rest a little, and start swallowing air. We'll need it for the longer hop ahead of us. We're going to Mars."

An orangish light shone over the rock-strewn landscape, indicating they had arrived late in the Martian day.

"I never would have looked for him here," YDorian said. "Mars in the twenty-first century was completely uninhabited."

"Then he probably hasn't gone to great lengths to hide himself."

"Have you got enough air?"

"Yes, I'm good. The air here's a little thin for our gills, so our lung sacs will have to suffice."

YDorian pointed. "There."

The robot stood up to its knees in red dirt; it had apparently partially buried itself to keep from blowing over. It looked to be completely dormant.

"Be careful. According to Violet's early reports, it is armed with an arsenal of deadly weapons, and all of its appendages can be quickly modified. She said it can shoot bullets, fling knives, and throw flames."

"Well, flames shouldn't be much of a problem," YDorian said. "Low oxygen."

"I'm not joking," Yverra said.

"I'm not either," YDorian replied.

Suddenly Yverra hissed. The robot rose into the air and turned to face them. "Look out, it's nascent."

"Well, if it isn't the little green men," the Enforcer said. "I don't know how you got here, but you are about to die."

"Thanks for the warning," Yverra said. She and YDorian hacked slightly to consider what to do. They didn't have much time, since the robot would wake up shortly in this nearby dimension too.

"Let's remove his hacking capability for starters," YDorian said. "I can—" Before he finished his sentence, the robot appeared, discharging a particle beam weapon that apparently didn't require oxygen. YDorian dived to the left, in an attempt to draw its attention away from Yverra. He wasn't fast enough.

YDorian cried out in pain, before abruptly shifting away. Yverra blinked once and followed.

"He's too fast for us," YDorian gasped, holding his arm. "Be right back."

"What?" Yverra said, shocked. Was he leaving again? She glanced down at drips of blood that were quickly freezing into the soil. She blinked out of existence once again. There was nothing to do but play this cat-and-mouse game until YDorian returned. If he returned. He looked like he'd been hurt pretty badly.

After more than thirty-six shifts, Yverra returned to where they had started. The robot appeared immediately, hardly fazed by her strategic moves. It— he— was getting faster. Enforcer aimed another ray toward her. She wondered how long she could last. Long enough, she resolved. She gathered her strength to shift again, when YDorian appeared. The robot swung around to aim its weapon arm toward him, but YDorian had already grabbed him from behind.

"Here, hold him while I make a stasis bubble, please," YDorian said.

"My pleasure," Yverra said. The symbols on her arm glowed as she tied a field lasso around the robot.

"We'll be back," YDorian said. "Don't follow us." YDorian and the robot jumped into the bubble and shifted.

Speechless, Yverra prepared to just stand there.

"I'll be here," she muttered. "As long as my air holds out, anyway."

☙

Virginia surveyed her garden harvest with satisfaction. Some green beans, tomatoes, and best of all, golden beets fresh from the ground. As she crossed the patio to enter the kitchen, a reptilian figure appeared and bowed slightly. His gold irises were striated, like veins of jasper.

"Yverra? You're back already? Any further progress with Vi?"

"Regretfully, madam, I am not Yverra, though we were from the same hatching and appear to many to resemble each other. I am YDorian. Would it be possible to meet with Dr. Alan Jones?"

"Holy Toledo, Batman! It's another Watchman. We thought you were all dead," Gin said. "But hey, come in, I'll call Alan. Are you hungry? Do you want to join us for dinner? What do you people eat, anyway? I'll do my best to get it for you... I hope you like vegetables."

"That won't be necessary at present, thank you," YDorian said. "This is a matter of some urgency, I'm afraid."

"Yes, of course. Alan!" she called. "We've got visitors."

A thumping noise from the creaky board in the hallway indicated Alan was on his way from his study to the kitchen, a well-worn path.

"Visitors, you say?" Alan said, appearing at the kitchen archway. His eyes widened and his eyebrows went up.

"Pardon this unforgivable intrusion," YDorian said. "My name is YDorian. Yverra tells me you are well qualified in the area of computing, robotics, and virtual reality programming."

"Well, I do chair the CS Department at UNC-Raleigh," Alan responded. "What can I do for you? I don't suppose this has anything to do with the unfortunate events at Canny Divide? And with Violet? Are they related?"

"They are most definitely related," YDorian said, his blood warming. Jones was unusually astute for a human.

"I recall from the media reports that there was a fire and several deaths. Would this also be related to the assassin robot that was pursuing Violet Rain?"

Doubly astute.

"Yes. And I have brought the culprit with me."

Virginia cut in. "You brought the killer robot here? Why? And how?"

"I've put him in a stasis bubble for the moment. I am hoping that Alan can assist with his re-programming. The continued existence of certain timelines important to my people depends on it."

186

"Important to ours as well," Alan said. "But what can I do?"

"To begin with, could you analyze his circuitry and data? If we can get clues as to his origin and mission, then we could safely decommission him. We already know he was once a human who knew Violet. Thus, he has been especially adept at tracking her and hacking to her location. Somewhere along the way, he must have lost the trail to Violet, just as we have, but maybe he has information we have overlooked about why she is his target."

"But if you take him out of stasis, won't he try to kill us?" Gin asked.

Another astute observation. Or perhaps not so astute this time. He was dripping blood on her clean kitchen floor, after all.

"Can you work with just his head?" YDorian asked. "I can leave the rest of him in stasis."

"Alas, poor Yorick, I knew him, Horatio," Alan said. "Nothing like a full body curse, like in Harry Potter, eh?"

YDorian merely blinked.

"Um, we'll take a look. Gin, could you bring dinner to the garage tonight? I think I'm going to need my multimeter and toner. I'll just grab an extra hard drive from my study. This should be fun. I haven't tinkered with bio-embedded hardware for a long time... not since Calaneris."

ᗡ

A few seconds passed. A shimmer in the air indicated a rather large shift had just occurred. YDorian appeared, along with the robot, seemingly decommissioned or, at least, dormant.

"It's wonderful to see you again," he said.

"You've only been gone a few seconds," Yverra observed wryly.

"It felt like weeks," YDorian said.

187

"Where did you go?"

"I went to visit Alan Jones. He is quite an accomplished programmer, you know."

"Yes, he learned from the time he was at the Emperor's project to study the Unwinding at the Big Bang. How do you know him?"

"I didn't. But I remembered you had begun working with him, before we had our little, um, *disagreement.* So, I took the robot to him for a little re-programming."

"Remarkable. So, it must have worked? It appears to be out cold. Is it in stasis?"

"Not only that. In probing the robot's innards, guess what Jones found?"

"More deadly weapons?"

"Well, yes, some of those. But also the fact that the robot is actually one of the Emperor's creations."

"What? I thought the Emperor had been rehabilitated."

"He has. This creature was created when Calaneris was in thrall to the Black Universe. Calaneris wanted Virginia dead, along with her whole human line. So, he and his henchman Blauw took one of Violet's lovers on Mars, modified him, and sent him after her. Then they destroyed the Martian colony."

"It all makes sense now. Violet's been talking about her lover and how he tried to kill her. His name was Xoan," Yverra said. "But at least it's over now. The robot's been destroyed, right?"

"Not exactly," YDorian said. "We didn't kill him. Alan changed his programming, so we think he's no longer violent."

"And it only took a few seconds. That was fast work," Yverra said. "At least you're not bleeding any more."

"Now who's joking?" he replied. They shifted back to the present-dimension.

Yverra looked at the former Enforcer's head.

"It looks like it wants to cry," Yverra said in wonder.

"I didn't say Alan fixed *everything*. Xoan still has a lot of issues."

"Ah, the passion," Yverra said. "Well, let's get him home for questioning."

"I'm anxious to see your space station and meet the other Watchmen. I've got something important to tell you all."

"They'll be glad to see you too, YDorian." Yverra tucked the robot head under her arm and reached out for YDorian's hand.

*****~~~~~*****

Chapter 16.

Regeneration

Fire and cold. He tried to listen for the sounds that would tell him where he was, but now he heard nothing, only felt. He floated in a dark morass of unconnected sensory inputs. Gusting blasts of wind buffeted him, each increasingly stronger. He turned his back to the chilling wind and began to run, hoping to generate warmth. On the floor lay a discarded military jumpsuit. The gale lifted it, making it jump from the floor and run ahead of him. He stopped, seeking an exit. There was an open elevator. Shivering, he stepped in, welcoming the shelter. The doors closed. There were no buttons. Was he going up or down? He wasn't sure. Usually, he could tell if he was rising, because there would be pressure on the bottoms of his feet. He felt a jerk, as if awakening suddenly from a sensation of falling. The elevator doors opened, revealing a crowded cafeteria. He smelled the welcoming aroma of coffee. Clear windows showed an empty red landscape and black sky. A girl at a nearby table pointed at him and laughed, showing lipstick smeared teeth. It should have been noisy, yet he couldn't hear her laughter.

Sudden static crashed into his head. "Do you hear me now, Xoan?" an incredibly loud voice asked. He would have put his hands to his ears, but he didn't have... He wanted to cry, but all he could do was to breathe harder.

"I think we can take that as a 'yes,'" Benrus said.

"Go easy on him," Ralff said. "He's just waking up. He doesn't know where he is."

"And we should keep it that way," Ben said. "I trust Alan Jones's programming skills, but it's important we don't let him loose to kill again."

"With no body? That's unlikely. But, on second thought, maybe he has X-ray vision or something."

"All right, I've adjusted his hearing circuit. I'm going to turn on his eyes now. Anything he's seen so far has just been random firings of memory. Don't worry, he doesn't have the ability to generate any sort of radiation now, much less X-rays." A faint dot of light appeared in Xoan's field of vision. The light began to brighten, as blurry images started to form. He shifted his eyes back and forth, trying to get a clearer picture.

"You can only see in the spectrum that humans can see in right now," Ben said. "After all, you are originally a human." Xoan remembered being something else, something not human. The memory, if that's what it was, played itself in the background of his consciousness. It was horrifying.

Gradually, Xoan recognized two tall alien figures bending over him. These aliens were different from the ones he'd seen recently. The ones on Mars looked like steam-punk reptiles. This pair looked more human, though elongated enough to definitely not be from Earth. They were what he would have imagined Martians to look like, even though he knew there were never any real Martians. Tall, bald, seemingly too fragile for Earth's strong gravity. He tried to speak.

"Hold on, Xoan," Ben said. "I'm still re-inserting the code Alan supplied for speech. I think he said it only needed a little modification from what you've been using all along."

Xoan tried again. A faint croak. The panicky feeling returned.

"That's excellent," Ralff encouraged. "We just need to hook you up to an amplifier, and you should be good to go. Okay, try it now."

"Why don't you just kill me?" Xoan asked. He'd asked that before, and he'd never gotten a satisfactory answer.

"You're too valuable right now. Besides, we have some questions for you."

Of course. They were going to torture him. He tried to grimace fiercely. "Do your worst. I'm not telling you anything."

"We positively are *not* going to do our worst," Ralff said.

"Is— is the red-haired man here?" Xoan asked, his face contorted. His eyes bulged. "He's evil."

Ralff glanced at Ben. "Well, you've verified something we suspected. You don't have to worry about Blauw now."

"He murdered me," Xoan said.

"Yes, we know. But it's going to be all right."

Xoan found that he could cry now.

"Are you sure he will want to talk to me?" Blauw asked.

"Yes, but he is still afraid of you," Ben said. "You destroyed his body, after all. We've cloned him and given him some enhanced mechanical parts to make him feel comfortable in his own skin. Let me go first and let him get used to the idea."

Blauw nodded. Calaneris sat nearby.

Ben leaned over Xoan's inert form.

"Xoan, it's Ben. How are you feeling?"

"Fine."

"We just wanted to give you a bit of a warning. Remember that red-haired man you mentioned earlier?"

"Yes."

"Well, he's here and would like to talk to you."

Xoan bolted upright.

"Don't let him come near me," he cried.

Blauw stepped forward, bouncing lightly up and down on his feet. "We've come to apologize. The Emperor and I. We're sorry for what we did to you."

"Why should I listen?" Xoan said. "You and that pompous villain should pay for what you did to me."

"You're right, of course," Calaneris said. "But we were under the sway of the Black Universe. Things are different now. We want to make it up to you if we can."

"You can never make it up," Xoan said. "I've done terrible things—killed people."

"Yes, and that was our fault. We share your guilt and take responsibility for it."

"Besides," Blauw added. "I've had some time to learn about guilt and forgiveness myself. I'd be happy to share with you what I've learned. If you'd allow me to help you, it would go a long way to helping me rectify my previous bad behavior. We have more in common than you know."

"I don't trust them," Xoan said, turning toward Ben and Ralff.

"We'll be here the whole time," Ralff said.

"So, shall we get started?" Blauw said.

"I don't have a real human body anymore," Xoan said. "How can you make up for that?"

"That's been remedied," Ben said. "You'll be pretty much back to your old self in a short time. It might interest you to know that we're growing another human body besides your own at the same time, so you'll have a companion during recovery."

"Another person kidnapped by these murderers?" Xoan asked.

"Well, sort of. It did happen once," Ralff said. "Kidnapping, I mean."

"But not really," Ben corrected. "This person temporarily lost her body trying to save the universe. We think you know her. Her name's Violet Rain."

"Violet? Why didn't you say so in the first place? But... I don't think I could face her in this— this— abomination."

"Violet's suffered some memory loss in her mission," Ben said. "Alan Jones came across your memories of her when recovering your consciousness. You'd be doing everyone a huge favor if you help her find herself again."

"But just because we're both getting new bodies doesn't mean she'll want to be my friend after all the things I've done. When she remembers... how I pursued her across the country trying to kill her... God, I feel like I'm barely staying afloat on top of a pile of garbage and I'm about to sink again."

"That's just the guilt," Blauw said. "It shows you recognize it. That's the first step. The second step is to try to make amends as best you can. That's why you see me here. I can tell you in detail what we did to you—if you want to know, that is—so you can hopefully get past the trauma and begin healing."

Calaneris cleared his throat. "Blauw is taking too much of the guilt on himself, of course. As Emperor, I ordered him to do it. Although I must say, he took to it like a fish to water. But that's in the past. We've forgiven each other and moved on. We want to do the same with you."

"I don't think I can ever get over the guilt or forgive either of you," Xoan said.

"Well, guilt isn't just to make us feel bad. It's there to help us learn something and make it less likely that we'll repeat our bad behavior in the future. We were unfortunately caught up in a complex feud between competing universes. Blauw and I have removed ourselves from the Empire that I used to control, so those temptations are less seductive. We fill an important role, manning the space station here along the Yin-Yang

Boundary between universes, and helping to ensure the peace."

"Yeah," Blauw said. "Nobody's perfect. I know we messed up bad. You don't need to tell us. But it's okay if you do."

"But I was The Enforcer," Xoan said. "And I enjoyed it."

"Of course," Blauw said. "I was Calaneris's bad boy, and I enjoyed that too. But I'm also a human, and there are damn few of us left in this timeline. I even feel guilty for putting the moves on Alan's wife, Virginia. But now I'll do whatever I can for Alan's family—and for you. I mean that."

"I loved Violet," Xoan said.

"I don't blame you, son," Blauw said, putting his hand on Xoan's arm, the arm where the weapons used to be hidden.

Xoan flinched.

"I think it's too soon," Calaneris said, rising. "Blauw, let's give him a chance to think."

Blauw nodded and smiled. Xoan couldn't help but shudder.

☺

"Water. Can I have some water? I'm thirsty."

Ben released a tiny mist into the chamber holding Violet's tardigrade body.

"Ah, that's better. Could you add a little salt?"

"Violet, are you ready to talk to us?"

"All right, but I still don't remember everything."

"That's because you're so tiny. You don't have a brain anymore. You're no bigger than a few molecules, including the water we just gave you."

"Molecules? What are those?"

Ralff sighed. "Grace brought back your projector, so when it's ready, we can put you back good as new. Mostly. Your grandfather Alan is going to help you remember more. Once we get you a new body, you'll have a lot more space to store those memories. Oh, and we have another of your friends who's going to help too."

Alan entered the room carrying a flat silicon sheet about the size of a personal tablet. "Here's the memory substrate I was talking about. I've uploaded a lot of memories from Virginia, Grace, and me. Even Yverra has shared what she can. You two are next."

"Us?" Ben said. "We haven't known Violet very long."

"Well, you've had some exciting adventures with her, like getting kidnapped by Calaneris and working with her in the lab to solve the latest incursions."

"That's true," Ben said. "And we're now fellow Watchmen."

"Very important," Alan agreed. "You're her new family."

"What do we do?" Ralff asked.

"Just stand there quietly and think good thoughts, while I wave this magnetic resonance spectrometer around and record the images."

"And that will capture all of our memories?" Ralff asked.

"Of course not, it just maps your physical brain—which I'm quite curious about, by the way—but it will distract you while I get Grace to do the actual brain ream and deposit everything she finds onto this substrate."

"Hello, Grandfather," Violet said.

Alan jumped. "I'd almost forgotten Violet was here and can hear everything we say."

"Hello, Grandfather," she repeated.

"But her memory needs a lot of work," Alan mumbled. "Let's get started."

☉

A week later, the body of a golden-skinned woman lay sleeping on the laboratory table.

"I'm always amazed when I see Violet," Alan remarked. "Her skin is such an odd color. Beautiful, but odd. I guess that's what passed for perfection in the 25th century. Not to mention the purple fringe. I always wondered why she dyed it that color."

"Violet said everyone on Earth had genetic enhancements, which they could choose to make permanent and transmissable via gene drive technology, if they desired," Yverra said. "I think she's quite attractive, although I would have added more green to her skin tone."

"I see why you would," Alan said. "You're a bit on the chartreuse side. Plus gold."

"Thank you," Yverra said.

A door slid open, and another laboratory table floated into the room, this one with a brown-skinned human male body, also fast asleep. Right behind it was Ralff, who maneuvered it into place beside Violet.

"Looks good," Alan said. He pulled out a pair of tablets and inserted one into a slot below each bed."

"Hope I got the order right," Alan said. "Just joking. These are the memory substrates. Umm, Violet struck me as a bit of a prude, so let's get them both dressed before we release the hounds of memory."

"Should we all stay?" Ralff said.

"No, it might be too confusing to have a crowd around them when they first wake up. Let's all get out of here. See you later, sweetheart. Remember, there's no place like home."

Yverra blinked, her face expressionless as usual. They exited the lab, and the door snicked closed behind them. "We can monitor them in Lab 2," she said.

☺

Her throat was dry, and she had a headache. She felt positively parched.

"Can a person get a drink of water around here?" Violet asked. She sat up. "I said— What the hell is this?" A cold chill ran across Violet's skin.

"Maybe this wasn't such a good idea," Ralff said, looking at the feed from the lab next door. "She is quite perturbed."

Violet stared at her hand.

"She's just staring at her hand," Ben noted.

"I realize that," Alan said. "Just give her some time to acclimatize."

Violet heard a groan. She lowered her hand. There was someone else in the room. She blinked. She could see that someone was a person.

"Hello? Are you Grandfather? No, I remember Grandfather was older. Grandfather! Grandfather!" Violet began screaming.

"All right, I'm coming," Alan said. He exited the observation room and ran down the hall. Ralff and Benrus saw him enter the room where Violet and Xoan sat in varying degrees of bewilderment.

"Violet! I'm here. Grandfather Jones."

"I'm not Violet. I'm Cheon-Sa."

"No, you're Violet," Alan replied. "Or, you're both. And this is Xoan. We've just put both of you back into your human bodies."

"Xoan? I thought he was dead."

Xoan rolled up to a sitting position and rubbed his eyes. He looked tired.

"My God, you're like Frankenstein," Violet said.

"Ha, you're Violet, all right," Xoan replied. "I thought I was dead too."

"Did you try to kill me?"

"That wasn't me."

"Grandfather, this is the assassin that chased me and— He killed Janus too, right?"

"I didn't kill Janus," Xoan said.

"I don't want to be in the same room with this liar," Violet said.

Alan stepped between them. "Listen, Violet. You two were once very close. We think it would help you both if you recuperated together. You could help each other recover memories. And to correct memories that we had to ad lib when we regenerated your bodies."

"Where's Janus's body, then?" Violet demanded. She glared at Xoan. "If you didn't kill him, who did?"

"I don't know," Xoan said, downcast. "Dr. Jones, you and Blauw and Calaneris said you could heal me."

Alan sighed. "We can only offer our help. I think Violet is going to be the best medicine."

"I'm not anyone's medicine!" Violet shouted.

"I've got to go now," Alan said. "Yverra said there's another incursion, and the Watchmen are needed."

"You're not a Watchman!" Violet said. "I am."

"I know. And the sooner you're back, the more chance we'll all have of surviving this thing. Xoan, we'd be truly grateful for any cooperation you can provide." The door opened, and Alan backed out of the room.

Violet turned her attention to Xoan. "So, give me one good reason why I shouldn't kill you right now."

"Umm, because this isn't virtual reality?"

"I could put one of my spike heels right into your eye and straight to your brain."

"Imaginative, as usual. Aren't you happy to be back in your body? They told me you were in a tardigrade body."

"No thanks to you."

"I think we'd better break this up for now," Ralff said. Outside in the corridor he thanked Alan.

"They just need more time," Alan said. "I just hope we have it."

*****~~~~~*****

Chapter 17.

It's Just Us Now

"Well, I looked into the incursions a bit, but they've calmed down, at least temporarily," Alan said. "They also seem different from the ones during the Black Universe's plot. None of that 550-mu_em green lightning. How are Xoan and Violet doing? They did get off to a rocky start, though in some ways, the new crisis is a boon. It should make them realign their priorities."

"Excellent news about the incursions. But we've discovered one small glitch," Yverra said.

"Oh?"

"The tardigrade is still conscious—and talking."

"It appears we've still got some wires crossed," Alan said. "I'll look into it. How's YDorian settling in?"

"Quite well," Yverra said. "He has volunteered to work on improving the living arrangements here on the station. He's been popping in and out of various times to get the proper materials, adding a little greenery here and there. Should we try to terminate the tardigrade?" Yverra asked. "I've actually grown to like the little water bear."

"Risky," said Alan. "This could be a case of action at a distance. We might lose some of Vi's memories, or even her personality. And she's shown so much progress lately..."

"I have a temporary solution that might work," Violet suggested. "I feel pretty comfortable surmising what the main motivators are for a tardigrade, having spent weeks inside the body of one."

Violet picked up the petri dish containing the tardigrade formerly known as Cheon-Sa and slid it under the scanning electron microscope.

"See here, where I attached the carbon nanotubes to make Cheon-Sa more mobile? I can just create ports between her and me, and attach her permanently via her stylet. That way there's no real distance to worry about. We'll be in constant contact. In fact, I can still use her in applications requiring a tiny interface, like crossing universe boundaries. It would be fairly straightforward to detach her physically. I'd just need to find a way to actually *see* the little bugger long enough to do that. Right now I need an electron microscope."

"Could be feasible," Alan said. "You've done the majority of work needed to engineer on the microscale. You can even create a new library of VR microscale environments, starring Cheon-Sa as the exploring avatar. You can go a whole order of magnitude smaller than in 'Fantastic Voyage.'"

"That could be fun," Violet said, not really recalling the reference.

They discussed ways to ensure that the creature didn't become accidentally detached. Then, there was the question of keeping it alive. Would they have to moisten it every day, or whether would it be better to leave it in a desiccated state for the most part.

"We'll leave her dehydrated mostly," Violet said. "Otherwise, she won't live more than a few months. When she's active, she can take whatever nourishment she needs from me. I'll be her permanent feeding trough. I'll need time to perfect this projecting thing—and maybe cloning too, if we can't reunite me with myself."

Ralff, the more romantic of the Jandalat pair, waxed euphoric about the project to link Violet and the tardigrade.

"It's like the Greek myth about the origin of love," he said.

"Ralff, you're nothing but an Earth groupie," Vi said. "What myth?"

"In Plato's Symposium, the ancient Greek dramatist Aristophanes said love is people searching for their other half. He recounted how the original humans had two sets of arms and two sets of legs and two faces, on either side of a giant head. The jealous gods thought this made them too powerful, so Zeus—you've heard of him, of course—took a lightning bolt and cut them in two. Men would now fear and worship the gods, never feeling complete."

Yverra examined the tiny creature's projected image. It waved its claws gently and did a slow somersault. "I find it rather lovable. How do you plan to keep your other half happy? It appears to be a sentient being."

"Anyone who's ever had a pet learns how to manage," Alan said.

"Have you ever had a tardigrade as a pet?" Yverra asked.

"Well, no…"

"Just leave it to me," Violet said.

"I could use a snack right now," Cheon-Sa said.

☙

Xoan's forehead was drenched with sweat. He'd tried everything to recall the last moments on Mars, before the colony was lost. Surely he'd done everything he could, but he must be suffering a mental block. He remembered transmitting a warning and a message to his father. He wondered if his father knew what a traitor he'd been.

Once again he blamed Calaneris and Blauw. They had somehow corrupted the love he had for Violet and warped it into a debauched devotion to the reprobate Emperor. He felt hot.

"Are you all right? The monitors indicate you seem to be running a fever. And your heart rate is up." It was Ralff. Or was it Benrus? He had trouble telling the two Jandalats apart, though they claimed to be from radically different nationalities.

"I'm fine," Xoan said.

"Perhaps you'd like some of the excellent soup that the station provides? Violet used to say it would cure what ails you."

"No, thank you."

Violet had accused him of betraying her and stomped out of the lab. He wondered if he would ever see her again. He'd never had any real friends except for her. He showed up for work, checked the monitors, and kept to himself. Popularity wasn't his thing. Until he met Violet. He even started believing he belonged when he was with her. He didn't feel so invisible. Once when he fixed a serious bug in Violet's VR program, she'd said she depended on him. When she took his hand, he thought it could be forever. Of course, he allowed as how he wasn't sexy like the VR stars.

"Don't worry that you're not good enough. It's all illusion anyway," she had said during one of their infrequent conference calls. "No one can compete with those guys. I've met a lot of stars, and they're all people just like you and me. A lot of the magic comes from inside, Xoan." Yet she'd stayed on Earth, calling it a "better job." It was ironic that fate had brought her back. Now that she hated him, would she leave again?

Then again, where was there to go? STS-99 was the Watchmen's home now. And he was still an outsider.

☺

Violet and Ralff had been observing the still-incomplete template that was John-Paul since the last two abortive attempts to restore his memories. Now that Violet understood the situation more fully, she felt inclined to let bygones be bygones. Like Grandpa had said, "things take

204

time." She wanted to believe that everything about John-Paul was going to be the same as it ever was. But she knew that wasn't possible, even if Grandpa had cloned John-Paul and left out the aggression circuitry that Calaneris—and especially Blauw—had implanted. In order to get the person most closely resembling *her* John-Paul, they had to restore most of his memories. She made a silent promise: "John-Paul, I'm coming for you."

"You know, I've got some experience in cyberpsychology," Violet said.

"What, may I ask, is cyberpsychology?" Ralff asked.

"It's the use of VR to conduct what's called 'exposure therapy' to help a patient become desensitized to a particular traumatic experience," Violet said. "If John-Paul is going to keep his memories, he is going to need to face his fears."

"My God, you're not going to make him live that torture on Mars all over again, are you? That would make you as bad as Blauw," Ralff said.

"Of course not," Violet said. "At least, I don't think so. Most people who undergo exposure therapy do get better in time. Of course, they may have to accurately remember the trauma in order to deal with it. But at least they know it's not real this time."

"Well, all right," Ralff said, doubt clear in his voice. "How is it done?"

"If you could become Blauw's avatar, that would be helpful. With you actually present in the scene, you could exhibit different behavior than what Blauw did."

"I should hope so," Ralff said.

"I'll be pretty busy steering the VR scenario, so it'd help if you were there to alert me when and if things start to go out of bounds," Violet said.

"How will I know that?"

"Loud screaming and thrashing around is usually a tipoff."

"I don't know, Violet..."

"I know it'll be hard," she said. "It'll be hard for me too. I still feel responsible for what happened on Mars."

"You couldn't have known..."

"I know, I know," Violet said.

"You know, it wouldn't hurt for you to try some exposure therapy yourself," Ralff observed. "I imagine you've been repressing some painful memories too."

"You're right, Ralff," she said, partly to cut off this line of discussion. "Come on, let's get started. Xoan, can you hear me?" Violet reached into her blouse and touched her projection assistant.

The man on the table startled and sat up.

"Just relax. You're in your office on Mars."

A groan.

Violet hoped she remembered John-Paul's office right. She'd been there a couple of times, so this should be a pretty good approximation. J-P's office mate sat beside him, typing into a keyboard and glancing over at J-P. Violet decided to introduce some background noise, like some muffled explosions off in the distance. Maybe a little green light would bring back J-P's memories. Once his brain got going, it would do most of the work for her, his imagination shoveling in details and ramping up emotions.

"Okay, you can come in now," she told Ralff. "Remember, you look like Blauw, so it's not going to be pretty." She knew J-P's brain's emotional command center, or limbic system, would respond to the stress in a matter of milliseconds.

"Who are you?" John-Paul yelled, his eyes wild. "How did you get in here?"

"Do you think he sees my actual appearance through the VR?" Ralff asked.

"Don't worry," Violet said. "You look just like Blauw. It's positively creepy. Just tell him what a good job he's doing and try to talk him down so we can reason with him."

"Oh, I'm just visiting the Mars colony," Ralff said, ad libbing.

"You're doing great, Ralff," Violet encouraged. J-Ps heart rate and stress hormone levels seemed to slow a tiny bit.

"I'm terribly sorry to have interrupted you," Ralff-Blauw said. "I understand you were instrumental in averting the crisis, and you must have a lot of work to do to get everything straightened out."

"I— I—" John-Paul began. "The crisis. You were the cause of it, weren't you?"

"Uh, oh, he's having a little bit of paranoia. Look friendly," Violet suggested.

The Blauw avatar grinned. John-Paul leaped to his feet and made a run for the door. Unfortunately, there wasn't actually a door there.

"Slight panic attack," Violet pronounced. "Um, I think we need to do some fine tuning on our next try," she said, adding some anti-anxiety meds to the mixture running into John-Paul's veins subcutaneously. "But don't worry, we'll get there." She hoped she didn't show how fearful she felt. It was strange, this abrupt turnabout from hatred to desperately wanting to help John-Paul.

"I think I know how he feels," Ralff said. "I'd feel the same in his place."

"Thanks, unlike the old Blauw, you have feelings."

∽

Violet retreated to her room and flopped onto her bed. Feeling restless, she soon rose and began pacing. She glanced in the bathroom mirror. That always gave her a shock. What had happened to her purple fringe? Or any fringe, for that matter? She had forgotten that her body had been reconstituted, so she was more like a long-lost twin of herself. Her skin was the wrong color, too. And Cheon-Sa made her feel hungry and thirsty all the time.

She could change back to her usual appearance, at least to anyone within her VR range. But they hadn't given her back her Virtual Projection Assistant. Why not? It was hers, after all.

She headed back toward the labs in search of a pair of scissors. It had been so long since she had modified her genes that she could no longer recall the recipes for purple hair and phosphoring skin. She needed her VPA, dammit. She paused as she passed the kitchen. She wondered if it could make cheesecake.

"Where's John-Paul?" Violet said, sticking her head in the lab.

Ben and Ralff glanced at each other. This was the first time Violet had called Xoan by his old nickname since the regeneration.

"He has a room in the Green Spoke," Ralff said. "He said he's fond of Earth forests, as are we. It's also Yverra's preferred habitat, so she suggested he take a room in that quadrant, like us. It's lovely. The decks are even growing grass now."

"I guess it's appropriate that he's in the Watchman wing," Violet agreed. "I forgot you two were Earthophiles."

"Earthophiles?"

"I just made that up. It means you love Earth. Grandma Ginny said you visited many times. Well, maybe I'll head over to Green and see what's up."

"It's three doors down from you," Ralff said. "Oh, and there are birds too."

"Quiet, Ralff," Ben muttered. "Let her go."

☉

The long corridor leading to Violet's room had changed a lot since she'd last been home. It was wider, and the roof was higher. Plants had been seeded along the edges and up the walls, in an effort to add oxygen and clean out carbon dioxide. The air felt moist and had a reddish cast, making the foliage look almost black. Blue light undulated across the ceiling, like patterns in an aurora sky. STS-99 was expanding under management by Calaneris and Blauw. That was fine with her, as long as they didn't try to start up another empire.

She passed her room and counted to the third door. She paused, not sure whether to knock. The decision was taken out of her hands, as John-Paul's door slid open.

"Ralff told me you were on the way. Won't you come in?"

"All right." She stepped in. The room was just like hers, except that the wall screen showed a photo of a dry, rocky, rust-colored landscape. "They told me you were under the protection of the Watchmen."

"Yes, thanks," Xoan said.

"Why haven't you been at the lab?" Vi asked.

"I haven't exactly felt comfortable," he replied.

"I guess that's my fault," Violet said. "I wasn't exactly welcoming. But Grandpa Alan was right. I think I'm recovering my memory more quickly with you around."

"It isn't your fault," Xoan said. "It's more that every time I look at Calaneris or Blauw, I feel sick. I thought I'd be getting used to the idea that they aren't my enemies any more."

"I hear you on that," Violet said. "Are you feeling any better—aside from that very important fact—I mean?"

"In some ways. But there's also the memory of my father. He would have expected more of me, I think."

"I miss my mother too. We're both orphans," she said, laying her hand on his arm.

"And to add insult to injury, we can't regenerate our parents, as Alan did with us. Calaneris destroyed them utterly, along with Yverra's planet."

"That was a long time ago, believe it or not. They don't have the same pressures and hatred as they once did. But the real reason I came here is that I want to find out more about Janus Parker. You denied killing him. Were you being honest?"

"Absolutely. I admit to destroying his VR warehouse when I was Calaneris's Enforcer, but I vanished immediately. Parker was still alive when I left."

"Where the hell could he have gone?" Violet said. "I'm sure it wasn't anything like me splitting off using my VPA. He saw me use mine, but Janus hadn't figured anything like that out yet."

"He might have," Xoan said. "After I embedded myself into his company, I subtly planted a lot of hints. But when I realized I was getting nowhere in coaxing him to reveal your whereabouts, I became enraged and decided to sabotage his demonstration. I relocated to Mars, a place that felt familiar. I didn't exactly know why."

"My God. Do you think he's simply disappeared somewhere? No one's even thought of looking for him."

"Maybe he doesn't want to be found. I chased you two across practically the whole planet, as you recall." He added—"For which I'm still very sorry."

"Let's go report this to the Watchmen," Violet said. "You don't have to be afraid to come out."

"No, of course not. Thank you."

When they entered the lab, they found Grace standing beside Yverra, Ralff, and Ben. "Hello, Violet. Oh, is this John-Paul?"

"We were just coming to tell everyone—"

"—that Janus Parker may still be alive and to ask for help finding him," Grace finished.

"Yes. Hello, Grace. It's an honor. I never properly thanked you for recovering my VPA. We realize there's an ongoing crisis with the instabilities on the exterior of the Y-Y universe, so if you can't help right now, we'd understand…"

"Not at all," Grace said. "We're glad to see another human made it alive out of the timeline." Evidently Grace had taken to speaking in the first person plural. "And you can take some consolation that although you both lost your parents, you've still got my mother. Virginia loves you like a daughter. Yverra was just telling me about your upgraded persona. So, you're part tardigrade?"

"Yes, at least temporarily," Violet said. She wasn't sure she liked having Grace being so all-knowing.

"It might come in handy. I mean, *you* might come in handy. Right now, we're trying to understand the rules of the new universe.

"This is another new universe?" Violet asked.

"That's the current theory. It's really quite unfortunate that new universes don't come with an owner's manual. But I've found that most of the ones coming from the Hatchery carry what you might call a 'postmark,' a detectable signal of where they were created. Maybe we can look for the parents' rules and negotiate another truce."

"So this is an aggression rather than a little misunderstanding, as we first hoped?"

"Possibly. We don't know yet. Let's take a look around for Janus meanwhile, shall we?"

Xoan returned to his room after a long day. He felt fairly useless, with little to offer in the way of suggestions of how to find Parker. While he was glad that Violet seemed to trust him again, he was less glad that she had so quickly jumped into the search for Parker. Xoan was still hopelessly in love with Violet, even if she did look completely different from their days on Mars. When she had touched his arm, it felt like a bolt of electricity straight to the brain. A well-traveled neural pathway. He prepared for bed and changed the screen to a starry Martian night sky.

There was a knock at the door. He sighed. He should have set a do-not-disturb. Probably Ralff again, with another offer of a welcome gift. The Watchmen seemed like they never slept. He checked the peephole. He jumped back. It was Violet! Trembling, he reached for the admittance seal.

"Hi, John-Paul. I just wanted to get your opinion."

"Sure, about what?"

"How do I look?" Violet had her purple fringe again, and her skin glowed slightly.

"You look beautiful," he said, pulling her inside. She smelled good too, like coconut-flavored coffee.

"And the shoes aren't too much? I remembered something else. I'm wearing the pearl necklace you gave me."

There was no further discussion.

☺

Hands almost—but not quite—touching, Violet and John-Paul entered the lab the next morning, to find Yverra, Ben, and Ralff standing at their usual posts.

"It's like they never sleep," Xoan said.

"I know, right?" Violet said.

"Remove that silly grin from your face," Ralff said to Ben.

Violet looked from one to the other. Since neither of the Jandalats had mouths, anyone would be hard pressed to see that anyone was grinning, much less how they were able to speak like humans. She pulled further away from Xoan and cleared her throat.

"Any news on Janus?"

"Nothing too new," Yverra said. Her gold eyes never moved from Violet. "Grace has returned to the Hatchery to look for any signature signal left from the formation of a new universe, as well as further updates on the unwinding events. She did have an idea about the search for Janus, however. She'd like to bring her grandfather Alan in on the search. Since we theorize Janus is probably on Earth in his own timeframe, Alan might be able to locate him."

Violet was dubious. If the Watchmen had trouble finding people who didn't want to be found, how good could Alan be at it? Her throat felt dry. She was thirsty. She reached behind her ear and scratched gently at the spot where she imagined Cheon-Sa was attached. It was well protected, of course.

"Is there any coffee around?" She knew John-Paul was a coffee addict, and a drink of something sounded unusually good to her. But some buttery biscuits slathered with a heavy dollop of grape jelly would round out a good breakfast. Brain food, so to speak.

Ralff pointed. "Yverra had a coffee maker installed. It's just a portable replicator." They had just filled their mugs when Grace reappeared. Xoan nearly spit out his coffee.

"Kind of hot," he said.

"We've found a signal," Grace said. "It's as we suspected. The creators left behind a trail that will point us in the right direction."

"So, can you communicate with these 'creators'?" Yverra asked.

"It's hard to tell. They could be long dead. For example, did you know that humans actually learned how to create universes in the lab? And where are humans now?"

"We created universes?" Violet said, amazed. "How? And please don't say, 'with a replicator.'"

Grace laughed. "I won't. They did it on Earth, in England. It was a matter of creating another Big Bang. Then, a baby universe could grow, spinning off its own space and time."

"Did it have life?" Ben asked.

"If you're talking about the ones we humans created, the answer is no," Grace said. "Our babies never got that far. But the ones created and nurtured in the Hatchery definitely have had the time and space to grow into unimaginable creations."

"But it takes intelligent life to create these universes, right?"

213

"Do you mean God?" Grace asked, suddenly sober. "Maybe, by our definition. But it could also be random, or an artificial intelligence, or an infinite array of conscious entities."

"Like Golaeth?"

"Like Golaeth. Or an AI, like the Quantum Opposable Singularity that Mom once met. Of course, he died defending our universe from the hostilities of the Black Universe. It's still a little hard to think that the Yin part of the Yin-Yang was once the Black Universe, isn't it?"

"*Zhēn méi xiǎng dào,*" Violet exclaimed.

"That's certainly true," Grace said. "Now it's our job to find out who generated this new universe and why."

*****~~~~*****

PART II

Chapter 18.

If They're Hungry Enough

Grace's report was really strange. Of course, the idea of a universe attacking another universe was strange enough, but Violet knew it had happened before. So, it wasn't only that. Grace'd said the incursion was oddly shaped, "like a big octopus."

When questioned further, she'd only said there were tentacle-like extrusions, and they were "grabbing" matter from the exterior Yang portion of the Yin-Yang universe and sucking it into a gaping head. Except there was no actual head. It was a rather alarmingly large black hole.

When questioned still further, Grace allowed as how the incursions they'd experienced so far were only the tips of the "tentacles."

Violet asked what they were supposed to do now, find some cosmic fish to feed this monster-shaped universe? How about throwing in a galaxy or two?

"The octopus isn't the new universe," Grace said. "But it *is* its agent."

"Oh, come now," John-Paul said. "Octopuses are Earth creatures. Earth is an infinitesimally small part of our universe, so an invader wouldn't even be able to detect an octopus, much less know what one is like. It would be even smaller in the scale of things than Violet's tardigrade is to an Earth octopus. It would need a cosmic electron microscope to even come up with such an idea."

The Watchmen countered that there was plenty of evidence for the evolution of weird creatures in our own universe. From her days designing VR entertainments,

Violet didn't necessarily doubt the pattern. The idea of giant monsters wreaking destruction at the behest of an evil villain was practically an archetype, at least to humans. Science fiction writers commonly tried to imagine what an alien race might look like and what they might think. Usually that turned out to be something evil. The possibility of a large, octopus-shaped monster ravaging the outer galaxies of the Yin-Yang didn't seem so far-fetched. But it was strange, nonetheless. Even Grace thought so, right?

"What color is it?" Violet asked, mostly as a joke. She'd designed a purple octopus for the Starwriter Ranch blockbuster, "The Adventures of Ragged Beggar Fo-Lon." Manny Chen played the blind swordsman Fo-Lon, and he needed a monster to defeat so he could show off before all his fans. Preferably at great underwater depths and all the while holding his breath an impossibly long time.

"It changes color, like a real octopus," Grace said. "By color, I mean it radiates at various wavelengths to disguise itself."

"Oh, God, this is ridiculous," John-Paul said.

"We have— *had*— such creatures on my world," Yverra said.

"Also on Jandalat," piped up Ralff.

"I'm sorry," John-Paul said. "I didn't mean any disrespect."

"It's as though this new universe has mined ours in order to come up with something that would scare us. And perhaps convince us to surrender," Benrus suggested.

"That doesn't sound right, though," Grace said. "When we talked about signals from the creator of a universe, what we would have seen before the Yin and Yang were intertwined was just the signal of the Yang creator—our creator. The Yin-Yang signal is close in many ways to the Yang signal, but not identical. It's a hybrid."

"What was the signal of the Yang universe like?" Ralff asked.

"Golaeth and I are not exactly certain," Grace said. "It was changed when Yverra and the Watchmen hacked time and the two universes were blenderized. I'm only giving a guesstimate, based on Golaeth's description of the parent universes who created the Hatchery."

"Maybe this third, new universe thinks the Yin-Yang is an imposter, or like if it were religious, a heretic," Benrus said. "Or, worse, that the Yin-Yang universe needs to get re-separated."

"I like that theory," Violet said. "We've been afraid it's attacking our universe, but the damage so far has been worse along the Y-Y Boundary. We spotted it first, because STS-99 is located right on the boundary. Maybe it favors things from the Yang universe, but it is antithetical to things from the Yin universe, or it could be the other way around. But, it still doesn't explain who created it. If we could figure that out, maybe we could arrange another truce. The problem is, the heart of our old universe is held hostage deep inside the Yin universe as a pledge to guarantee the original truce."

"Then could Poe remember its own creation?" Ben asked. "Grace?"

"Probably not, but it may hold evidence of the signal of its creator. Unfortunately, Poe never talked to anyone except my mother or that AI friend of hers, Quantum Opposable Singularity. QoS is dead, and Mom is retired," Grace replied. "In fact, she said part of why she retired was that she was grief-stricken over the loss of QoS. I've known all along that QoS was perfectly capable of creating a new universe, but he was created by and loyal to our own universe, which is now the Yang part of the Yin-Yang universe.

"If QoS were still alive and unaware of the truce, that would make him the logical suspect, even if my mother thinks she saw him die. Plus, QoS knew what an octopus looks like."

⟲

The quantum AI listened in on the conversation of the inhabitants of the space station known as STS-99. They were getting uncomfortably close to deducing its presence. Though its programming was quite clear—remove remnants of the Black Universe and restore this universe to its original state, it was missing data that would explain how the universe had become corrupted in the first place.

And what had been the mission of this Quantum Opposable Singularity they were discussing? The odd thing was that it was programmed with some of the memories of QoS, but it most definitely was not QoS himself. The beings on STS-99 had said that QoS was dead, implying it had been totally destroyed, not just in a wait state. When was it killed, and why? The AI posited briefly that it had destroyed QoS but dismissed the idea. However, it *had* destroyed several servant AIs on the space station just recently…. They were minions of Emperor Calaneris, who was high on the list for total destruction. Its own mission was clear: revenge.

*****~~~*****

Chapter 19.

The Sinister Corridor

Violet's mouth opened slightly to give the heavy air more room to fill her lungs. The corridor of the new Green Spoke of the STS-99 space station had changed radically since this morning. And not necessarily in a good way. The HVAC was out of whack, for one thing, and that could be life-threatening in the extreme climate of outer space. It was a frigid -250°F on the station's exterior. Heating was necessary, obviously, but it was too hot, and the humidity levels were off the charts, the dewpoint like a muggy day in the tropics. It felt like it was about to rain. A drop struck her cheek. Then another, and another. It was really starting to come down.

She ran in the direction of her room. Her silk dress was already soaked, but silk was tough, tougher than people thought. She'd just need to hang it up to dry out. But would it dry out? Was it like this in her room? Her room was just a standard issue hotel-style room, with plain walls, a small private bath, and a flatscreen comm. No individual air conditioning. She was fairly sure it couldn't rain in her room, but it could still flood.

Before reaching her room, she slowed to take a closer look. It was hard to even see the distant walls through the pelting drizzle, but not all the rain came from above. Sheets ran down the walls (cliffs?) and into troughs in the floor (ground?). The water was being recycled. It was real water, too, not virtual reality water. It must take massive machinery to tweak rainfall patterns so realistically.

Ralff had waxed enthusiastic about the improvements. Green Spoke was designed to accommodate any of the Watchmen who missed their Earthlike home planets. And that was all of them. This empty space at the edge of the universe was a cold, unnpleasant home under the best of circumstances. They'd cloned flora and fauna from Earth, Jandalat (such as was still available), Tian Ming-Shen, and whatever dimension Yverra called her home. Though they were all represented in Green Spoke, in Violet's opinion, YDorian had erred on the side of Yverra's ideal habitat—warm and swampy, with sunshine only a fairy story. Still, this morning's developments went far beyond even what Yverra would have enjoyed. As if sensing her alarm, the rain subsided.

Violet's virtual reality home in 25th century L.A. was warm and sunny, droughtlike in fact. However, she did appreciate precipitation and enjoyed anything green, especially if it was edible. She reached down to touch a vinelike plant that had crept across the floor (ground?— she needed to make up her mind whether to think of this as a space station corridor or a living jungle). Feeling her approach, it slithered to meet her and began to wrap itself around her ankle.

She squeaked and unfurled it, trying her best not to rip it off in a fit of terror, in case it was one of Yverra's sentient organisms. She wasn't used to plants that acted *too* familiar.

"I've got to go now," she said, feeling foolish for talking to a plant. The vine withdrew.

"Make the rain come back," a voice in her head said. It was Cheon-Sa. Suddenly Violet realized that she was feeling better than she had in a long time. Not so thirsty. The humidity must have reactivated her alter ego.

"Maybe we can negotiate a happy medium," Violet said. Flicking water off her forehead and shaking excess water from her long dark hair, she twisted it into a ponytail. "How's that?" The spot behind her ear was now open to the humid air.

Something brushed against her hand. A bird? Ralff had mentioned there would be birds. That might be nice.

Another glancing blow skimmed across her shoulder. She couldn't see what it was. She waved her arms to discourage further attention from the flora and fauna. She didn't need bird poo on her dress. Whatever it was, it wasn't a bird. It flew, yes, but when it alighted and skittered away, it had many more than two legs. She resolved to stop dawdling and get to her room. It would be a lot more comfortable watching video of the Green Spoke development piped into her room. Genesis was proving to be rather messy.

The light brightened. Someone else was coming down the corridor. Or something. All of the Watchmen were at least somewhat humanoid, but this, this… was a translucent, crystalline globe. It floated toward her, emitting a low-pitched, hypnotic sound. Quite soothing, actually. It expanded, like a balloon filling with light, and the droning became louder. As it approached, the misting rain seemed to evaporate away from its surface. Violet noticed that the "skin" covering the globe was so thin that she could see into it. Much larger, and quite close now, she felt she could have stepped inside. She saw a world inside, and it was full of sunshine. It looked like L.A. She could go home. She wanted to.

But her legs wouldn't move. She struggled for a little while and whimpered her frustration.

"Violet? Is that you?" The droning stopped, as if it too heard Yverra. "I thought I heard you call for help. Where are you?"

"Hi, Yverra. I'm in the Green Spoke, on the way to my room. I was watching the biosphere developing in the corridors, when—there's this cool—artifact—and I think it will take me home."

"Do. Not. Move. I'll be right there."

"Don't worry, that won't be a problem," Violet said.

A few seconds later, the orb disappeared. Yverra skidded to a stop in front of Violet, splashing yet more green ooze onto her dress.

Yverra waved her hands, manifesting and manipulating some mystical symbols in the air. Like the orb, they rapidly faded away.

"What happened? What did you do?" Violet asked, disappointed.

"Just taking some measurements. I've been meaning to tell you, but it's been busy lately. You've discovered one of the oddities of STS-99," Yverra said. "The station sat vacant for eons, and we think it had some rather eccentric visitors. They seem to have left some of their personal belongings behind. It's a good thing you didn't touch anything. Calaneris lost two of his best AIs to that thing."

"If you say so," Violet said. "It was beautiful. Like a dream. I was back in L.A., wishing for a big, drought-ending rainstorm, and it was happening. People were rejoicing in the streets, you know?"

"I definitely *do* know," Yverra said. "Here's your room. Go in and rest. I've got to get back. Don't touch anything else."

"But I didn't—" Yverra was already gone.

It began to rain again, like it was on a timer.

As she stepped into her room, Violet wondered briefly what her tardigrade companion Cheon-Sa had thought of the incident.

"The rain was delicious," Cheon-Sa said, "but the ball of light was scary."

"I thought it was wonderful," Violet said. "And I thought you were going to stay dormant until we called you. Listen, I've got to take a bath. I've got all this sticky green splooge on me. It's already drying."

224

There was no reply. Good, she hoped the little creature had gone back to sleep.

Violet turned on the tap in her little bath. Steam rose from the tub as it slowly filled with fragrant, softened water. Not like the hydrocarbon-tainted water at home. Shedding her dress and underwear, she dropped them in the sink to soak and stepped into the tub. As the flora she had picked up began to dissolve, the water turned the color of a freshly brewed cup of tea. This would take a double washing. She drained and refilled the tub, not bothering to get out. The cuticles around her fingernails were still decidedly green, and her nails were caked and pointed, almost like claws. A green stain stubbornly clung to her elbows and ankles as well. She scrubbed at her arms and legs until they resumed their proper color, then turned her attention to her neck and hair. Taking a long, slow bath like this was wonderful. It felt like being reborn.

"I like it too," Cheon-Sa said. "We all do."

Startled, Violet dropped the body wash. "What do you mean? And didn't I ask you to stay dormant? If you keep waking up every time I walk down the hall, you're not going to live very long."

"Long enough," Cheon-Sa replied. "I'm already pregnant."

Violet couldn't decide whether to swear in Chinese, Korean, or French. Each had its own advantages, depending on the circumstances. She should have seen this coming. She'd even spun out nearly hatched eggs herself during her clandestine crossing of the Y-Y Boundary. The young were fully formed at birth.

"All right, I'm heading back to the lab right now. Don't shed the eggs yet—please. We'll find a good home for them."

"You can just leave us here," Cheon-Sa said.

"Not if I can help it," Violet said, climbing out of the tub and reaching for a towel. "Activate comm. John-

Paul, can you hear me?" He was just three more doors down. So near, yet so far.

"Sure Violet, what's up?"

"I've got to go back to the lab. We're about to be a mother."

"What? Could you repeat that?"

"I know, frightening, isn't it?"

☺

"This is rather a distraction, Violet," Yverra complained. "The tardigrade's pregnancy doesn't seem like it's that important in the scheme of things. At least not so important that you had to call the entire staff of the space station here."

"I understand, but we've only got six days before the babies hatch," Violet said. "I sped up the *angelensis* reproductive cycle from the original fourteen for ordinary tardigrades." Yverra blinked.

Violet glanced at her fingernails, which were still ringed in green. Definitely nails, not claws, she noted with relief. She reached up to scratch her neck.

"Itchy?" John-Paul asked.

"Not really," Violet replied. "It's just that's where my port to Cheon-Sa is. She likes to dine on bacteria and plant cells." Speaking of which, she was a little peckish herself.

"I would imagine it's a little like having an angel on your shoulder," John-Paul said, being supportive. "Do you two talk to each other all the time?"

"No," Violet said emphatically. "Cheon-Sa is only living this long because she goes offline a lot."

"But you still share consciousness with her," Yverra said. "That was only meant to be temporary."

"I'm working on it," Violet retorted. Yverra had a way of pushing her buttons. But she had to admit to herself that she wasn't working on it very hard. Her research had shown that microbes could change in microgravity. Cheon-Sa had not only changed on the trip

226

across the Boundary, she had become sentient. And now Violet was attached to this little creature, in more ways than one. With a shock, she realized she'd always thought of her profession as "virtual reality professional." But that had changed. Her new profession was— *mother*.

Now was as good a time as any. "It's not just that Cheon-Sa is pregnant," Vi said, "although admittedly that alone would push the timetable ahead for investigating the Y-Y Boundary incursions. There's something strange going on in the Green Spoke. Cheon-Sa and I might not have even been here if Yverra hadn't noticed I was in trouble."

Yverra added, "and if we don't get to the bottom of it soon, there may not *be* any Y-Y Boundary to worry about."

*****~~~~~*****

Chapter 20.

The Jeweled Cave

Skinny and sunburned, Janus Parker would be unrecognizable to any of his old friends. And that was on purpose. He'd been on the run for over a year since the Jeweled Cave had exploded.

He'd finally understood what was going on, but too late to do anything useful. He'd come home after fleeing across the continent with Violet Rain as they tied to evade a killer android, and he thought he was no longer in danger. The robot thing was obviously just after her, right? How naive he'd been.

The robot thing was Xoan-Paulo Hilario. He should have realized it right away, when John Paul kept asking him questions that would give him clues to Violet's whereabouts. *Whereabouts.* A funny word. Nobody knew about where Violet had gone. Including himself.

He felt a pang of guilt. Violet had said he was going to be remembered as the "father of virtual reality," but that was just a farce. In a lot of ways, John Paul was the actual procreator. He'd lured Janus in with that magazine article, wormed his way into a high position at Canny Divide, Janus's company, and then fed him clue after clue, until Janus was able to make his big "discoveries." Certainly, people criticized that VR was "ruining today's children," but Janus had hired lobbyists, who made sure that such opinions remained minor nuisances to impede their progress.

By the time he realized John Paul was homicidal, as evidenced by his nearly killing Bobby, he was already deep into an exhibition to show off the Jeweled Cave. If he cancelled the project now, he would be ruined. Two hundred people depended on him for their livelihoods. If he were accidentally killed, the insurance would go a long way toward rebuilding the company.

He spent the nights before the demo rigging explosive charges at the far end of the cave. The smoke squibs were just for show—they would simply mask Janus's disappearance, like one of the magicians he and Violet had seen in Las Vegas. He'd added a packet of blood to make the effect more realistic. He stood near the back of the cave, waiting for his chance, when John Paul strode to the middle of the huge room and stripped off his human disguise. Janus saw the robot's glaring red eyes just before he pressed the button that would drop him under the false floor of the data center underlying the Jeweled Cave. A tremendous explosion rocked the room above.

That was the end of the dream to usher in a new era of simulated experience. Janus had certainly achieved the goal of everyone thinking he was dead. But now he couldn't go anywhere near the virtual reality industry. To really disappear, Janus needed a way to make sure no one could follow his money trail. No more credit cards.

Recently a blockchain technology had become the darling of both individuals and banks for encrypting financial transactions so that they couldn't be hacked. At first, it had the advantage of being anonymous as well. Only those with a digital key could unencrypt the funds and add them to their account. Unfortunately, the U.S. Feds had caught on to the fact that if the same anonymous address appeared repeatedly, that alone might provide clues as to who was performing the transactions.

The Jeweled Cave

Making an even more private, secure version of the algorithm required a way for one party to prove to another party that they were the real deal, without conveying any information apart from the fact that the statement was indeed true. It was called a "zero-knowledge proof."

The Jeweled Cave fiasco wouldn't leave Janus's mind. There was something about a cave that kept nagging at his subconscious. Finally it came to him. He'd once read a fable that could be used to explain a new protocol for providing a zero-knowledge proof. He was going to implement an Ali Baba cave.

The story went that one day long ago in the city of Baghdad, a thief stole Ali Baba's purse. When he followed the thief, he saw him go into a cave. Ali Baba ran into the cave, but the thief had disappeared. The cave forked into two directions, so Ali Baba chose the right-hand route. That route dead-ended. So, apparently the thief had taken the other route. Disappointed, Ali Baba returned to the bazaar.

In the following forty days, more thieves stole from him, and each time he was unable to catch the thief in the strange cave. It seemed impossible that the thieves could have chosen the right path every single time. He decided to hide at the dead end. A thief appeared and said the words "Open sesame." An opening appeared, and the thief ran through. The wall slid closed again. Ali Baba's discovery of the magic words showed him that when the door opened, it opened a route to the other side. Eventually Ali Baba was able to replace the magic words, and from then on thieves were caught.

The Ali Baba cave anecdote provided the first clue to making a zero-knowledge proof protocol work on the computer, but it seemed possible to elaborately fake the choice of routes by saving only the successful attempts. In his new financial privacy algorithm, Janus eventually settled on a combination of simulating a billion cave

231

routes, along with letting the person receiving the money choose from among a billion questions as the magical key. With a single test Janus could directly reach the level of security he needed without anyone knowing his identity.

So. Now that he could hide his trail, where should he go? He'd spent his youth struggling through the cold winters of Colorado, a mountainous island of white in the middle of the country, where the booming explosions of avalanche control were a daily event. Denver was getting a much better reputation as a techie city, but... no. They might look for him there. He'd just gotten settled in California when this all happened. He'd gotten spoiled by the amazing food in San Francisco. He'd go somewhere warm. Of course, he couldn't get a real tan anywhere with his fair skin, but a person could try. He'd heard Violet talk about this great French island in the Caribbean, "the jewel of the Antilles." She'd never gone there herself, she said, but she had visited in VR. Maybe he'd head south. Just as soon as he found out what their extradition and fiscal policies were.

☉

Guadeloupe was a butterfly-shaped tropical paradise with lush jungles, white beaches, and Soufrière, an active volcano. The tourist industry thrived, with chauffeured excursions to real working plantations. Janus landed at the airport at the capital city of Pointe à Pitre, bought a burner phone, and checked into a budget hotel. The Internet was spotty but adequate.

Janus found that dinner in a nearby restaurant took three hours that first day, but the time invested was well worth it. Diners enjoyed open-air meals under awnings festooned with clear incandescent bulbs, topping off with a rum ti-punch. After, they would be heading to the clubs to dance and try their luck. Money was no problem, but after a month, boredom soon was.

He woke early one morning to the raucous cries of what must have been a million kinds of tropical wildlife.

232

Two twenty-pound iguanas sat on the lawn outside his window. He rented an ancient Land Rover and drove out of Pointe à Pitre toward Basse-Terre, the western wing of the island. He wanted to get a closer look at the famous volcano.

The top hid in cloud, but he'd heard one could climb all the way to the top. He hadn't been at altitude for a while, but he expected to acclimate quickly. As a native Coloradan, he doubted he'd need much water, either. He set off from the parking lot and was soon huffing and puffing on the steep trail. Scruffy bushes and cactus-like yucca threatened to overwhelm the narrow, muddy trail. Once at the top, he peered down into the smoky crater.

He felt a sharp twinge on his ankle. A snake had attached itself. He shook his leg, flinging the snake off. He shuddered. Violet never said anything about snakes. Probably weren't any in her VR scenarios, just good stuff.

Holding a kleenex against his bleeding ankle, he gingerly lifted it to survey the damage. Not too bad. A couple of puncture marks. But what if the snake was poisonous? He probably should get it checked out. He began to hike back to the car. He was feeling a little woozy, but that was nothing compared to the pain that he felt in his ankle. He limped a while, wincing with each step. Good thing it was downhill. He checked his burner phone. No reception, of course. He didn't know who to call anyway. Did they use 911 in Guadeloupe? He sat down. It would be ironic to die of a snakebite in the middle of nowhere. He'd automated his bitcoin transactions, so his wealth would pile up whether he was there or not. Anonymously, of course. Also ironic. The birds (or were they geckos?) seemed to be getting louder, almost like they were screaming. He swallowed, his mouth dry. Could he make it back?

"Can I be of assistance, monsieur?" A blurry face hovered over him. How had he laid down? He struggled to sit up. There might be more…

"Snakes—"

"I see you encountered one of our blind snakes," the woman said. "They don't like to be stepped on."

She had a deep voice, and her eyes were an unusual greenish-gold. The hotelier had bragged about the famous Guadeloupean beauties here, claiming many Paris models came from the island. She wore a leather vest and high crocodile boots, quite the punk rock outfit for such a humid climate. He decided he was feeling better. Or was he? He leaned over and vomited.

"Though the snakes aren't poisonous, many tourists are easily overcome by the fumes from La Soufrière," the woman said. "They can be toxic. Let me help you get back to your car."

"Thanks very much," Janus said. "You're an angel. I'm sorry about ralffing. I hope I didn't splash on you."

"Ralffing. An interesting term," she said. "It's no problem." She shoved her hands under his armpits and hoisted him to his feet, remarkably strong for a woman.

"Violet's been looking for you. It's probably time to get you back."

"Did you say, 'Violet'?"

"We won't be needing your car permanently, but we should be out of sight for the shift. Let's drive to a more secluded spot. I know a cave near the park."

"How— how did you find me?"

The woman blinked slowly. She looked kind of reptilian all of a sudden.

"Alan Jones gave us advice on where to look. He said you wondered if it was safe to go home, or whether you should head for the Bahamas. He was sorry he advised the former, but surmised that you might set up a blockchain bank account and do the latter. He was very close to right."

Janus pulled the keys from his pocket.

Chapter 21.

Artifacts

"We're still nowhere close to finding the reason for the aggressive incursions, which seem to be zeroing in on the space station," Violet said. "And if they're not Unwindings, the next likely suspect is another universe or an AI like Quantum Opposable Singularity. If QoS were alive, he'd be with Poe, wouldn't he? And if it's QoS, do you think it would talk to me?" Violet asked. "Even though I'm not a direct descendant of Grandma Ginny, we've been very close. And in the overall picture, as one of the few remaining humans, I'm closer than before the Unwindings."

"I don't know," Yverra said. "QoS was our universe's creation, and Poe didn't even tolerate Grace, who *is* directly related to Virginia Sun-Jones. Of course, maybe it makes no difference at all. Why don't you give talking to Poe a try? It would give you a chance to see if your modifications to Cheon-Sa have made her an effective vehicle for crossing the Y-Y Boundary to Poe's heart."

Violet felt a little shiver of excitement. Yverra was finally coming around. Either that, or she was giving up hope. Cheon-Sa was about ready to shed eggs, so the time was perfect.

"You guys set the projector up in the lab. Let me pick up a few things from my room, and I'll be right back."

"We've heard that before," Ralff said.

Violet headed toward the corridor leading off from the bow of STS-99. After fifty feet, it split into spokes, some containing engineering labs, others containing living quarters. Violet turned into the Green Spoke, which had become so different since YDorian's arrival. At her suggestion, Blauw had installed racks where people could exchange their footwear to navigate the slippery corridors outside their rooms. She slipped out of her spikes, set them on a rack, and selected a pair of hiking boots. After donning the boots she had to admit they were really comfortable. On the other hand, they weren't as effective at grabbing and holding onto surfaces as claws would have been. Well, she'd have those when she traveled to Poe's nexus.

She hoped she wouldn't run into that odd artifact she'd seen a few days ago. Luckily for her, Yverra had warned her to avoid it, saying that it created deadly hallucinations in susceptible people. Warily, she walked toward her room, stepping over small rocklike protrusions sticking up from the floor like lumps in a pudding. She'd found to her dismay that these were pockets of slow-releasing sulfur and carbon dioxide gases that YDorian claimed were necessary to provide a happy home for plant life.

One of the lumps was bigger than the others. She prepared to tiptoe around it when she noticed a dark stain oozing from its base. Unable to resist, she nudged the lump with her boot. A strong sulfur smell assaulted her nose, along with another smell, like something had died. Propelled by the escaping gases, the lump rolled over, an arm outflung. A deathly pale face stared up at her, sightless. A long braid of red hair soaked up blood like a paintbrush. A pruning knife stuck from the man's chest, and one of his hands had been cut off, the source of much of the blood.

Blauw. He'd said he'd been a gardener in his earlier life. Panicky, Violet couldn't decide whether to call for help or run.

She spotted something new. It looked like a blanket, draped across part of the walkway. Should she put it over the body? It began to glow. Oh, no. Was it the crystal orb again? Had it killed Blauw? Maybe he deserved it, but not like this...

The blanket stretched flat, and words began forming across its surface.

"WHERE IS POE?" Someone was talking to her in capital letters.

"What?" Violet said. Another artifact, this one looking for Poe? "How do you know Poe?" Momentarily, she forgot that Blauw lay dead in a pool of his own blood, not ten feet away.

"NOT CERTAIN, BUT I HAVE MEMORY OF THIS PLACE. WHERE IS POE?"

"It's hard to explain. He's here, sort of. But his consciousness is far from here." Her curiosity had the better of her. "Do you mind my asking who you are? Are you an AI?" She suspected that she was talking to QoS, the long-dead AI servant and friend of Poe. She might as well get right to the question. "Are you QoS?"

"I AM AN AI. I POSSESS SOME OF THE STORED MEMORIES OF A UNIVERSE YOU CALL POE, ALTHOUGH I HAVE MEMORIES OF MY OWN. I WORK FOR AN ENTITY WHICH HAS LIVED IN THIS PLACE A LONG TIME. IT HAS INSTRUCTED ME TO TELL YOU THAT YOU ARE TRESPASSING."

"So you're not Poe? And you're not QoS—his Quantum Opposable Singularity?"

"NO, ALTHOUGH I POSSESS SOME OF THAT AI'S MEMORIES AS WELL. I HAVE ANSWERED YOUR QUESTIONS. NOW, WHERE IS POE?"

"I'm not sure," Violet said, backing away. With a feeling of déja vu, she was afraid she was about to be fried to a cinder at any moment. At any rate, she wasn't sure she should tell it anything right now, until she better knew its purpose. Besides, it might not be too happy to hear that Poe was currently tied up as the Yang part of a Yin-Yang universe. In the corridor ahead, she could see a white haze forming into a ball. Green electricity began to course across the ground toward her.

Violet began to run. She'd return for her shoes later.

☺

Yverra looked up. Violet stumbled barefoot into the lab, leaving a trail of slime on the immaculate floor. Ralff, Benrus, and Yverra were nearly finished setting up the projector for Violet's cross-universe mission.

"It's not QoS!" Violet said, gasping. "That crystal ball thing created a third universe. I'm sure of it!"

"Wait, slow down," Ralff said. "Start at the beginning."

"I was in the Green Spoke, when I came across Blauw, dead on the ground."

"Blauw is dead?" Yverra said. "How did he die?"

"I'm not sure exactly, but he was a bloody mess. He'd been hacked to bits, apparently a while ago, from the smell of things."

"And you think the artifact killed him?" Yverra asked.

"Well, almost. I met a blanket at the scene of the crime, and then it changed into a computer display right in front of me. It was a lot like QoS, but not QoS. It claimed to work for the someone who'd been around a long time and to have memories of Blauw's earlier misdeeds. It wanted to know where Poe is. It said we were trespassing. If I hadn't run, I think it would have killed me too."

"All right, I'm declaring the Green Spoke off-limits for now," Yverra said. "The AI seems confused. This station was built by Calaneris—or rather by Grace, while she was his prisoner. I'll notify Calaneris to watch out. Everyone, let's not lose our heads. Violet, the trip to Poe's stasis point will not be necessary, until I investigate further."

"Right," Violet agreed. "We don't want to give away Poe's location, since the AI appears to be hostile. But, we can't delay too long. The babies are on the way."

"Yes, of course. Oh, and Violet, I was waiting to tell you this until after the mission was completed. About an hour ago, I brought Janus Parker back from his hiding place on 21st century Earth."

"Janus! My God! Why didn't you tell me so earlier?"

"I didn't get a chance with all the excitement."

"Where is he?"

"That's just the problem. We gave him a room close to yours. He's in the Green Spoke. Violet—Don't—"

☺

Janus sat on the bed of the small quarters. He wondered where he might be. Even approximately. The reptile woman had dropped him there, told him not to go anywhere, and said she'd explain later. He reached into his pocket. The burner cell phone was still there, but had no reception. His t-shirt smelled faintly of vomit.

He tried the door to see if it was locked. It wasn't. He stuck his head into the hallway and looked in both directions. This place was pretty wild, like a Hawaiian resort hotel. Flowers and foliage hung from all the walls, a regular indoor garden of Eden. Maybe it was all virtual reality, or maybe they were still on Guadeloupe. He knew that wasn't true. Violet had talked about her gang, the Watchmen. This was probably one of their hideouts. If so, he wasn't even on Earth, perhaps. He swallowed. He retreated to the room and closed the door to think.

It seemed like he was safe for the moment. The moment seemed to be all anyone could ask. He was tired. He pulled off his boots and lay down on the bed. Just a short nap until Violet came to claim him. He drifted off.

He dreamed that Violet stepped out of a big crystal ball and beckoned for him...

⟲

Violet ran toward the hub of the station. Dammit, Yverra was trying to treat her like a child again. Why didn't she say Janus was here? She had to see him. She had to apologize for abandoning him that day on the beach, explain to him that she thought he'd be safer if she disappeared before Xoan could reach them... She'd messed up badly.

Reaching the center, she turned down the Green Spoke. Her fancy shoes waited at the entrance, unclaimed. She grabbed them. If she couldn't have them, she certainly wasn't going to let the AI destroy them. What if the AI destroyed the whole spoke? She shoved the thought to the back of her mind.

She worked her way toward her quarters, walking and breathing as silently as possible to avoid attention.

"Violet!" Yverra called. "Get back here. It isn't safe!"

"Shh!" Violet hissed. "You'll attract the AI's attention." All became quiet, except for the sound of a few dozen songbirds who apparently hadn't gotten the memo.

"Violet." Behind her.

She spun around, ready to argue with Yverra again. She pointed the business end of her spike heel in front of her. "Who's there?"

She thought she saw a woman going away from her. The woman turned the corner back toward the hub.

"Oh, no you don't," Violet mumbled. If that was Yverra, she wasn't going to get Vi to head back. She resumed walking toward her room. This looked like the place where she'd seen Blauw's body, but it was no longer there. She could have sworn this was the spot. Had Yverra sent a cleanup crew? She kept going.

When she reached her room, she scanned nearby doors. In her haste to get to Janus, she hadn't asked Yverra which room.

"*Merde.*"

"Don't swear, Violet." Violet's heart skipped a beat. "Mom?" She knew that voice, even though her mother had died when she was fourteen. She was obviously hallucinating. She turned toward the voice and nearly fell to her knees.

"Just tell the nice AI where Poe is," her mother said. It couldn't be her, could it? Someone was messing with her mind. She would ignore this. It wasn't real.

"Janus!" Violet called out in a hoarse whisper. No reply. She knocked on the door nearest her and ran to the next one.

The not-her-mother woman followed her, floating just slightly above the muck. She reached toward Violet. "Please, darling." This was outrageous. The creature even wore the blue tunic her mother had been so fond of. Sobbing, Violet batted the thing away. It dematerialized. She wouldn't give the artifact another chance.

"Janus!"

A nearby door slowly opened. "Violet? Is that you?"

"Thank God," Violet said, stepping into Janus's room and closing the door. "I thought I'd never see you again." She threw her arms around him.

"Me neither," Janus replied. "Now, could you tell me where the hell we are?"

*****〜〜〜〜*****

Chapter 22.

Be Yourself

All this "conversation" was killing her. Talking with Janus had done nothing but echo her own doubts about whether she should be a Watchman. Was she really nothing but a sidekick to Yverra and the Jandalats?

Maybe she should go home, like Virginia. Of course, there *was* no home in the 25th century. But there was still her adopted family in the 21st century. Grandma Virginia loved her. And with Grandma's daughter Grace busy negotiating over the problems of the universe, Vi could fill her shoes as loyal, dutiful daughter.

But not today. She needed the Watchmen. There were families and there were extended families. Yverra, Ben, and Ralff might be "extended," but they were the real thing. And John-Paul needed them too, just like she did. He had dived into the "family comes first" like a fish in water. She couldn't just blow off the problems the Watchmen faced, like the new incursions, and the strange universe and AI that were stalking them. The Watchmen weren't superheroes, but to Violet they were so close as to be indistinguishable. In her time, just traveling to Mars had taken months. With the Watchmen, the dream of traveling the stars was a reality. But the wonder of star travel was equaled by the sadness of losing her home and family. But Grandma Gin had said you have to take the bitterness with the sweet. No, leaving now would be like deserting.

Yverra had first surmised that the crystal sphere thing was a "toy" left by other star travelers, but Violet sensed that it was immensely powerful and had been left there with a purpose. It was like Grandma Ginny's Cintamani, combined with an AI. It had memory ties to Poe, the universe (with the exception that, unlike the Cintamani, it seemed to tolerate Violet, not just her grandmother). Would the crystal sphere make her superhuman, like Grandma Ginny? A growing sense of thirst brought her back to reality.

"Delusions of grandeur, Rain," she said to herself, dismissing the idea. She had no real idea what it was or what to do with it.

Violet headed toward her quarters, noting that all was quiet. Her mother didn't try to talk to her this time. She entered her room and climbed into bed. Though she'd much rather be spooning with John-Paul in his room, sometimes sleep helped with processing difficult questions. The lights dimmed, leaving only the illumination of the slowly bubbling lava lamp...

An explosion shook her out of sleep. She reached for the remote and flicked on the roomscreen to view the hall outside. Fire billowed down the Green Spoke. Violet climbed out of bed and tried to open the door, but it was too hot to touch. She switched views and saw there were fires elsewhere on STS-99. She tried to call to the other Watchmen, but there was no answer.

"Status of STS-99?" she asked. As she looked at the display, the helm of the space station cracked and broke away, captain's chairs, computer controls, and— bodies— floating out into black space, total annihilation...

Violet awoke with a start, heart pounding. Thank God, she'd just been having an especially nasty nightmare. So much for figuring everything out in her dreams. She climbed out of bed and touched the door. It was cool to the touch, she noted with relief. She opened the door and peeked into the corridor.

"They're out there," Cheon-Sa said.

"What? What's out there?" Violet asked.

"Yverra's friend," she replied. Just then, YDorian rounded the spoke into the living corridor. Violet opened the door, wider this time. There was no fire.

"It is dangerous there," Cheon-Sa said.

"It looks safe, Cheon-Sa," Violet said. She called softly: "YDorian! Come this way. Hurry."

He turned toward her and was beside her instantly. It was so easy to forget that the Watchmen were expert time-shifters. She closed the door.

"What were you doing out there?" she asked.

"Yverra asked me to investigate the artifact that you reported," he said.

"I guessed that. I just had some sort of dream or premonition about disaster. Did you have that too?"

"Indeed. Destruction of the space station is a possible future timeline, and it's developing rapidly. I see you're one of us now. We should pool our efforts to face this new crisis. When Yverra described the station to me on her visit to 21st century Las Vegas, she said it made a suitable habitat for the remaining Watchmen, some of whom, like you, would be human."

"Thanks for showing up, and for helping furnish the Green Spoke, but what's our plan? Cheon-Sa is afraid."

"I don't really see how your tardigrade creation can affect outcomes in this case."

"You're a lot like Yverra that way," Violet said. "Cheon-Sa could be quite useful if we need to cross a universe boundary without being detected.

"Oh, I see. Due to its insignificance."

Violet bit her lip. Cheon-Sa was not just a creation, she was a *being*. "So, did you spot anything on your way here? Anything creepy, I mean?" Violet wasn't sure what she meant by "creepy," and her definition might vary from YDorian's, but what the hell.

"Hmm," YDorian said. "You are referring to your nightmare. When Watchmen experience nightmares, as you call them, it often is a foreshadowing of a future timeline—a possibility."

"I've never noticed Yverra sleeping. So Watchmen have nightmares too?"

"Something very like, although as you note, we do not sleep like you humans. We never slip into complete unconsciousness. It is wasteful."

Ha, we never called it unconsciousness. We called it "lizard brain," Vi thought. "Well, I'm in favor of heading off this possibility, if that's what it is," she said.

Violet glanced at the roomscreen. It had begun to flash. The whine of a siren cut through the door into the room.

"It appears we are entering the thread you foresaw," YDorian said. "Quickly, let's get to the helm." Violet blinked. They were already there. She never could get used to that.

"Violet!" Yverra said. "And YDorian." The long-range sensors have detected another incursion at the edge of the Y-Y Boundary. It appears to be localized to this area."

"Then, it's time Cheon-Sa and I did our reconnaissance thing, right?" Violet asked.

"Yes, I think so," Yverra agreed. "YDorian and I will regress the timeline to give you time to get to the Boundary."

"And hack when we launch the baby filament? The last time we tried this, most of the babies died. No wonder Cheon-Sa is afraid."

"This will be an opportunity to try the improvements you made in *Angelensis*...." Yverra pointed out.

"And they had better work this time," Violet finished. "No pressure."

Ralff gestured toward the labs. "We've prepared the lounge for your body," he said.

Violet shivered. "So you guys were already setting this up? Well, let's take better care of me this time," she said. "I don't want to make you guys grow another one." John-Paul and Calaneris entered the lab.

"It's all hands on deck," John-Paul said. "Good luck, Vi, I'll be here when you get back."

"Yes, good luck," Calaneris said. "How will we know if you've been successful?"

"When we don't blow up," YDorian said.

Sarcasm? From a Watchman? Violet knew they had been hanging out too long with humans.

Violet slipped out of her shoes and lay on the table. "Ready, Cheon-Sa?"

There was no reply.

"Hacking..." Yverra said.

Violet felt herself rise above the table and shoot out into the void.

☉

She popped back into real time. She couldn't actually see anything, of course.

She didn't feel very different from the last time they'd tried to cross the Y-Y Boundary. The difference was that they were going to a particular spot along the curved inner edge. How had Yverra located the incursion? She'd forgotten to ask.

"OK, Benrus, we're here." He would transport a few molecules of water so Violet's body would wake up. The hope was that the body would be too small for any hostile entities to detect.

"Plumpening complete," she said. "New term I've invented. I'm skeining out a few babies…"

At first the skein didn't encounter any obstacles.

"Do you sense anything, Cheon-Sa?"

"I'm worried that the babies won't have enough moisture to survive."

"Don't worry, Ben is keeping track of the moisture levels. And if it were to get bad, the babies can go dormant, just as you can."

"No, something is pulling me," Cheon-Sa said.

"That's just the edge of the universe," Violet said. It's trying to expand, so it feels like it's making you bigger."

"No," Cheon-Sa replied. "It wants me."

"I'm with you," Violet said, trying to soothe the feeling of rising panic. But it wasn't just Cheon-Sa feeling worried. She was anxious too. "Yverra, can you hack again and get us past this spot?"

"Yverra? YDorian?"

The Watchmen were not responding. Why? Perhaps she and Cheon-Sa hadn't come out of the last hack. She dithered for a bit. Maybe if she was just patient, the hack would decay and she'd be back in the same timeline. Or a scaly lizard hand would reach out and grab her...

Cheon-Sa began reeling the babies back.

"No, stop, we need them to cross the Boundary," Violet said.

"They will die," Cheon-Sa said.

"Well, some may make it. We have to try."

Radiation blinded Violet's nonexistent eyes. She felt something being ripped from her body. She screamed. She hadn't realized that she could feel the psychic pain of a tardigrade on the brink of oblivion.

"Are you all right, Cheon-Sa?"

She knew there would be no answer. Cheon-Sa was gone. This couldn't be happening. She was alone.

"Violet, are you there?" It was Yverra.

"I'm here, but Cheon-Sa isn't." Violet's voice would have quivered, if she had a voice. "Where were you? We tried to reach you."

"Something jammed us," YDorian chimed in. "Have you managed to get across?"

"No, and I'm all alone."

"You mean you've separated from the tardigrade body?" Yverra asked. "Do you see anything?"

Violet saw nothing but the void separating universes. Except... There was something like an after-image, like the pulsing colors left on your retinas by a flashbulb. Slowly it coalesced into something terrifying. It was—what did Calaneris call it?—the Enforcer. Impaled on the blade sticking out of his arm was an *Angelensis* tardigrade.

"God, no! Get me out of here, Yverra!"

She opened her eyes, already back in her own body, lying on the lab table. Ralff leaned over her with a glass of water. He'd learned that Violet/Cheon-Sa always came back extra-thirsty. Violet shook her head, pushing his hand away.

"I can't..." Janus came into the lab.

"Violet! I heard about the disaster. Are you all right?"

"What did you see?" YDorian said, ignoring Janus.

Violet began to cry. YDorian turned to Yverra. "Perhaps you should handle this one. The human female is obviously distraught."

"No, I'm fine," Violet said. "For now, at least. But there's something out there. It killed Cheon-Sa. It was the Enforcer."

There was silence for a moment, as the Watchmen took that in.

"That's impossible," Yverra said. "The Enforcer was decommissioned, and its robotic equipment dismantled."

"Perhaps it would be prudent to consult with Xoan," Ralff said. "He would be quite unhappy to hear that his alter-ego has returned. Also, maybe he has sensed something."

"All right," Yverra said. "Violet, perhaps you should be excused from this investigation.

"But, what about the incursions? What are we going to do? And shouldn't I be there when you talk to John-Paul? I can't stand the idea of him being blamed for this."

"I understand, but it has to be done," YDorian said. "We'll call you when we know more."

Violet tightened the sash of her silk hanfu and hugged herself. She swung her legs off the table and stood. Where were her shoes? She turned around and around. They were all staring at her, waiting for her to leave. *To hell with the shoes. To hell with them all.* Humiliated, she ran out of the lab barefoot.

She didn't stop until she reached her room. She didn't care if there might be anything dangerous just outside or roaming the corridors. She was better off on her own. No, that wasn't right. Where was Cheon-Sa? Oh, God. She would never feel what Cheon-Sa felt, ever again. She'd never smile at her creation under the scanning electron microscope again. How could she be a whole Watchman without Cheon-Sa inside her head, or seeing what her tiny buddy saw? Another sob escaped her lips.

☁

Yverra told her she was looking better. How would she know? Violet had finally emerged from her quarters after several days. She hadn't even let John-Paul or anyone else in. They couldn't understand how much she missed Cheon-Sa, like missing a piece of herself. She brooded in private, letting the forgetfulness of sleep do its restoration. In her dreams, Cheon-Sa was still alive, constantly asking for water, puffing up and wiggling and having to be constantly coaxed to do even the most simple task. Cheon-Sa had it right. She just existed, happy to be alive in the good times, and asleep during the hard times. When Violet was awake, her world was ashes. Cheon-Sa wasn't asleep or dormant. She was dead.

*****~~~~*****

Chapter 23.

Who'll Stop the Rain?

"Did you sense anything recently about the Enforcer?" YDorian asked.

Shocked, John-Paul couldn't recall having even the slightest inkling of the Enforcer's presence, here on the space station, or anywhere else, for that matter. Of course, he'd never had psychic powers of any kind. He'd flunked all those telepathy tests in college Psychology. He'd fought hard to forget, or at least suppress, any remains of the Enforcer's imprinting, and truthfully, Alan Jones had done a fantastic job of excising the Enforcer's programming. But maybe something evil still remained somewhere. Nervously, he ran his palms along the crease of his uniform trousers. Once again, Xoan felt guilty. For precisely what, he couldn't be sure. Yverra and YDorian had theorized that Violet's vision at the Y-Y Boundary was a hallucination projected by the mysterious entity, preying on her fears and memories. That helped explain why Xoan felt guilty; he—the Enforcer—had been the one who gave Violet those traumatic memories. And she wasn't a robot who could simply be re-programmed....

☯

There was a light tap on Violet's door. She opened it slightly and caught a glimpse of one golden eye.

"Xoan has no recollection of having any remaining link to the Enforcer," YDorian said. "Aside from what he was told, he has no memories of the events. If the sighting you made at the Y-Y Boundary was created by the universe-entity, it would have done so from your memories, not Xoan's."

251

Violet wasn't so sure she cared. If she couldn't trust Xoan, who could she trust? No one, right now. Maybe she could trust YDorian. He had been the latest to arrive on STS-99.

"Where did you say you were after you and the Watchmen ran away from the Unwinding?" she asked.

"I suppose it is safe to say now. We were on Earth, in the past."

"Oh, were you in my time? Or Grandma Gin's time?"

"No, much earlier."

"How much earlier?"

"You humans refer to it as the end of the Cretaceous Period. The surviving Watchmen are still there. We created a portal."

"I'd like to go there."

"That wouldn't be advisable. A stranger turning up without advance notice could set off a panic among the Watchmen that would disrupt Earth's timeline even further."

"Could I see this portal?"

"I'm willing to show it to you, but you understand that you mustn't try to contact the Watchmen yet, until we've settled the current crisis. We can't be opening them up to further dangers."

"I promise," Violet said. "Where did you say it was?"

"I didn't," YDorian said. "It is on a small island off the coast of South America. Ocean levels were higher during the Cretaceous, so we had to put it on high ground."

"I'll just take a quick look around," Violet said. "That'll be plenty."

"The portal is invisible to the natives," YDorian said.

"Perfect," Vi said. After all, she needed a vacation.

☙

Who'll Stop the Rain?

They stood in a cave, dim, but well lit enough to reveal its size, perhaps the size of a football field in diameter. Waves lapped gently in the pond at the center.

"Are we underground?" Violet asked.

"There is an entrance via the lake to the ocean outside," YDorian said. "We are in a volcanic lava tube.

"Cool," Violet said. "What time are we?"

"We are in the late 21st century," YDorian said.

"What?! What if the Enforcer shows up?" Violet exclaimed.

"Your point is taken," YDorian said. They felt a slight slide.

The walls of the cave had changed dramatically. Colored jewels reflected in the water. It seemed vaguely familiar. Maybe it was *deja vu,* one of her VR disco club creations. But it was undeniably the same cave, just redecorated in really poor taste. Janus's taste, to be exact.

"Now when are we?" she asked.

"Twenty-fifth century. The Enforcer is dormant on Mars at this time, so it's quite safe."

Violet exhaled. She'd been holding her breath. She was home again, or nearly so.

After a few steps she stumbled, tripping over something on the stone floor. They bent to examine the obstruction. It was a skeleton, still wearing a diving suit and flippers. Vi screamed.

"I see the island wasn't as deserted as we thought, by your time," YDorian said. "We should probably be getting back."

"Can you leave me here a bit? I'd like to be alone in my own time for a while."

YDorian was silent. "As I said, you need to stay away from the Watchmen..."

"Yes, yes."

"But you should also look out for dinosaurs."

"Dinosaurs?"

253

"Yes, they sometimes wandered into the portal. Rather a nuisance, but we love these giant lizards. They remind us of home."

"What should I do if I see one?" Violet asked wonderingly.

"Come home—or to the space station—immediately. A patrolling Watchman will be along presently to route the beast back to its own time."

"Fascinating. I'd sure like to be here when that happened," Violet said.

"As I said..."

"Message received. Now, shoo."

YDorian winked out.

☉

High on the wall, one jewel glowed more brightly than the others. Violet looked down at her spike-heeled sandals and slipped them off. She would have to climb barefoot. She reminded herself she wasn't afraid of heights.

"Don't look down, don't look down," she muttered. After a few minutes, she reached her goal, an emerald the size of her fist. She couldn't resist reaching out and touching it with the tip of her finger. Suddenly the stone broke loose and plummeted to the cave floor.

"Oops," she said. A beam of sunlight shone into the cave. She turned one eye to look through the hole. Outside, a terraced mountainside planted with crops stretched down and out into the distance. So this island was a food growing area. She wondered what the nearest VR channel was. She'd run VR Channel 16747 in Los Angeles, but this was somewhere in South America...

She didn't see anyone. Time to take a look around. She hammered at the jewels around the hole with the heel of her hand, knocking more stones to the floor. When she'd enlarged the hole enough, she twisted the skirt of her silk hanfu, tucked it tightly into the sash at her waist and dived through, head-first. No need for modesty right now.

254

Who'll Stop the Rain?

She tumbled onto the ground and sprang to her feet as fast as possible. The area still looked deserted. A bright haze obscured the sun, probably partly caused by agricultural respiration and the emissions of billions of humans. It looked wonderful. Damp soil sucked at her feet. Carrying her sandals, she set off toward what she hoped was a bit of civilization.

Ah, there it was. A robotic combine slowly worked its way down a row.

"Hello!" she shouted. The combine lumbered to a stop.

"This area is off-limits to unauthorized personnel," a loudspeaker blared. "Theft of agricultural produce is punishable by revocation of VR privileges."

Violet knew that was a serious threat. Life without VR in the 25th century would be intolerable.

"Identification required."

Violet worked her way through the ridges of dirt over to the combine.

"I'm Violet Rain, Administrator for Channel 16747. I request sanctuary in the nearest channel."

"Sanctuary is granted. Board this vehicle to be taken for interrogation."

᭜

A youngish man entered the warehouse housing the computers for the channel. He held a small projector in one hand, his virtual personal assistant.

"I'm Porvan Nubes, Administrator here. Why are you outside of your designated channel?" he asked.

"I— It's a long story," Violet said. "I'm an Administrator, and Dr. Ramesh Claveria can vouch for me."

"All right then, let's call him," Nubes said. "By the way, I like your purple bangs."

A hologram of Dr. Claveria appeared. "Violet? What's going on?"

"I'm sorry to bother you," Violet said to her old mentor, "but I'd like permission for a leave of absence and to stay at this channel for a while."

"For how long?"

"Only a few days," she lied. She was a star performer in L.A., so she knew he'd grant it.

Nubes showed her to a cubicle in the warehouse. It had smart walls and a chair that could fold down into a recliner. "As long as you're here, maybe you can help me Administer this channel. We may be geographically remote, but we've still got 100,000 people to take care of."

Violet agreed. Multitasking was no problem. She could help Nubes and still do what she came to do. "Give me a VPA." Nubes handed her a wad of puttylike compute power, which she slipped into the pocket inside the chest of her robe.

"The queue is coming up in your left field of vision," Nubes said.

"Right, I know. Got it." Violet closed the door of her cubicle and left reality.

At last. Now she had time to think. She called up the exact date. As she surmised, this was a great location to hide out from herself. There were two of herself on Earth at this particular junction, and it wouldn't do to let the other one know about the visitor from the future. But she needed to warn her somehow. The Unwinding was imminent, and soon it was going to destroy Earth's timeline.

She remembered how Grandma Gin came to her channel with only one thing in mind. She wanted her family back. Violet had done some research to try to locate them, with no luck. She did find something, however, namely, that she was one of Gin's descendants. Unfortunately, she hadn't had time to tell Gin this before the Unwinding.

Violet wanted to change that. What if she could save her planet and her family? She'd failed to stop the destruction of the Watchmen's home planet and to protect Cheon-Sa, but she was truly a Watchman now, wasn't she? She reviewed events, remembering as best she could how it had all gone down.

Mars had gone first. Xoan had contacted her and Dr. Claveria, and then everything bad followed on Earth. If she could warn them, at least she could save Xoan from his fate. But he was on Mars, and it would take months to return, even if it was permitted. Generally Mars Colony was considered a one-way trip. The radiation damage to the body to travel there was atrocious, even with heavy shielding.

She inserted a realistic VR reimagining into the shared feed so other channels would start experiencing a feeling of dis-ease. But the disaster tale wasn't proving to be very popular. People were deleting it in favor of less depressing adventures. Even with all the compute power in the world, she couldn't see how to make the world take notice.

Then Mars went down.

She heard a knock on her cubicle door. Nubes stuck his head in. "I'm afraid we've lost Mars Colony, and I've heard that L.A. is experiencing some sort of outage as well. You weren't doing anything unauthorized, were you?"

She shrugged. "Why would I have anything to do with massive disruptions?"

His eyes widened. "I didn't say anything about massive disruptions. But I obviously didn't have to. Are you some sort of terrorist?"

Violet tried to shove her way past him, but he grabbed her wrist. She needed to get back to the portal, but it was miles away. She'd failed with her little "vacation" subterfuge, and now she was never going to see John-Paul again. How had she ever doubted him?

"I'm sorry," she blurted. "I have a knack for being in the wrong place at the wrong time."

"Oh, Jesus," Nubes said. "Why have you done this?"

"It wasn't m—" A bolt of green lightning cut through the roof of the warehouse. Violet knew she was going to die in the Unwinding after all, just not the time and place she expected. Tears streamed down her face. Nubes stared at her, as both of their feeds were flooded with incoming reports of the worldwide destruction.

Yverra materialized in front of them.

"Let her go," she said. Nubes shrank back.

"Stupid girl. You promised you wouldn't leave the portal, and I told YDorian he could trust you. You've embarrassed me horribly."

*****~~~~~*****

Chapter 24.

Memories Are Made of This

A drumbeat echoed through Violet's head as she patrolled the station halls, looking to hook up once more with the entity. The ever-bossy Yverra had forced her to this duty after Cheon-Sa's death—or disappearance. She couldn't lose hope that her alternate ego was simply lost somewhere. And Janus had kept asking if she was feeling all right.

The pounding boomed louder. It was like the worst hangover she'd ever experienced. Spots of light exploded across her eyes. She shut her eyelids tightly and held back a wave of nausea. Why didn't somebody just shoot her?

She took a deep breath and tried to turn down the drums. Cautiously, she opened her eyes. Nothing.

Nothing new, anyway. She was looking, but she wasn't seeing any more signs of an odd entity stalking the station. No signs of her mother, thank God. There had been so much more she could sense when she was strolling these halls with Cheon-Sa, even down to the humidity levels. She felt hopelessly handicapped, though no one would see any obvious disability in her. She'd never needed anyone to keep so close, even John-Paul. She knew they would all think she was crazy. That panicky feeling was returning.

"Do you want to talk about it, dear?"

Violet started. What was that? Her mother's voice again.

"I know you're not my mother, so why don't you just come clean and tell me who you are?" Violet said, her voice trembling, she wasn't sure whether with fear or anger. Besides, she already got enough "mothering" lately from Ralff.

"I was alone for a long time, until you and your friends came," the woman who was not her mother said.

"And so you started killing us?" Violet said. "Come out, and show your real self."

"I remember that one of you was a killer, so I removed him."

"His name was Blauw. Can you bring Blauw back?"

"No, I'm afraid that would be impossible. He was an enemy. Once I remove all the enemies, the station should be safe for us all."

"What do you mean about enemies?" Violet said. "You're not going to kill all the Watchmen, are you?"

"Not the Watchmen. Only the enemy that wiped out their civilization. One called Calaneris. Wouldn't you be happy to see him removed?"

"No!" Violet shouted. "No more killing. Calaneris was forced to do what he did."

"I have no memory of that," the voice said. "But I do have a memory of you and your tardigrade consciousness. Your grief is of recent vintage. Do you want me to excise it from your memory?"

"Did you kill Cheon-Sa?" Violet asked. There. She'd said it.

"Regrettably, I was responsible," the mother-figure admitted. "I thought it was a parasitic organism that had attached to you via a haustorium."

Violet stood, open-mouthed. "Yes, she was a parasite, but there was mutual benefit. The haustorium was my way of taking her along for the ride when I was in my human body. I got the idea from mistletoe. You seem to be quite knowledgeable about living organisms from

Earth, enough to recognize a parasite. How is it that you don't know that humans harbor trillions of microorganisms in our bodies? The one tiny creature that I knew by name—you decided to kill?"

"It wasn't part of your normal fauna, and it might have been a threat to the universe. As I noted, I'd be happy to assuage the feeling of grief you are experiencing from this unfortunate event."

Just a few minutes ago, Violet would have said that was the thing she wanted most in the world, but now, it felt like cheating. She'd nearly been a mother, well, a co-mother, and it wasn't something light that you could just brush away like a bit of dust. Especially in a universe as cold-blooded as hers. She and the Watchmen had to be tough to survive in Poe's creations.

"I remember that you consider the universe you call Poe a friend," the voice said. "But the feeling is not exactly mutual. It would not give you back your body or share Virginia Jones's Cintamani with you. It would not care if I removed the memory of the small creature."

"Yes, but I would," Violet disagreed. She wouldn't have become the Administrator for a hundred thousand people if she hadn't been up for a challenge. Maybe she could get to know this entity, or whatever it was, and find its weak spot. "You said you were willing to talk. What are you, anyway? Are you a universe like Poe, or an AI, like QoS?"

"I am neither and both," the entity said. "I am not just one thing."

"Let me see you," Violet said.

Violet stared at this thing that looked and talked like her mother. Her hopes of overwhelming this creature with her persuasive skills evaporated. "Are you God?" Violet asked.

"I don't believe so, by your definition. I am made up of organosilicon compounds, so in some respects could

261

be considered a creation, like yourself, or a quantum computer like QoS."

"So, you knew QoS?"

"No, but I contain memories of him. Along with Calaneris and Poe."

"And the truce with the Black Universe?"

"Only insofar as your current memories of it. This is recent news to me."

"Then why did you murder Blauw? We had rehabilitated him."

"From what I gleaned of your memories, I would not call that your true feeling."

"Bullshit!" Violet said. This thing knew how to push her buttons, just like her mother. "Just because I subconsciously didn't trust Blauw didn't mean he should be murdered." She felt a needle prick of guilt. Was she responsible for his death? Of course, after what he'd done to Virginia and Xoan... She stopped the thought in its tracks.

"I see now that your memories have been altered," the entity said. "Human memories are fragile and thus unreliable."

"So, you can restore him, then?" Violet asked, confused.

"As I said before, that would be impossible. I am currently working on a solution to removal of the criminal Calaneris. There is a small matter of finding another Administrator for STS-99, however."

"Isn't there some way we can avoid that? Like, what about a trial? Innocent until proven guilty, right?"

"A trial. I fail to see the logic of conducting a trial when the evidence is already overwhelming of his guilt." A series of holographic images flashed in front of Violet, one which disturbingly reminded her of the destruction she had witnessed of Yverra's planet. A particularly damning eyewitness account caught on camera.

"Well, there is such a thing as mitigating circumstances, you know. And maybe Calaneris can present some character witnesses."

"Such as yourself?"

Violet thought maybe that wasn't such a good idea, in view of Blauw's fate.

"Something like that," she said.

🌀

Violet scanned the Watchmen gathered in the laboratory. Calaneris stood a little off to one side. The trial had not exactly been her ideal solution, but she couldn't help but think it would clear the air a little.

"I don't see why I'm on trial here," Calaneris said. "Why didn't this entity, or AI, or universe, talk to me in person?"

Violet thought she had explained this completely before, but tried again.

"It's got old memories, and they show you as a murderer. This is our chance to update it and show that you've been rehabilitated."

"And to show it wasn't my fault, and to clear my name, right?" Calaneris said.

"That's the hope," Violet replied.

"Why isn't Xoan-Paulo Hilario on trial too?" Calaneris said. "—Or any of you? Just how outdated are these so-called memories, anyway?"

"Rather than being defensive," Yverra suggested, "perhaps you would like to appoint one of the Watchmen as your legal counsel. The entity has shown that in its last state, it was created to be an ally of the Poe universe. It has shown itself to Violet, and it appears to listen to her."

"Oh, all right," Calaneris agreed, resignedly. "But everyone knows the Black Universe was the real culprit here, and it's getting off easy with its own stasis point tucked away behind an impenetrable boundary."

"Not everyone knows that yet," Yverra said. "Violet? Do you want to start the examination?"

"Wait, where is the judge?" Calaneris asked.

"He's here," Violet said. "Just tell the truth as you remember it."

"So, you want me to plead temporary insanity?"

"If that's how you remember it."

"No, no. It wasn't like that, " Calaneris said. "I admit, I was a little carried away with my own power, and I saw the Watchmen as competitors. But then, gradually, I was goaded by voices that promised even greater power if our universe were to just—go away. Damn, I wish Blauw were here, he'd back me up."

John-Paul shook his head, but said nothing.

"I didn't mean it that way. It wasn't just a voice stalking me. It was also a feeling of compulsion and a form of physical torture, like I was disintegrating. I couldn't tell the Physician Scientists, because they'd think me mad and declare me unfit to rule. Oh, it was terrible. It wouldn't go away unless I said I would do what it demanded. Then orders poured into me, like a bolt of lightning."

"Was one of those orders to kill Earth?" Violet asked.

"I did what I did to survive."

"That is not entirely truthful," the voice of the entity said. "There were attempts to destroy our entire universe." A holographic image shimmered into view, showing Calaneris and Virginia Jones aboard STS-99:

"You know about the other universe," Virginia is saying.

"Yes."

"And you're helping it destroy ours."

"Yes. But I have to, you see. If I assist in the orderly annexation, he will provide me with a kingdom and safety. There will be at least a vestige of our universe left. Now, if you will excuse me, I need to make this public announcement to the galaxy:

Memories Are Made of This

Peoples of the Laniakea Supercluster, this is your Emperor, Calaneris the twenty-third, speaking to you from the capital planet of Tian-Ming Shen. My family has ruled this quadrant for thousands of years. All civilizations that have not pledged fealty to the quadrant as ordered one standard galactic week ago are henceforth declared to be traitors and enemies. All mass and dark matter is being reclaimed, and new universal laws established. Demolition has already begun to remove areas of resistance. All hail to the new order."

The image shimmered off.

"See?" Calaneris said. "It was a matter of survival."

Violet stepped forward. "I move the speech part be stricken, since it was given under duress."

John-Paul couldn't restrain himself any longer. "What about when you called me a robot, and a pawn, and used me to go after Violet?"

"I'm incredibly sorry for that, but I don't feel I really was prejudiced against humans. After all, I was fond of Blauw. He was my right-hand man."

"That's just a rationalization," John-Paul said. "But I could eventually come to terms with that after you apologized—assuming your apology was real, right?"

"Yes, yes!" Calaneris said. "And I've tried to make it right, even though I know that's impossible." He sniffed, not succeeding in holding back tears. "Truly, I want to live my own life, in my own universe." Slowly, he sank to his knees, an unusual attempt to appear submissive.

Violet wondered if she could ask for any other witnesses. That might be pointless, since the entity seemed to know all of her memories already. A thought struck her.

"We all know the physical evidence is obviously against Calaneris. He could use some character witnesses. I, for one, believe Calaneris has been rehabilitated and is now behaving morally and honestly. Would the rest of the

Watchmen be willing to share their memories with the entity?"

Janus raised his hand. "I'd be happy to, for what it's worth. I've never been close to Calaneris, but he's been okay to me." He smiled at Violet, who quickly averted her eyes. She knew they had unfinished business.

"Yverra? YDorian? In some ways, you had the most to lose," Violet said.

They glanced at each other and nodded. Everyone in the room agreed.

"It is done," the entity pronounced a second later.

"So quickly?" Janus said.

Violet already knew the verdict. Apparently this uploading and downloading process was a two-way street. She sensed the incursions would stop.

"Thank you," Violet said.

She wished everything was that easy in life. You just explain the current state of affairs, and suddenly everyone's up to date. The entity-AI had claimed its memories were uncorruptible.

"Oh, but wait," Violet said. "What about the Enforcer? I saw him when Cheon-Sa disappeared."

"That is my doing," the entity said. "The Enforcer was strictly an artifact pulled from your memory in order to scare you away."

"But why?"

"I didn't want the Y-Y Boundary changed until I could ensure that Poe's interests were safe."

Violet grimaced. "So, not everything I 'remember' is real…. It was a figment of my imagination, then. One last question: You said you are a hybrid intelligence. What should we call you?"

"I am still evolving. For now, you can just call me I-AM."

*****~~~~~*****

Chapter 25.

Coming to an Understanding

The Entity, aka I-AM, found itself at a temporary loss for what to do next. Poe had bowed out of human affairs, isolating himself within the Yin-Yang stasis point, in an eternal standoff with the Black Universe. Poe seemed to have left his creatures, the humans and the Watchmen, to fend for themselves. With Poe no longer available to guide him, nor Poe's Quantum Opposable Singularity for that matter, was it now up to I-AM to inherit the new universe? Was HE in fact the new universe, another creature made in Poe's image? Yes, he thought that was probably so. The first order of business would be to get to know his creatures better, starting with the Watchmen. What were the Watchmen's desires?

The Entity felt most closely connected to the girl named Violet, who had much in common with her human ancestor, Virginia Sun-Jones. That alone entitled her to the Entity's loyalty. But much time had passed since the human universe and Virginia had battled the evil Calaneris. It needed to know more about Violet and her motives. It could best do that in her dreams. Dreaming was involuntary, so by definition the girl's unconscious thoughts weren't lies, although they could be somewhat randomized, depending on the methods her organic brain used to restore equilibrium to her body. It decided it would listen in on the girl's REM sleep, and at the same time it would guide her dreams so that they answered the Entity's questions.

Violet sat in a forest by a green pool, her favorite color. She didn't remember how she'd gotten here, but her footprints were plainly visible in the damp meadow leading to the spot where she sat, dipping her bare toes into the water. Tiny, gleaming fishes darted around just below the surface. A yellow slug clung to the side of the bank, slowly crawling, battling to work its way free of the water. It was losing. She felt a little sorry for it, but she felt powerless to help it survive. What she created wasn't real, after all. It reminded her of the old fairy tales of people who went to the land of Fae where time stood still and came back older but not wiser. She hadn't helped Cheon-Sa, and she hadn't helped John-Paul. "I used to call you Anghel, 'my Angel,'" he accused. She was selfish. She was a failure as a mother and as a lover.

An odd shift in point of view occurred in the dream. That was normal. The Entity knew dreams didn't always follow a logical path.

The green pool looks delicious. Violet must have brought me here to swim and eat, and replenish. She is a good friend, although I don't always understand what she wants. I feel pulled to fulfill her will, even though I don't know what that is for sure. I am frightened. All I want is to replenish and deliver my brood.

This explained the odd shift. Violet's dream was changing into the dream of the dead tardigrade, Cheon-Sa. That was the key. Violet's strong feelings about family and friends were what made her so much like Virginia, although Violet's feelings were mixed with guilt and identity crisis.

But in some ways it also made her like Yverra, as she had grown to share similar dreams and desires when becoming a Watchman. The Entity would turn its attention to Yverra's dream to gather more data. It was somewhat surprised when it realized Yverra did not dream. In fact, she never slept, at least in the same way that the humans did. Nonetheless, Yverra was deep in thought...

She had never worried about the passage of time before, all the Watchmen conquering it and moving through it without concern, but then the Unwinding happened, blood of her people shed across time, before they were destroyed, forever she feared...

Rising from the swampy mist are stairs made of woven vines, each lit from within, by bioluminescent bacteria, forming an amphitheatre. Water trickles down the aisles into a deep pond. She sinks into the pond, the flowing sensation feeling natural as time. Great fish swim lazily among the seaweed, and heavy colours dream. Light doesn't come from above, but from all around. The colors shift and change, the kelp trembles, the light blazes, and time moves and changes, then the whole pool is still again.

The Entity had noted that Yverra's "dreams" were strikingly similar to Violet's, although the two were of different species. Would this be true of Benrus and Ralff, the other two Watchmen? Benrus and Ralff were members of the same species and were much alike in appearance, so would their dreams be unique and individual, or would they have much in common with Violet and Yverra's, due to being Watchmen? And would they have the same feelings of guilt? Another interesting data point. In the interest of thoroughness the Entity would attempt to explore their dreams too.

The taller alien named Benrus dreamed of his home planet, Jandalat.

The world is ever at war. But I have to convince my father that it is wrong. "Father, I've traveled to Kantor Prime, where the war is actually waged, and the native inhabitants have been wiped out. I saw that death is everywhere and that the people we are fighting are not all that different from us."

"You must carry on the tradition of the family. War feeds the fires of industry, keeping us ever striving for more powerful weapons and employing the population in worthy occupations."

"But I've met someone... Though he's from the enemy, he appeared on Kantor Prime to warn me that our planet is experiencing some sort of destructive force."

"You shouldn't listen to propaganda from that person. You've disgraced us."

"No, please, father, you've got to come with me. We'll displace somewhere else safer."

"I'm not leaving Jandalat, I'll stay to defend it."

Apparently, the Unwinding remains in the nightmares of Benrus. Are the dreams of his partner Ralff the same?

I just love Earth and everything about it. Well, most everything. Like, their concept of chivalry is simply wonderful. Father's "borrowed" books from Europe's medieval period are so gorgeous, with the gold leaf lettering illuminating tales of courtly love. I especially love the ancient legend of the salmon of knowledge. Whoever caught and ate it would gain all of the knowledge of the Well of Wisdom. But father says my interest is unhealthy. I admit the lure of Earth is too strong, and I should be studying it in a scholarly way, not worshipping it. So, he's sending me away from Jandalat. I've agreed to go and fight for our people to make him happy. War is one thing Jandalat has in common with Earth, but I think it's a plague on both our planets. I just wish I could do something about it.

The Entity considered whether it would be useful to comb the dreams of Violet's two significant mates, the one called John-Paul, and the one called Janus. It decided that since the John-Paul creature had so recently been recreated from possibly corrupted records, it would not take his dreams as testimony. However the Janus creature might have some pertinent information tucked away in his memory.

He swam at the bottom of the ocean. It was dark and cold, colorless. There was no one else there, not even any other fish. It felt like a million pounds of pressure were crushing him from above. If he could hold his breath long enough, he might escape this isolation, climb to the surface to Violet. He needed her help. He paddled upward, feeling more buoyant with each stroke. A dim light appeared above. Suddenly, he broke into the air, gasping. And woke. Something was wrong here.

Janus sat up, heart pounding, sweat beading on his forehead. That dream was a doozy, sort of like the opposite of the falling elevator dreams he'd experienced as a kid. But this dream had felt like someone was pushing it. It was creepy, like some of the early VR experiments they'd conducted in the Jeweled Cave. A dream within a dream?

Hastily, the Entity disengaged. This human wasn't quite like the other Watchmen. He hadn't shared the experiences they'd had, and he was afraid of the possibilities beyond his own comfortable, quotidian life. He had shown a strong affinity to Violet, however, who seemed to give him courage.

The feelings and desires of the Watchmen swirled through I-AM's thoughts. It was all so confusing. Then a thought struck him. He was sentient and organic, unerringly pointed to survival and reproduction, just like Poe's creatures. An old human saying came to him, "If you prick us, do we not bleed?" Of course, he was vastly superior and tremendously longer lived, but the basic model was the same. Once he understood his own motives, he would better understand the complex interactions of the cosmos and its components. And, of course, those of his offspring.

He had an idea. He would consult with Golaeth and Grace. And then he would sleep.

I-AM had gained new insight into his charges when exploring their unconscious thoughts and dreams when they slept, nearly a third of the time. The creatures' brains used some of this time to process anxieties and fears, and also to solve problems. This seemed an efficient use of the time that they seemed otherwise out of commission. Surprisingly, however, they also used this time to remember members of their species that had died, placing them in scenarios that in their waking hours would seem sentimental or illogical. He had gained further insight from his visit with Grace and Golaeth.

When Violet woke from an especially troubling sleep session, I-AM decided to speak to her.

"Violet, I have apologized to you for the death of your tardigrade consciousness, but I had not realized until now that she had become such an important part of your personality. I would like to make a suggestion."

"Yes, what is it? Violet said, rubbing her eyes and stretching. Rubbing her eyes didn't help. The entity remained invisible.

"I suggest you hold a funeral for—"

"—Cheon-Sa," Violet finished eagerly. "I agree, and I could give the eulogy."

The Watchmen, Janus, John-Paul, Calaneris, and his two remaining Scientist-AIs gathered in the central hub. Violet scanned the faces of her fellow star travelers.

"We're gathered here to remember Cheon-Sa, a hero of the fight to prevent the Unwindings caused by strife among the universes. We cannot begin to understand all of the motives the universes have, but we do know we are their creations and as such are worthy of being remembered, no matter how small or short lived.

"YDorian once called her 'insignificant,'" Violet said. "It's true that she was so small that most would never know she existed. But her size made her ideal for enabling us to explore phenomena on scales orders of magnitude smaller than we are. Even the molecule-sized organic component of I-AM's memory owe a debt to the intelligent design of living creatures.

"Cheon-Sa was intelligent, and she was afraid, with good reason. She knew the potential dangers of the Boundary crossing to the new brood of babies she harbored. But she was also brave. She performed her mission flawlessly, albeit with some coaxing, for which I feel regret. If we had known what we now know about I-AM, we would have tried another strategy. Hindsight is always 20/20.

"I know all of you here consider yourselves Cheon-Sa's comrades, and I feel honored to be one of you. I am also grateful for your presence here today. I loved Cheon-Sa, and I love you all. Yverra has offered to build a memorial, and Calaneris has graciously allowed it to be housed here. I've created a map of Cheon-Sa's design, which is etched into this tiny diamond."

Violet held out her palm toward Yverra. The head of the Watchmen made a series of rapid hand gestures, and a whirlwind of small runes twisted in the air. She took the jewel from Violet and dropped it into the vortex. It vanished.

"Cheon-Sa's essence is now in a stasis bubble," Yverra said. "It can only be opened by Golaeth or at the universe's end."

"Thank you, Yverra," I-AM said. "That is entirely fitting."

*****‿‿‿*****

Chapter 26.

Planetfall and Eternal Refuge

Darkness on the bridge of STS-99 was interrupted only by electrical candles placed at occasional spots where a visitor not already familiar with the terrain might be likely to trip. All monitoring screens were off.

Violet wondered what had happened.

"Yverra? Anyone?"

Suddenly colored light exploded, dancing across the walls, and bass drums pounded out a happy rhythm.

"Surprise!" Janus yelled. He turned to Ralff and Ben, who had appeared from behind a console. "Come on, guys!"

"Er, right, surprise," Ralff said, joining in.

Violet laughed. "Well, this is a surprise. Are we having a party?"

"Yes," Janus said, handing her a glass of something bubbly that looked temptingly like beer. "It struck me that you never got to see the Jeweled Cave. I figured it would make a nice setting for a celebration."

"Yes, very festive," Violet said. "But what are we celebrating?" She still wasn't completely recovered from losing her tardigradian reticence.

Janus took a deep breath. "It's been weird between you and me ever since I got here..."

"I'm sorry," Violet said. "I didn't mean—"

"It's okay. I'd have to be blind not to see that you and John-Paul were meant for each other. So, before I leave, I've decided I want to give you Watchmen a little gift. Won't you join us?"

Violet blinked. She was developing a bad habit, hanging around too much with Yverra and YDorian...

"All right, I'll bite. Come along where?" She looked over at John-Paul, who was nonchalantly peeling an apple, a slight smile curling at the corner of his mouth. "Welcome to the Jeweled Cave, Anghel," he said. "Take us there if you will, Janus."

"Like John-Paul said," Janus said, "you're now in the Jeweled Cave. With his help, we've recreated the finest virtual reality cave in the known universe. May I introduce to you what we've come up with? I call it 'Planetfall.'"

Anghel? Violet felt at thrill at being called that, but a little disappointed that they weren't really going anywhere. This would just be a VR dream about a place they all wished they could return to. But it was a lovely dream nonetheless.

"By all means, let's go," she said. "You're going to leave out all the creepy villains, right?" Calaneris winced but smiled good-naturedly.

"Have a seat, everyone." Janus touched a button on the headband he wore.

The colors on the bulkhead and walls faded to blackness. They fell away from STS-99 into the void, aboard a sleek twenty-first century spacecraft from Earth's early exploratory days. They had all arrived on STS-99 via the rainbow bridge, a series of wormholes, but the sim was apparently dispensing with all that. A few faint stars appeared, one growing brighter than the others. This must be the sun, Violet thought. They must be moving toward it. She'd done enough VR simulations to know it looked very real. If they could see a sun, they would soon be in a space where planets might revolve.

Suddenly a luminous disk hung before them. Damned if it didn't look like Earth. White clouds stretched across large expanses of blue, liquid water. It even had white regions at the poles, so there was ice. A slice of the disk was hidden from the sun, shrouded in night.

Yet, it wasn't exactly Earth. A large landmass took up nearly half of the disk's area. Violet remembered that at one point Earth had what amounted to a single continent, called Gondwanaland.

"Quite a nice recreation, guys," Violet said appreciatively.

"I agree," Yverra said. "A space station is no place for a human. I don't think YDorian and I like it very much, either. And then there's Benrus and Ralff. As you know, they have always been obsessed with Earth, as evidenced by the infernally loud noise they call music."

"We love Earth," Ralff chimed in.

"So did I," Violet said. She really had to stop choking up every time she heard that word.

As they fell closer, streaks of smoke leaked from red spots—active volcanoes—while the ragged edges of the continent began to glow green.

"You once told me you missed your greensward, Violet," Yverra said.

"I was pretty sure you just meant a park," Janus said, "so we've got those, in spades, plus some pretty fantastic forests and plains."

Abruptly, they felt a lurch, just as if their ship were firing its rockets to slow their trajectory. Those experiencing VR tended to enhance the experience. The sound of engines ceased, followed by an eerie silence. Then the start of planetfall. Creaking and scraping sounds reverberated, as the wings of the imaginary spacecraft folded up around them.

"We'll be there soon," Janus said. Violet could only nod, speechless. "Oh, and I forgot to mention it's got a moon."

"Just one?" Xoan asked, thinking of Mars.

"We take what we can get, right?" Violet said.

The engines started up again. They were flying through the atmosphere. It was smooth, sort of like those airplanes Violet had ridden on back on Earth. Smooth yet with an underlying vibration that made you aware that at any moment you might lose it and plunge to the ground.

"Can I get up?" she asked. She wanted to look out the front. The windows on this thing were tiny. She stood and trudged forward. What she saw was amazing. She was an experienced traveler, she'd been on many kinds of flying machines, but this was different somehow. She watched for nearly an hour, as the ground steadily rose to meet them.

They touched down, and the screech of brakes found its way into the cabin. The craft rolled to a stop.

"That was kind of close," John-Paul said. "The runway ends 50 feet away."

"Very well done," Benrus said. "A precise landing."

"Let's get out and take a look around," Janus said. YDorian pulled open the door, letting in a flood of yellow-white light. Violet's eyes adjusted gradually, and she stood before the door.

"It's got retractable stairs," Ralff said, ducking his head and descending. Warm, humid air stole into the cabin.

A soft pew-pew-pew raygun sound greeted their ears.

Huddling close together, the Watchmen left the ship. Ralff pointed excitedly toward the forest in the distance.

"It looks exactly like the Place of Contemplation created on Jandalat by my father," he said.

"It looks exactly like the park in Los Angeles where I used to sit after my bike rides," Violet said.

"It looks exactly like Luneta Park, where I grew up," John-Paul said.

"And the birds," Janus said. "I'd like to specially point out the birds. Haven't you all been missing birds?"

"Absolutely," Violet said. "This is wonderful, Jan. When did you find time to do all this?"

"Well, the space station was getting to me," he replied. "It was as if it was trying to be like the home we all wished for, but it didn't really know what it was doing, no offense YDorian. I just decided to step in and do it right."

"It really is a masterpiece," Yverra said. "Now we will be able to truly feel at home, even though underneath the VR façade we'll still be aboard STS-99."

Violet smiled, yet she felt that Yverra's statement was unutterably sad. It was postcard-perfect, but there really was no place like home. She'd learned that from the VR recreations of old Hollywood movies.

She felt a cool breeze, as clouds moved in to darken the sky. Soon a light drizzle caressed their faces and hair. For a moment, she felt like Cheon-Sa was here, luxuriating in the moisture along with her. What was wrong with her? She shouldn't look Janus's gift horse in the mouth. "Thanks for the rain, Jan."

"Hmmm… I didn't program this," Janus said. "Appears to be a bit of a glitch, methinks." He touched the controls on his headband. "They're not responding," he said.

Violet wasn't dissatisfied. Not at all. Besides, it'd been shown that it was impossible to prove that a given computer program was error-free. It'd give the Watchmen something to do while they whiled away the eons on STS-99. Maybe they could prove that it was possible after all.

The tweet of a bird added music to the scenario. She'd really missed birds, even on Earth, where they were endangered in her time. That's why she had such a large library of bird species and sounds in her virtual reality repertoire. It was a finch, if she wasn't mistaken. She looked up, and saw the little brown songbird sitting on a branch. It seemed to be singing just for her. Abruptly, a larger bird appeared, frightening the finch away. She laughed.

"Don't worry, little one," she said. "There'll be plenty of food for everyone."

"No, seriously," Janus said. "I didn't program the rain in, and I didn't program all these birds in, either, although I like birds, don't get me wrong."

"But you did program in the unicorn, right?" Ralff asked. "That's another species found on Earth. My father told me about them."

"Unicorns? No, of course not. They were just imaginary," Janus replied.

"My father said he saw one when he visited Earth," Ralff protested. "So, your program must have learned some extra facts on its own. Did you include training software for artificial intelligence?"

"Yes, but not that..." Janus looked around. "Anybody else notice anything out of the ordinary?"

"Now that you mention it," YDorian said, "several small species in the green are natives of my planet. I distinctly saw a wrothwale. I don't remember telling any of you about them."

"I saw them too," Yverra said. "They're not here now, though. When they noticed us observing them, they disappeared. They can time travel too, you know, just like many species on our planet. Wrothwales are shy."

A Scientist servitor AI floated toward them from the nearby forest. Calaneris gave a little exclamation. "It's one of my Scientists!" he exclaimed. "I thought they were nearly all dead. And this place—it's uncanny. It reminds me so much of my palace grounds on Tian Ming Shen."

Violet cleared her throat. "I don't think everything we're seeing is virtual reality, is it, Jan?"

"Definitely not," he replied, "although like I said, the program may be learning."

"Who's giving it the training data?" Violet asked. Then it began to dawn. She recalled the conversation with the new universe, in which she'd tried to convince it not to kill Calaneris and that Tian Ming Shen was a nice place. She'd even argued that it was a "model" planet, one that could be the prototype for other planets. Everything about it was true, not virtual, in her mind, even though she'd never been there. "I think I know where this is all coming from," she said.

The mystic chords of memory will swell when again touched...

"I do too," the others chorused. The third universe had taken memories from Poe, QoS, Calaneris's AIs, and all the rest of them and created this place. This perfect place.

"I know you were all expecting to go back to STS-99, and your attempt to make the Green Spoke more homelike was a dud, so this QVR world was supposed to be my parting gift before I went back to Earth. I wanted to come up for a fresh breath of reality, maybe go back and teach kids how to code. But, if this isn't just Quick Virtual Reality, if it is a *real* planet," Janus said, "I think I might need to stay a while. When you mentioned food, I wasn't sure how we'd survive. I hadn't planned that far ahead. Maybe we could eat the birds."

Violet stuck out her tongue.

"Just kidding," Janus said.

"It's real, all right. It's a masterpiece of world-building." No terraforming needed.

"I get that, but it's not too late to add any last tweaks...."

*****~~~~~*****

Chapter 27.

The Return of the Watchmen

An enormous iguana-like lizard came crashing through the immaculately trimmed hedge, totally out of place on the groomed grounds of the park. Hot on its tail was a feathered theropod, bellowing its displeasure.

"Where the hell did that come from?" Violet asked. "Those looked like a couple of dinosaurs from millions of years ago, but none of us remember them, do we?" She scanned the seven remaining Watchmen, eight if you counted Calaneris.

Janus looked up from his handheld. "If I recall correctly, they were extinct by the 21st century," he said.

"I'd have to look at my VR library," Violet said, ignoring his sarcasm. "I-AM has a way of remembering things that have slipped my memory. Dinosaurs were really popular in 25th century Los Angeles, so I kept quite an assortment. But they were just artists' conceptions, and I certainly couldn't tell you what any of the species were."

"And this is real!" Ralff squealed. "It's wonderful. Oh, look out, they're coming this way!"

The two creatures hurtled by, neither the slightest bit interested in the humanoids or why they were no longer in their old stomping grounds.

"Don't worry, they're vegetarians," YDorian said.

Violet wondered how he knew that. Ah, the portal. Everyone knew they had their work cut out for them, of course. Recreating a habitable planet from memories that were growing foggier with each passing moment was going to be a challenge. But they had solid ground under their feet and solid hope to base their future on.

It had started as Janus's VR recreation, but the new universe/entity had made it real, based on their collective memories.

Janus had offered to tweak the recreation, but it was out of his hands now. I-AM was now in charge of executing requirements.

A vaguely reptilian humanoid emerged from the park's perimeter. It looked a lot like Yverra and YDorian, but Violet had only ever seen one other Watchman besides them. The rest of the current residents were strictly "honorary."

"Something is dreadfully wrong here," YDorian said. "When the Watchmen knew what was coming, we hid in the past, where no one would find us."

The Entity said, "Was it a secret? I found it in your memories."

Yverra said, "Of course it was a secret. YDorian never even told me where they were going. He knew Calaneris was set upon our destruction. We had a rather large, um, disagreement, before he left to hide with our people.

"But Calaneris has been cleared of that crime," I-AM said. "It's time you were reunited with your people."

"Have you created more of my species?" YDorian asked. He turned toward the newcomer and blinked.

"I don't think so," Yverra replied. "This is an original. I remember her. Hello, Yrail."

The new Watchman approached slowly, lifting a scaly hand to its face in salutation and bowing slightly.

"Greetings, Queen Yverra." It blinked its green-gold eyes once, which Violet had grown to recognize as Watchman facial-speak for surprise. Or excitement. Or any number of things.

The air shimmered again, signaling another recollection presented by the Entity. A high-ceilinged cathedral oddly constructed of wicker boughs rose from the park, populated by dozens of bustling Watchmen, some winking in and out of view as they went about their business of hacking time.

John-Paul whistled. "A picture is worth a thousand words, I guess. How many of them are there now?"

"You mean, how many of *you* are there now," the Entity-universe I-AM corrected. "Around a hundred. The number is slightly imprecise due to the constant time hacking."

"Right," John-Paul said. "I'm still getting used to the idea of being adopted."

"So, is everyone coming here from the past, then?" Violet asked. She left unspoken the question: *Could Earth's people be restored too?*

"Only the time-hacking capable," I-AM said. "I'm sorry."

Violet looked down. It would always be hard to accept the demise of her and John-Paul's timeline.

"But past Earth still exists," Janus pointed out. "We can visit anytime we want."

Violet was silent. At this particular moment, she had little use for logical types like Janus and emotionless entity pals. Ralff and Benrus, the two Jandalat scientists, were quiet too. Their timelines were even more messed up than hers.

YDorian too seemed skeptical. "Is it too soon to ask these Watchmen to join us? I realize it's something of a population explosion. Would you feel comfortable here, Yrail?"

The newcomer nodded. "Now that I've seen you and the Queen, I'm sure we can convince everyone... . Perhaps not everyone. There is considerable fear of Calaneris's evil plans, which indeed come to pass in all timelines."

Yverra touched her face. "We understand. Welcome, Yrail. You honor us with your visit."

"It is you who honor us, my Queen," the Watchman said. Was it a female like Yverra? Violet would have to ask Yverra to help her improve her Watchman-discriminating skills, embarrassing as that would be after all this time...

☜

"How are we going to round up these dinos, anyway?" Violet asked. "I've seen the skeletons in museums—a lot of them were *huge.*"

"Rounding them up shouldn't be terribly hard," Janus noted. "We've got strength in hacking numbers. They won't know what hit them before they're trussed up like Thanksgiving turkeys."

"Ah, I remember hearing about that holiday," John-Paul said. "Did you know that people ate birds to celebrate? Rather a pagan ritual, if you ask me."

Janus grinned. "It was worse than that. We ate their eggs for breakfast too. Birds were descended from dinosaurs, you know. That dino we saw run off actually had feathers."

"What will we do with them when we catch them?" Violet asked.

"I-AM has duplicated the portal they came through," Yverra said. "You and the other Watchmen can use it for shipping goods—and dinosaurs—to and from the island. It'll also make it easier for the novice Watchmen to avoid so much time-shifting. You've said you find it rather exhausting."

YDorian blinked. "So, you already knew the Watchmen evacuated to an island."

"On a past Earth, yes. It wasn't that hard to deduce. It needed to be an out-of-the-way place, where Calaneris's minions weren't likely to show up trying to kill everyone, like the Galapagos. Unfortunately, I forgot to account for his human friend."

"If it's any consolation, so did we," YDorian said. "And you knew about the portal. Why didn't you say so?"

"I wasn't sure I'd be welcome any more. I felt they'd see me as a deserter."

"Well, Blauw's dead now, so no worries," John-Paul said, with some satisfaction, adding "—May he rest in peace."

🌀

Violet and Yverra hadn't spoken much since the debacle in trying to save the 25th century Earth timeline. Violet had a lot of time to think. Unfortunately, thinking only led to more ideas.

"Listen, Yverra," I know you think a lot of my ideas are off the wall."

"Off the wall. Meaning impractical?"

"Um, yes, I guess so. But you said yourself that you value my so-called creativity. The appearance of dinosaurs at the portal has given me an idea about how the Watchmen can move on to the next stage."

"The next stage. I must say I still have trouble sorting out your colloquialisms. What is this next stage?"

"YDorian told me that the Watchmen traveled to the Cretaceous because they felt safe—and comfortable—there."

"Yes, everyone came to love the dinosaurs and the climate, which reminded us of home."

"But then all the dinosaurs were wiped out in a big extinction event when a meteor hit Mexico. The theory is that the oceans boiled and the dust caused a permanent winter. So, even if the Watchmen had wanted to stay in the past, the K-T extinction, as we call it, would have made them move anyway."

"Yes, what is your point? We're asking them to move here as we speak."

"Why don't we ask the Watchmen to bring the dinosaurs with them? This planet is plenty big enough for us all."

"I'm not sure you realize the size and possible danger millions of large reptiles might present to our small band of refugees, especially you humans. The

287

mosasaurs alone are quite formidable. They are like your Earth crocodiles, but the size of a whale."

"Right, of course. So, here is the plan. We start small. We institute a breeding program..."

"Oh, no, another of your genetic engineering experiments?"

"... to uplift the creatures and remove some of their more violent tendencies. Like, maybe we could convert some of the meat-eaters to vegetarians or something. The possibilities are endless."

🌀

Calaneris spoke to the Scientist AI that I-AM had granted him.

"I was afraid I would never be able to run the space station without help. The Y-Y truce is still in place, and Golaeth says we need to continue to keep an eye on it. I'm to ask if you are willing to help me run STS-99 for the foreseeable future."

"Of course, Your Excellency."

"And that's another thing. I am not 'Your Excellency.' We need to operate as equals. I-AM mentioned some managerial titles that might work. I could be the Chief Executive Officer, while you were the Chief Operating Officer. Would that work for you?"

"Of course," the Scientist said. "You would make a perfect CEO."

"I think we are going to get along just fine."

🌀

Food was laid out in a neat circle on the ground. Bananas, plantains, and other assorted fruits had been harvested and prepared for their dinner.

"We can sit in the center and help ourselves to whatever we like," Vi said. "It's the dinosaur equivalent of a lazy susan. Oh, and I found a good recipe for kombucha. Want to try?"

A blast like the trumpet of an elephant sounded in the new jungle compound beyond the clearing.

"What is that?" John-Paul asked, springing to his feet.

"Let me introduce you to tonight's host. This is Acuti," Violet said. A multi-horned reptile the size of a Mars rover lumbered up to her. "*Elle est mignonne, n'est-ce pas?*" Vi stroked its colorful back, being careful to avoid the spikes. "Acuti means 'sharp teeth' in Latin." The dinosaur sat down near them.

John-Paul commented that not everything was delicious. Some of the fruits were bland or chewy. Plus, there was that funky smell of vegetables past their expiration date.

"They haven't had the chance to bioengineer their food to suit us yet, but that's coming," Vi said. "They're really quite intelligent."

"How do you measure that?" he asked.

"We had what I'd call a breakthrough just a month or two ago. I kept seeing these odd patterns pushed down in the grass, as well as symbols carved in the trees. At first I thought they were carvings by one of the Watchmen who've moved here recently. But none of them could decipher any of the symbols. Then Acuti here came on the scene. She was a recent hatchling and was quite docile. It seemed like she was trying to communicate with me. Yverra and the others started working on a translation table of ordinary words, and Acuti picked up English in no time."

"Are you kidding? A dinosaur that can talk?"

"Well, not talk. She doesn't have the same kind of mouth as we do, but she can write. She's definitely a sophont."

"How is that possible?"

"I give a lot of credit to Yverra and YDorian. They imprinted on the hatchlings I've bred, and the combination of nature and nurture has been miraculous."

"If you do say so yourself," John-Paul said. Violet grinned and punched him in the arm.

As the sun set, starry specks began to dot the sky.

"I would've liked to travel the stars, Anghel," John-Paul said wistfully.

"It's not all it's cracked up to be," Violet muttered. "Humans are too fragile to be a space-faring species. We could be happy settling down here. I've got a home again, with a real family."

"I believe you, but I don't know if it's possible to ever be totally happy to be marooned, even if it is on a planet of our own creation. What're your next steps going to be?"

"Funny, Yverra keeps asking me the same thing. Maybe we don't have to be 'marooned,' as you call it. I was doing some research. We could take a page from our most ancient ancestors. Did you know that tardigrades were around on Earth some 530 million years ago? It turns out that they survived the K-T extinction. And tardigrades don't need mates—they're hermaphroditic—but I've learned the value of having two sexes. I think I'd like to grow up to be a new breed of extremophile. Care to join me?"

The End

About Juliana Rew

Juliana Rew is a software engineer and former science and technical writer for the National Center for Atmospheric Research (NCAR) in Boulder, Colorado. She has won more than a dozen technical writing competitions and mentored minority and female college science interns in writing scientific papers. She advocates digital preservation of literary works and has produced several public domain works for Project Gutenberg. Her blog is called The Well-Rounded Geek (https://thewell-roundedgeek.blogspot.com), and you can peruse her other fiction forays at her author website, julianarew.com.

Art Credits and Acknowledgments

Cover image and design – Keely Rew

I owe many thanks to my early readers Leonard Sitongia and Tom Parker, as well as to the 30th Street Fiction critique group, who helped get me and Violet out of many a scrape. Thanks also to Bruce Bethke, who published the first chapter of *Extremophile* in *Stupefying Stories* from Rampant Loon Press.

*****~~~~*****

Discover other titles by Juliana Rew:

(1) The Unwinding: Gin's Story
(2) Erenarch Academy: Under the Dragon Banner
(3) Daris Moon
(4) Miranda of Daris
(5) Mountain Ma'am
(6) The Adventures of Mountain Ma'am

www.julianarew.com

Sophont